LOVE

AND

DEATH

LOVE
AND
DEATH

A MEG SHEPPARD MYSTERY

BOOK SIX

VICKY EARLE

ISBN: 978-1-78324-340-2

This book is a work of fiction. Any resemblance to actual persons, living or dead, events or locales is entirely coincidental.

www.vickyearle.com

Published by Wordzworth
www.wordzworth.com

This book is dedicated to
Leah, Deandra, and Alexis

1

Hit and Run

If only I could have let things lie. But I couldn't. I didn't realize how much anger was simmering inside me until it reached the boiling point. William was shaken by my sudden and unexpected outburst aimed at him.

Melissa, my half-sister, was the only one of the three of us who wasn't surprised. She knows me well—even though we've only been together as adults and for a relatively short time. But she's more devastated than I am, if that's possible, that the result of our altercation is William has left. And I don't know if he'll come back.

It was a mistake to let him take Jake, and I hope Kelly, my beloved border collie, forgives me for the loss of her buddy. She's pressing against my leg and gazing up at me with wide, dark brown eyes, asking for protection against the threatening rumbles of an approaching thunderstorm.

The weather reflects my sombre and agitated mood. Storm

clouds dash across turbulent skies and the trees sway to such an extent that I fear one or two will snap.

We leave the barn and reach the backdoor just as a few enormous raindrops pummel us, and as my mobile signals that Neal, my racehorse trainer, is trying to connect.

"Hi, Neal."

"Meg, I need your help." His voice is agitated and raspy. He can't simply be asking me to assist with chores in the backstretch. "Linda's being questioned by the cops."

"Goodness. Whatever for?" Linda is the most valued groom in Neal's barn and is assigned to my five thoroughbred racehorses. She's an excellent horseperson and a caring woman. I can't imagine why the police would be questioning her.

"You must have heard—that awful trainer Barton Woking was found in a ditch."

"No, I haven't. Did he have an accident?"

"He was hit by a vehicle. Linda told me he suffered brain trauma and died in hospital about an hour after he was loaded into the ambulance."

"But why is Linda being questioned?"

"No clue, but she's been vocal about him. He's a cheater and pushes his horses too hard. He's had a couple of fatalities this racing season."

"I know he wasn't liked."

"Even one of the television guys mentioned Barton's surprising results on air. He made it clear he thought Barton was a cheat. But nothing came of it."

"What about Linda? I still don't understand why she's being questioned."

"Can you come?"

* * *

2

Kelly and I clamber into the pickup, and I point it towards the racetrack. It should be able to get there without any help from me since we make this trip so frequently. But I almost forget where I'm going because my mind is still spinning. William is a considerate and kind person, but he decided I wasn't comfortable with the role of stepmother to Gabriel, his nephew. He led me to believe that his sister's wish was that we would raise Gabriel after she died, but later told me his cousin Maddy, and her husband, were to adopt him. And he decided it would be best if Gabriel left without saying goodbye. All these decisions were made for me. And rather than the passage of time helping me to heal, my resentment has grown and now I'm mad.

Do I want Gabriel back? I'm not sure. He's probably better off with Maddy, her husband, and their son who's older than Gabriel. But I'm surprised at how much I miss him. And I feel like a failure. I sort of want a second chance, but that wouldn't be fair to the boy.

Is there a possibility of reconciliation with William? Melissa thinks he's having an affair with Ramona, his assistant, who she believes has been infatuated with him for years. Oh darn, I've missed the turning.

I turn the truck around and arrive at the security gate. Perhaps I can help Linda and help myself at the same time by focusing on something other than William.

The inevitable rain resumes with large drops that hit my windshield and explode, reducing visibility in an instant. My wipers do their best to come to the rescue, but they can't sweep away the torrents of water fast enough.

I don't have my raincoat, so I run into Neal's barn leaping over a puddle already formed in front of the open door while dodging the waterfall cascading off the steel roof. The temperature has dropped by several degrees. Neal greets me and ushers me into his small, cozy office.

"Linda called. She'll be here in about ten. Coffee?"

"No thanks." Not only do I not drink coffee, but the burnt smell of the dark brown liquid threatens to turn my stomach. "So, Linda's being questioned about the death of Barton Woking?"

"She's terrified. That's why I called you.'

"The police must be treating his death as a homicide."

"I reckon."

"He's not a well-liked man. But why Linda?"

"It's got to be because she's been vocal about Barton, as I said. You know Linda. She cares so much about the horses and believes he was cruel. She's friendly with one of his grooms who he fired."

"I'd like to talk with him or her."

"Him. Les Joseph. Linda told me about him."

Neal's mobile rings. After about a minute, he tells me what I've already guessed—it was Linda, and she wants to meet with me, but not here. She'll be in a coffee shop near her home since she must be back to make her mother's dinner.

The rain thunders on the metal roof as I leave the barn. The water seeps through my fleece jacket and splashes over my running shoes as I dash to the truck. Kelly is peering through a steamy window. I should have opened it a crack for her. She ducks down behind the seat as I approach. She knows she must not be seen in the backstretch.

A text appears from Melissa, my half-sister. She needs to talk to me right away. Hoping it's not anything serious, I respond that I'll be at least an hour. She sends me three sad emojis but no desperate call for help, so I drive to the coffee shop in a steady rain that the wipers can handle.

Linda sits with her head resting on folded arms. A cup of coffee with the plastic lid off but nothing drunk sits on the table in front of her. I grab a small tea and sit opposite her. I leave my fleece jacket on but am conscious of its dampness and musty aroma.

"Hello, Linda."

She lifts her head and mumbles "Thanks for coming". Her cheeks are flushed and her hand trembles as she reaches for her drink.

The coffee shop is almost empty but the drive-through must be busy because the employees are darting about—making coffee, grabbing muffins, assembling sandwiches, and many other tasks.

"Linda, how did it go at Police Services?"

"It was scary. They said they had like a few questions, but I was there for over an hour."

"It's about the death of that trainer, Barton Woking, right?"

"They must reckon I hit him with my car. They've taken it for testing. That's why I said to meet here. I got a taxi. I can walk home from this coffee place."

"Couldn't Austin have picked you up?"

"He dumped me a long time ago. He wanted me to change my job."

"Why? I thought he was fine with it."

"He didn't like the hours I work. And he didn't like that I take care of my mother."

"Oh, I'm sorry to hear that."

"It's okay."

"About your car—the police obviously won't find anything." I smile, hoping to reassure her.

"There's a dent. Someone backed into me at the mall. Parking's a nightmare there."

"Did you get the driver's information?"

"I got out, but he took off. I don't know his licence plate."

"What did he look like? Colour of car? Model?"

"I don't know. I can't answer no more questions." She puts her head down again on her crossed arms and sobs.

"Linda, I'm here to help. I want to get on this right away so tell me what you can about Barton Woking."

She lifts her head. Her eyes are as red as her cheeks, but the tears have stopped. She turns towards the beeping coming from equipment behind the counter. Something needs attention but no one's reacting.

"He's, he was, a nasty guy."

"What do you know?"

"Most of it is what Les told me. Les Joseph was a groom in that guy's barn. Barton fired him because he asked the vet about something Barton told him to give to a horse. Les thinks it was something illegal."

"The police should question Les, then."

"No. I won't tell them about Les. Promise me you won't."

"If you want me to help you, I have to cooperate with the police."

"I'm not saying no more. I'm not going to like betray Les. He's a good horseman. I don't want him to get into trouble."

"I'll talk to him." Linda is not giving me much to go on. I'm certain she knows more than she's telling me.

As Linda and I walk towards her home, sporadic bursts of sunshine make the sidewalk sparkle. We exchange a few words about my five racehorses she cares for, but the conversation is intermittent, like the sun's rays, and most of the short and sluggish walk is silent.

I pick up the pace on my way back to the truck. Melissa must be getting impatient for our return.

*　*　*

Although fall has not officially begun, some of the old maple trees that encircle the farm have touches of red and gold. While I love the colours and the cooler days, I don't look forward to another long, icy, cold winter.

Melissa appears to be mimicking Linda—her head rests on her folded arms as she sits at the kitchen table. She lifts her head abruptly when the door slams behind me.

"Sorry. I didn't mean to bang the door."

She looks at me with such sorrowful eyes that I dump my stuff on the floor and trot over to give her a hug.

"Any news from William?" Her voice sounds nasal, and she sniffs. I hand her a couple of tissues. She's been crying.

"No, I haven't heard from him. What's wrong, Melissa?"

"Edwin told me I shouldn't have searched for my father."

"I thought you didn't want to because our mother said she'd been assaulted by him at the wife-swapping thing my detestable stepfather took her to."

"I didn't. But then I changed my mind. He was a Canadian official living in England, as you know." She blows her nose. "Since I now live in Canada, it sort of seemed the right thing to do. I just wanted to know who he was, but that led to this awful woman contacting me."

"Oh, who?"

"He's dead, by the way. But he has a granddaughter who's related to me, of course. She lives in England, not Canada, but she says she's coming to visit. She sounds awful."

"When?"

"Next week. She said she'll come as soon as she can get a flight. Honestly, I don't want her here."

"I suppose you won't tell her not to visit?"

She plonks her head down again and Kelly puts her snout on Melissa's lap.

"This doesn't sound like a catastrophe, Melissa. There's something else, isn't there?"

She raises her head slowly. Misery is all around me at the moment as well as eating away at my insides.

"Tell me and we'll do something about it. We're not going to let things get us down. Come on, Melissa. I'll do what I can to help."

"You can't do anything. It's about Edwin."

"Oh."

"Yes, 'oh'. It's so awful. I can't even talk about it."

"Is he sick?"

"It's nothing like that."

"You're going to have to tell me."

"He wants to move away from Vannersville. You know he's been teaching at the veterinary college. Well, he's been offered a post in Edinburgh."

"Scotland? He's going to accept?"

"It seems like that." Cooper jumps up onto the kitchen table and Melissa picks him up and puts him back onto the floor. I'm sure Cooper can sense when people are upset just as Kelly can.

"So, you'll go with him, of course." My heart sinks into my stomach which rebels. Losing Melissa would tear me apart. Even William's leaving is nothing to how the loss of my beloved half-sister would affect me. If Melissa goes to Scotland she won't come back. They'll start a life as a newly married couple, or perhaps get married there, and that will be that.

"I'd have to leave you, this farm, the animals—the life I love. And Milkweed Farm that you're giving me and Edwin as a wedding gift."

"Giving *you*."

"I don't know how I feel. I'm confused and stressed. I thought we'd make plans together. But he's made our plans."

This sounds much like how William made plans for Gabriel without consulting me, although he may believe I have no legitimate right to be consulted on the future of his nephew. But Melissa is Edwin's fiancée.

"What can I do for you?"

"Just talking to you has helped a bit. You're not going to investigate the death of that creep, Barton Woking, are you?"

"He may have been a creep, but whoever killed him shouldn't

get away with it."

"Well, I don't care. Besides, I thought you didn't take on cases that weren't related to horse welfare. He was abusive to his horses."

"Neal told me he was a bad actor."

"Yes, he sure was. He was suspended by the VRA at least twice for using illegal drugs, and once for using phenylbutazone on race day. Two of his horses died this season. Something rotten was going on in his barn."

"I heard about the sudden deaths."

"He was bad news, and I'm glad he's gone."

"Don't say that. You'll be taken in for questioning next."

"I heard Linda's been questioned. Everyone knows she loathed Barton. And he was hit by a car. Anyone can do that."

"Let's not jump to conclusions."

She rests her head down on her folded arms again and I'm at a loss as to how to console her.

* * *

Kelly misses Jake. She looks for him every morning. And Cooper often curls up on Jake's blanket as if he's waiting for his friend. I haven't put Jake's bowl or bedding away. Like Cooper, I don't want to think he's not coming back. There's a hole in our lives where Jake should be.

In the past, I've found that working on an investigation helped me put my personal issues into perspective. I hope that's going to work today. Kelly and I are on our way to meet with Les Joseph, Barton's groom, who was fired. He asked me to meet him at his home.

He lives in a thin, tall townhouse with about twenty concrete steps leading up to the front door. The linked buildings have flat roofs and dark brick facades. The long block of these houses reminds me of large, old, blackened warehouses in England. There's limited parking on the street which is lined with stunted trees. I'm so lucky to live on my beautiful farm. I have Frank to thank for that.

Les stands at the top of the steps and beckons me in. His white teeth gleam out of his walnut-brown face as he smiles.

"It's my day off. I don't get many."

"Thanks for seeing me."

"No worries. I'm just doing chores and vegging." His rumpled t-shirt has 'will swap brother for horse' printed on it.

"Do you have a brother?" I point at his shirt.

"Yeah, I do actually." He laughs. "This is his house. He's not a horse guy. He's a manager at Canadian Tire. Coffee?"

"No, thanks."

"Do I detect an accent? You're a tea person, right?"

"Yes, but I'm fine."

"Gotta make you tea. My mother brought me up right. I've got the real stuff—tea leaves, not bags. You'll like it."

"Okay, thank you." I follow him into the immaculate kitchen with its fingerprint-free stainless-steel appliances. A small window overlooks a narrow road that runs behind the townhouses. There's a door next to the window that must open into a single-car garage.

We sit on high stools on either side of a compact kitchen island.

It turns out, he's right. The tea is delicious—and served in an elegant bone china mug.

"You've got some questions, right? I heard you're a fancy investigator."

"I'm not. I prefer to call myself an amateur sleuth."

"Like Hercule Poirot?"

"Oh, goodness, he's professional and I'm not as clever or perceptive as he is. You've read Agatha Christie then?"

"Ah, I admit it." He folds his arms. "But you're the real thing.

What do you want to know?"

"Anything you can tell me about Barton Woking. You worked for him at one time?"

"Yeah. I'm ashamed of it now."

"Why?"

He uncrosses his arms and leans forward with his hands clasped in front of him.

"He seemed alright at first. I was glad of the work. But the longer I worked there, the more I saw and heard and the less I liked his way of doing business. To answer your question, Barton was a cheat."

"Do you have proof?" I wriggle on the hard stool.

"Nope. Even if I had, I wasn't going to be no hero and report him." He gulps about a quarter of his mug of tea. "I saw a tub marked 'Equine Top Performance' and asked him about it, like an idiot, and he said it came from the vet."

"That could have been true."

"That it came from the vet? Yeah, sure. And it did. But I asked the vet about it, didn't I? I was fired the next day."

"Oh".

"Have you checked Barton's stats? Like his suspensions?"

"No. All I know is what I've been told."

"Hercule Poirot would have." He laughs, takes my mug and refreshes my tea from a flowery Royal Doulton teapot.

"You're right. Give me the short version."

"He's been suspended six times in the past five years—four times for positive drug tests and twice for abuse."

"What about the horses?"

"What do you mean? The drugged ones were disqualified from their races."

"I mean, did they seem healthy?"

"The ones I cared for weren't too bad, but they had issues. I had to use ice boots on all of them, but that's not unusual. A couple of them were lame but he'd inject something on race days, and they'd pass the vet tests. There was other stuff. I got more uncomfortable the longer I was there."

"Did you meet any owners?"

"When I was around, his big owner was a guy called Knightscourt. Don't know his first name."

"Can you think of anything else?"

"Nope. I'm sure you'll give me a business card for when I think of something. Isn't that how it works?" He smiles and slides off the stool.

2

Stolen Horse

Kelly and I saunter from the truck towards our backdoor which flies open. A black ball of furry energy dashes towards us. Jake topples Kelly with his exuberant greeting, but she scrambles to her feet, and they tear around the outside of the house. They reappear, panting, as I walk into the kitchen.

"Is William back?" I ask Melissa. She shakes her head.

"Ramona's allergic to dogs, apparently."

"What has that got to do with anything?"

"Oh, Meg. You've been blind. I've told you before. Ramona's infatuated with William and always has been."

"I know, but I thought the feelings weren't reciprocated."

"Well, they're not only working together, they're also living together. William asked me to pick up Jake. They're staying in Ramona's flat until the renters move out of William's place above the office."

"He told you that?"

"He looked embarrassed. I felt like punching his face."

"Melissa!"

"Well, he's being such a twit. And he's put on weight. I can't figure them out. Perhaps Ramona likes being bossed around by him—she's been his assistant for several years."

My feet are like magnets and it's as if the ground is metal. I drag myself across the kitchen and stand by the table. I must look dazed. Melissa gives me a gentle hug and I wrap my arms around her warm body. My stomach feels as if miniatures of Kelly and Jake are scrambling around inside me, trying to get out. My emotions are in turmoil, but I can't tell Melissa that it's more about the possibility of losing her than about William's absence and his relationship with Ramona.

"What's happening with Edwin? Have you talked with him?" I don't recognize my quivering voice.

"I wasn't at work today and he's not texted me or called. I need time to think so I've decided to take tomorrow off. He has a vet student tagging along, so he'll be okay."

"Why don't you help me with this investigation?"

"Barton got what he deserved. But sure, since you asked." She rubs Jake's ears and pats Kelly. "We both need a diversion, don't we?"

* * *

With the two of us doing the barn chores this morning, we were back in the house in no time. We have each showered, are dressed in fresh-smelling clothes, and have thrown our horsey-scented outfits into the large laundry hamper.

The aromas of toast and coffee drift up the stairs, and as Kelly and I join Melissa and Jake in the kitchen a whiff of citrus is added to the mix—Melissa's hair hangs in damp strands below her shoulders.

"You must miss William," Melissa says as she puts a teabag in my mug.

"I do."

14

"But not as much as you thought you would, right?"

"You should be the sleuth, rather than me."

"Don't be silly. And you're avoiding the subject."

"That's because I'm not sure. Where's your engagement ring?"

"I took it off, just to see how it would make me feel." She passes me my tea.

"Thank you. And how do you feel?"

"Much the same as you. Not sure. What's the plan for today?"

I quash the tiny flicker of selfish hope that Melissa will break off her engagement and turn my focus on the day ahead.

The sun shines down on the four of us as we clamber into the pickup. There's a cool breeze but we don't need jackets. Melissa hops out to shut the gate behind us just as Neal calls.

"Meg, there's a guy who needs your help."

"Who and why?"

"Hang on. I wrote his name down. Here we go. Dirk Knightscourt. Someone's stolen his best mare that's in foal to the top Canadian stud, you know, Magical Black."

"That's weird. We're on our way to Dirk's place now. He owns horses that were being trained by Barton Woking and I want to talk with him."

"What a coincidence."

"I don't know. We'll have to see."

"They could be linked—Barton's murder with Dirk's mare being stolen?"

"Well, I'm going to keep an open mind. I've jumped to conclusions before—not wise."

"So, he knows you're coming?"

"No. I got his address from the owners' database. No phone number or email came up."

"I'll text you his number and let him know you're on the way. Linda got his contact info—she heard about the mare and is pretty upset."

"Thanks."

"What was that about?" asks Melissa as she slams the passenger door.

I fill Melissa in as we drive towards Dirk Knightscourt's house. The sun radiates its heat, and Melissa turns the air conditioning on. I welcome the cool air as it wafts around me and enjoy its soothing effect. Kelly and Jake are panting. I aim the vents towards the back and turn up the fan.

The gates to the Knightscourts' home are made of black wrought iron rods that look like spears, each topped with a gold-painted arrow-head. As we approach, the giant gates magically open and we head up the long, asphalt driveway which has a variety of strategically planted trees and shrubs on both sides. We leave the shade behind us and drive up to a grand, grey stone mansion, complete with turrets and leaded windows and a spectacular expanse of lawn all around.

"Peacocks!" Melissa shouts. "I haven't seen peacocks since I left England."

"And deer. Look, I think those are red deer. This Knightscourt guy wants to be an English aristocrat."

"I wonder what he's like."

We park the truck in front of an imposing front entrance. Tall, ornate white pillars soar up above us as we walk up wide stone steps. The large oak door opens as we approach, and we're confronted by a man dressed in baggy grey pants and a striped shirt open to the top of a paunch. A heavy gold chain with a medallion of some kind is nestled in the curly ginger hair that sprouts from his chest.

"Good. You're here. I'm Dirk. Well, come in. We haven't got time to muck around. Follow me."

He strides across the enormous entrance hall and turns into a room that must be his study or office. My eyes are briefly dazzled by an enormous glittering chandelier that dominates the middle of the room.

"Bobbie likes that blazing away all the goddam time. She's the wife. Sit down." He flops into a large leather armchair with brass studs decorating its edges. We settle on two uncomfortable chairs upholstered in rough cloth printed with peacock feathers. "Barton's been murdered. I can handle that. To be honest, I didn't much like the man. But my best mare being stolen—my god, what the hell's going on? And she's in foal to Magical Black. Did that trainer of yours tell you that? I've just had a chat with him."

"Yes, and…"

"It's outrageous. Damn disgrace. My security system went down. It's as if they knew it had."

"Could it be…"

"I know my staff—if that's what you're getting at. You bet I do. I can vouch for them."

"But…"

"Yeah, I know. I have lots of cameras. You saw them. You must have—if you're any good. But the whole system was down. And the alarms didn't go off to tell me."

"Was Barton…"

"No, as I said, I didn't like him. I didn't like the rumours of him cheating and he's been caught a few times. I was looking around for another trainer."

"Dirk, where's the tea?" asks a woman. I didn't know she was standing in the doorway.

"How should I know? That's your department. You probably guessed—this is the wife, Bobbie. These here people are investigators. They're going to find Bella."

Bobbie pulls out a mobile and texts someone. I don't know how she manages to message someone so quickly with such long fingernails.

"We're also looking into Barton's…", I say.

"His murder. Don't waste time on that. The police should do their job. But they won't want to find a horse. That's why I need you guys. I have lots of money, so spare no expense."

"The money…"

"You're not doing it for the money. You're doing it for the horse. I know about your animal welfare stuff. Good. That'll be a motivator. But I'll still pay. I settle my bills, not like some of those filthy rich people."

A tinkle of bone china cups and saucers precedes an elderly man carrying a tray. The silver teapot gleams in the chandelier's glow.

"Drink up. I want you to visit the barn. You know, the scene of the crime and do your sleuthing or whatever it is you do."

I've given up any attempt to ask questions and sip another delicious cup of tea. It may even be slightly better than the one I had with Les.

*   *   *

Dirk leaves us with the Stable Manager, telling us we won't get much out of him since he prefers horses to people. Orlando leads us around the stable, shows us Bella's stall, and points to a camera high up on the wall.

"Do you know what caused the security system to fail?" I ask.

"Cameras out," Orlando replies. He takes his baseball cap off and gives his bald head a hard rub. The black cap has an ornate, gold 'K' embroidered above the peak.

"Is the system working now?"

"Yeah. Mr. Knightscourt'll be watching."

"What made the cameras fail?"

"Unplugged."

"That seems so simple. But I suppose they were installed for the purpose of monitoring the horses, not to catch thieves."

"Both."

"Camera footage didn't show who disabled the cameras."

"No."

"I guess the thieves were lucky or had some way of not being seen or drawing attention to themselves when they unplugged the cameras.'

"Mr. Knightscourt is furious with the security company."

Orlando walks down the pristine aisle. No traces of hay, straw, grain, or manure. The rubber interlocking bricks look like new as if no horse or man has ever trodden on them. The barred windows are open and five young horses graze together in a large paddock. So, the barn must be used despite its appearance.

"Have you any idea who would take Bella or why?" I ask.

"Ransom."

"That could make sense."

*   *   *

Melissa and I drive past the peacocks who screech at us.

"He didn't have much to say for himself," Melissa says as she reaches behind her to pat the dogs.

"If you work for someone like Dirk, you'd get used to limiting your conversation. He won't let you get a word in edgewise."

"Do you really think Bella was taken for ransom?"

"I'm not sure. Dirk hasn't heard from anyone. He would have told us about that. I'm wondering if whoever it is plans to use the foal as a ringer."

"You mean substitute the foal, once of racing age of course, for a poorly performing horse with long odds, and make a lot of money on the bets."

"I know that's been done in the past. But it's not as easy now with microchips and DNA records. And even if a horse has great breeding it doesn't mean they'll be a great racehorse. They could be disappointed if that's their plan."

"I hope they know how to look after a pregnant mare."

"So do I. I'd like to know who Dirk's enemies are."

"A man with all that wealth is bound to have people who hate him."

* * *

My mobile vibrates and rings just as we arrive at the gate to the farm.

"Meg, where are you?" Neal asks.

"What do you mean?"

"Hector's racing in about an hour and I thought you'd drop by the backstretch."

"Oh, Neal, I completely forgot. We'll be there in half an hour. I'll see you at the rail."

He doesn't answer.

"Melissa, I've messed up. Hector's racing and I must go. Will you come with me?"

"I'll stay at the farm with the dogs. I don't want to go to the track right now."

"I get it. I'll just throw a different top on and be gone."

* * *

Neal's forgiven me. He knew I was at Dirk Knightscourt's place and could be tied up. But I did forget Hector's race and that has shaken me. I stand at the rail staring at the large screen that shows the horses being led in circles by their ponies behind the starting gate. Usually, I'm anxious about the loading process but I've got other things on my mind. I don't expect William to show up, but he part owns Hector with me. There's a story behind that but I don't want to give it any light, so I put a lid on it.

The sun is hot but there's a hint of cool in the breeze. I zip up my light jacket. I could have got away with not changing my top.

Strange shouts and chants drown out the general buzz of voices from the grandstand. Vannersville Racing Authority staff walk onto the track and head towards the starting gate which is on the other side of the large pond that dominates the inside of the oval. Neal turns up and immediately focuses his cumbersome binoculars on the scene.

"I thought this was going to happen," he says. "Have a look."

Several people are lying down on the track in front of the starting gate and a few others are milling around waving placards.

"What's going on?" I ask.

"Animal rights. They say horses shouldn't be used by people at all, not for any damn thing. And they're targeting horse racing right now."

"So, they've done this before?" I hand back the heavy binoculars to Neal.

"Yeah. But they've also broken into the backstretch and spray-painted a couple of trainers' offices. It was caught on camera, but security couldn't identify them."

"What's the purpose of that?"

"Their goal is to stop horse racing, but right now they're harassing trainers who they believe abuse their horses."

"Do you know which ones?"

"Primula Mokka. No one can make out why. She's one of the good guys as far as we know. And, ah, I see where you're going. Barton Woking. His office was one. These people reckon the penalties are much too lenient so trainers like Barton can continue to abuse horses. That's the way they see it. There could be others."

"How do you know all this?"

"From Linda. She tells me all this stuff."

"She has an uncanny ability to sniff out this sort of thing. Is Hector okay?'

Neal picks up his binoculars. "Yeah. He seems calm. And it looks like security has managed to clear the track. Amazing."

"It doesn't say 'slight delay' on the screen anymore."

"They'll load the horses into the gate now."

The loading process takes longer than usual because a couple of the horses haven't coped well with the delay and have become agitated. It's ironic that some horses have been upset by the animal

21

rights demonstrators' actions.

Hector stumbles as he comes out of the gate. Perhaps he was more disturbed by the delay than Neal thought. But he soon recovers and finds his lovely long stride. He moves from the back of the pack to about the middle as they gallop towards the turn. I must watch the enormous screen that looms in front of us because I can't work out where he is as they tear around the turn in a tight group.

Anything could happen with ten horses racing so close to one another. As far as I can tell, Hector is boxed in with horses on both sides and in front. The jockey holds him back so that he can maneuver to the outside and Hector puts on a spurt when he sees the open track in front of him. He passes two horses. The lead is shared by three thoroughbreds, one of which is Hector. Neal and I yell as loudly as we can to encourage him. I hope he can hear our shouts over the thunder of hooves pounding the track. The horses' loud rhythmic breaths get closer and then the runners charge past us and cross the finish line.

The announcer calls the unofficial order with Hector third.

Neal is handed a slip of paper. I can sense it's not good news.

"I'm sorry, Meg. I know you didn't want Hector in this race but it's the only one that was right for him."

"He's been claimed."

"I know the trainer. She's okay. Funnily enough, it's Primula."

"I don't think that's funny. You said she was one of the trainers the animal rights people targeted."

"Why don't you talk to her?"

"I definitely will."

As I drive home, I can't help worrying about Hector. Will he get the tender loving care that Linda gave him? Will they give him a chance to recover from this race before entering him into another? Will he have a nice farm to go to during the winter?

We'll miss him. Two teardrops escape and dampen my cheeks.

3

Missing Person

"You entered him into a claiming race?" Melissa almost yells at me.

"Neal thought no one would claim him because he's a gelding and getting older."

"But he's done well. That's stupid. Why did you listen to Neal? There are other races that aren't claiming ones. There must have been a suitable one."

"Neal said Hector would have had to wait for another two weeks for the right race, and he'd get antsy if he couldn't run."

"Are you sure it wasn't Neal that would have got antsy?"

"Melissa!"

"Well, he's an idiot."

"I don't think that's fair."

"I'm off to bed."

"Are you going to work tomorrow?"

"I don't know." She stomps up the stairs with Jake and Cooper on her heels. Kelly looks up at me with sad, brown eyes. The house isn't a happy place.

* * *

Melissa's bedroom door is still closed, and I've finished the barn chores. Kelly, Jake, Cooper, and I are in the kitchen milling around as I wait for the kettle to boil. It's as if it's on a deliberate work-slow protest. The morning sun highlights the fingerprints on the fridge which does nothing to lift my spirits—not that I care much about housework. The clicking of Kelly and Jake's claws, as they wander around, accentuates the emptiness of the room. I sit down on the floor with my back to the fridge and fondle the dogs' ears as Cooper snuggles up to me, purring.

Melissa shuffles into the room. All I can see are her fluffy slippers. I hang my head as she crouches down next to me. Jake sits next to her, and Cooper diplomatically rubs against each of us in turn.

"I'm sorry, Meg."

"You were right. I shouldn't have let it happen."

"Sometimes there's no choice. I get that."

"Well, it's done now. But I'm going to chat with his new trainer."

"Good idea."

"You're not going to work, then?"

"Nope. I can't forgive Edwin for accepting the position in Edinburgh without even thinking of talking with me first. So, I don't want to be around him right now."

"I see."

"I'm not sure you do. It means he doesn't love me. Not really. Because if he did, he'd have asked me, wouldn't he?"

"You have a point."

"If he'd asked and I'd said 'no', I didn't want to go, he would be going anyway."

"Perhaps."

"Well, he would. That's obvious. He's accepted the position."

"He could un-accept."

"There's been no mention of that, no concern for my feelings or plans—nothing."

"Oh."

"That should remind you of William. Before you say it—yes, I'm upset and I'd like William back here—but he didn't ask you about Gabriel, he didn't consider your feelings or plans, did he?"

"Well,"

"He didn't. You know he didn't."

"What are you going to do, Melissa?"

"The vet who's taking over from Edwin will be in the back-stretch tomorrow so I'm going to meet him and see what he's like. That might help me come to a final decision. I'm fed up with going around in circles like Cooper is right now."

We look at each other with faint smiles that brighten our faces. I pat Melissa's arm.

"Let's get some coffee and tea."

*　　*　　*

Melissa didn't want to come with me to the track because Edwin's going to be there. He's introducing his replacement to the people he'll need to know. We heard that this new vet was a partner in a practice in Alberta and has moved to Ontario to join Edwin's team at Vannersville Racetrack. Melissa doesn't know anything more about him and is apprehensive about meeting him tomorrow. Edwin plans to leave for Edinburgh in a few days so that he can find somewhere to live and get oriented before the fall term starts. I'm not sure what Melissa has said to him, but I rather think he believes she's going with him. I can't understand why he isn't connecting with her. Perhaps he's so excited about his new opportunity that he's not thinking straight.

Kelly is with me. It's purely selfish on my part. She could be at home with Jake, Cooper, and Melissa, but I don't feel like being alone. She's such a loving companion. Fortunately, she was eager to jump into the pickup and settled down on the back seat looking into my rearview mirror. I tell her she's beautiful.

We're on our way to see Primula Mokka and to give Hector some carrots. I can't help being concerned about what I'm going to find. Neal and Linda have such high standards I'm not able to imagine any other barn being able to match them.

Kelly lies down behind the front seats as I get out of the pickup.

A large horse with big bright eyes stands on a rubber mat as he's being bathed with a sudsy sponge. I walk past and enter a door to the barn where Neal says Primula has her horses. I ask a hotwalker where I can find Primula and she points to a woman who's giving a leg-up to an exercise rider. Primula strides out of the barn behind a grey horse with a streaked silky tail. I guess they're making their way to the training track, so I follow.

The dirt track is damp from the rain and has been freshly harrowed. The smell reminds me of a spring day on the beach in Devon, but less salty.

"It looks like perfect footing this morning," I say. "Hi, I'm Meg Sheppard. Neal may have let you know I'd be dropping by."

"Hello. So pleased to meet you. Yes, it's great today. You'll have to excuse me. I want to focus on Teddy. He's making good progress."

"Is he a two-year-old? He looks too tall."

"You're right. He was a late foal and hasn't filled out yet, but he's tall. All skin and bone. He keeps on growing and can't eat enough feed to put much flesh on his skeleton. So, he's not made his debut yet. I'm taking my time with him. I want him to be healthy."

"Lovely stride."

"I'm told he rides like a Cadillac, but I've not ridden him yet. He's lovely to watch and, so far, has been easy to train. He likes to work."

She picks up her binoculars and follows him around the track as he canters with long, floaty strides. His powerful neck is curved and his tail flows out behind.

"What a beautiful picture he makes," I say.

"Yes, he's magnificent. I'm pleased with him and enjoying watching his development—mentally and physically. I'm lucky to have him."

"Do you own him yourself?"

"I'm in a partnership with two others. Fortunately, we get on well and usually agree. I won't train a horse whose owners want to do things that are bad for the horse. And a common issue with owners of two-year-olds is they want to get to the races before the horse is ready. I'm sure you know some aren't ready until they're three."

Teddy is back to a trot and nearing the exit from the training track. The rider sits on his back, and he slows to a relaxed walk. Primula and I dodge some horse droppings and a few puddles as we return to her barn. It's hard for me to keep up with her brisk walk. She has the equivalent of the long stride Teddy has.

"I just want to check that Teddy's okay and then I'm sure you want to meet with Ginger Victor."

"Hector is his stable name."

"Thanks for telling me. We love him. He's such a kind guy."

"I was sorry he was claimed."

"The new owners have had their eye on him for some time. They hoped he'd be entered into a claiming race this season so I could put the claim in. Four others wanted him, so there had to be a draw."

"Wow. I should have realized there'd be a lot of interest in him."

We enter the barn and walk along the shedrow at a good pace.

"You probably don't know much about me, but I assure you he's in a good barn and he'll be well cared for—up to Linda's standards. Yes, she's known around the backstretch for being a great horse-woman. Here's Ginger Victor."

He nickers when he hears his name and pokes his head through the opening in the mesh stall door. I offer him a couple of the cut-up carrots I brought with me. Feeling his soft muzzle on my palm almost makes me want to cry. I don't like to see him in a strange barn with strange people. But he has his ears pricked and doesn't look stressed. I tell him he's the greatest and feed him a few mints.

"He'll be fine," Primula says. "We can talk in my office."

"Thanks." I pat Hector's neck and leave him to finish the rest of the carrots which I put on the clean straw just inside his door.

The rider has just returned to the barn, and he ducks his head as he and Teddy enter a stall piled with fresh, shiny, yellow straw. He jumps off the horse, tucks his crop into his belt behind his back, takes off the saddle and bridle, and dips the bit into the water bucket that awaits Teddy across from his stall door. Primula checks the horse's legs as the hotwalker clips on the lead-rein. The horse is led out to his bucket for a couple of sips of water, and then the cooling-off process starts.

"Good morning," I say to the hotwalker.

He smiles and returns the greeting. Teddy glances at me but seems unconcerned and walks off with his hotwalker. He doesn't look in the least bit tired to me.

"I do love that horse," I say, as Primula leads the way to her office.

"I'll tell you more about him in a minute."

Her office is one of several that are attached to the barns and encircle a concrete square that's used for bathing horses. I almost trip over a hose that lies on the rubber mat.

"Have a seat." Her office is full of paraphernalia. Her shedrow was so neat and organized that I didn't expect the chaos that surrounds us. "The mess is because I'm focused on the important things and because I moved offices just a couple of days ago. It was suggested I should move. They haven't been able to stop these animal rights people getting in and spray-painting my door. I was in one of the offices on the other side."

"They can easily find out where you are."

"I know. And security hasn't been able to discover how these people get in. Once they do, I hope they can stop it."

"Why are they targeting you?"

"Because they don't know anything about horses. You noticed that Teddy looks thin. To the unknowing eye, he looks malnourished, but, as you know, he's a young horse that's growing like a beanpole. I should send him back to the farm, but I want him to develop bone and tendon resiliency, and training is what does that best."

"Even older racehorses can appear thin. After all, they're athletes."

"A few are too thin, but that's my opinion and I know some can be hard to keep in condition. They burn too many calories. I'd offer you something to drink but I don't have anything plugged in yet and my shelves aren't up, and the cupboards haven't been moved yet."

"So, they spray-painted your office door because of Teddy?"

"I don't know exactly why." She crosses her long legs and studies her short nails. "You should talk with them. I'd love to find out. It was so hurtful because I take good care of my horses, and I can think of a couple of trainers I'd like to go after myself. I do have a theory, though. But I expect you want facts, not conjecture."

"Facts are great, but hunches and ideas are helpful too. What are your thoughts?"

"I can only think it's because Dirk Knightscourt was one of my owners."

"Really?"

"Are you surprised that he was one of my owners or because I think animal rights doesn't like him?"

"Perhaps both."

"I've not got much time, so I'll give you the short version." She pulls out her mobile, taps it and puts it back in her pocket. "Dirk is okay—I wouldn't have agreed to train his horses if he wasn't—but he got himself muddled up with Barton Woking. I assume you're investigating his murder and not the animal rights thing? But I could be wrong because you worked at the humane society, right?"

"Yes, I did. Actually, Dirk has asked me to investigate the abduction of his prize mare."

"Not Bella?" Primula leans forward with her hands on her thighs, her honey-coloured face contorted with what looks like pain.

"You know the mare?"

"I was her trainer. I recommended her to Dirk for breeding. This is confusing. Why would anyone take Bella? What do they think they can gain?"

"Ransom, perhaps, although as far as I know, Dirk hasn't been contacted."

"What if Barton's murder, Bella's abduction, and the animal rights group's vandalism are all linked?"

"It's difficult for me to see a connection, but I don't like coincidences."

"I think the animal rights group is behind all this." She sighs and crosses her arms.

"What would their motive be in taking Bella?"

"They're going after owners who had horses with Barton. Perhaps they thought stealing Bella would be an effective way of hurting Dirk. Or perhaps they thought he'd be convinced to get out of breeding racehorses. Or, as you said they may be after ransom—a whacky way of fundraising." She chuckles under her breath to suggest she thinks what's going on is preposterous.

"I'm not sure about any of that, but I'm doing my best to keep an open mind."

"Well, good luck. I do hope you get to the bottom of all this nonsense."

"Thanks. I'd like to find Bella sooner rather than later."

"Yep. That would be good. I must go—so much work to do." She taps my hand as she stands up. "Hector will be fine. We'll take good care of him. We love him already."

*   *   *

Linda's not in the barn. Neal says she's been so shaken up by her interview with police services and the fact that they have her car, that she's not come in. This is unheard of. She's such a diligent worker and passionate about the horses she cares for. I must follow up with her.

I visit with Fay, Basil, Rose, and Speed, and turn towards Neal's office with empty pockets. All the mints are gone.

Neal is so busy I decide not to intrude and return to the pickup.

Kelly sits on the driver's seat. I've been in the barn for a long time so she's grown anxious and isn't lying behind the front seats as she knows she should be when we're in the backstretch. I pat her as she dives behind me and out of sight.

My mobile vibrates and rings at the same time. I must have both notifications on. It increases the sense of urgency. Dirk's face fills the screen. He has his head tilted back and is peering down his nose with his eyes half-shut and his ginger eyebrows are arched as if he's surprised. He could afford to have a professional photo.

"Meg," he says before I can say anything. "You won't believe this, but Orlando's missing."

"How…"

"I know because he's not shown up this morning. He always shows up. And he lives down the road. I had someone check at his house. Not there. No answer on his phone. Gone."

31

"What..."

"What about his car? Well, it's still there. That's what's spooky about this. I'm freaking. And even Bobbie's feeling it."

"Do..."

"Yes, I do want you to look into it. I'll pay double. It must be something to do with Bella."

"Can..."

"You can come over any time. And it'd be a good idea to check out Orlando's place."

"Have..."

"I haven't told the police yet. I think you have to wait or something. Anyway, you can look after that. I'll leave it in your hands. Cheers."

And he's gone.

*   *   *

Melissa, Linda, and I sit at the kitchen table and play with our plates of lasagna and salad that Melissa produced from somewhere. None of us has an appetite.

"Thanks for taking me out of the house," Linda says.

"You've thanked us enough, Linda," I say.

"I love my mom, but I miss the horses and work. Sitting around listening to her going on about like taxes and teens and food prices drives me crazy."

"Why don't you go back to work?"

"Because they think I murdered Barton."

"No, they don't. Where were you when they think he was run over?"

"In the backstretch. I was in the barn feeding the horses. But no one saw me."

"You must have gone through security. I'll check it out and let you know. By the way, do you know who the animal rights people are who've been vandalizing some trainers' doors? I assume they're the same people who lay down in front of the starting gate the other day."

"I don't agree with that. It's not fair on the horses. But I get a lot of what they're saying."

"Like what?"

"You know, trainers who drug horses and hurt them."

"Very few trainers do that."

"But no horse should be treated bad. They should all get good care."

"I agree, but what those animal rights people do isn't helping."

Linda shrugs and moves a forkful of lasagna from one side of her plate to the other.

"I need to talk with them," I say.

"They wouldn't like murder anyone, if that's what you think."

"You know them then?"

"I've chatted with two of them."

"Would they abduct a horse to punish an owner they don't like?"

"You mean Bella. They don't know how to look after horses."

"How do you know?" asks Melissa.

"I just know." She shrugs. "I suppose I should get back to Mom."

"Give me the names of the two you talked with and then I'll drive you home."

"Ada Burkfield and Kenny Linseed."

"What's the organization called?" asks Melissa. "It's not that whacky Animal Equality and Freedom group, is it?"

"It's not whacky." Linda folds her arms and stares at her plate. "They care about animals."

"That's good," I say. "I look forward to chatting with them. Thanks, Linda, for the info."

On the drive back to her home, Linda's even quieter than usual.

Her round cheeks are flushed, and her chubby hands are clasped tightly in her lap.

"The horses must miss you. I know Neal does."

"Yeah."

"I'll do what I can to prove you weren't involved and as soon as possible."

She doesn't respond.

4

Dented Car

Dirk has phoned me twice this morning before I've even had a chance to have a shower. I can smell hay, manure, straw, and feed, mixed with my sweat. My hair and clothes need washing. While I like the familiar barn scents and I'll probably be visiting the track today, I need to look groomed—otherwise, I'll be upstaged by the clean, shiny, and well-cared-for horses.

Dirk didn't wait for me to do it and reported Orlando's mysterious disappearance to Vannersville Police Services. But he feels they haven't assigned it a high priority. He says he has other people doing the barn work, but he's growing more and more rankled about Bella's abduction and is sure the missing horse and the missing barn manager are linked to Barton's murder.

I don't know what to think.

Melissa left for the track and will meet the replacement veterinarian this morning. She hasn't said if she's decided about Edinburgh.

I'm doing my best to hide my emotions but the longer this indecision continues, the more challenging it is for me not to plead with her to stay—which would be entirely the wrong thing to do.

After my shower, Kelly, Jake, Cooper, and I wander into the kitchen. As I sip a welcome mug of tea, Kelly places her head on my lap and looks up at me with doleful brown eyes. Sometimes, I think she's more in tune with my emotions than I am. I pat her head and tell her everything will be okay, although I'm not sure it will be. She lies down beside me and snuggles against my chair. I open my laptop. My vision is blurred by tears I won't let escape. If I do, I'm certain I'll feel worse.

I take a deep, shuddery breath and start to do what William would have done well before this. I'm searching for information on Dirk, Bobbie, Barton, and Les Joseph, the groom.

Dirk has created his wealth from a chain of funeral homes. Knightscourt Funeral Services was established by his father and consisted of a single operation in Vannersville, but Dirk has expanded it to twelve operations in ten different communities in Ontario. It appears to be legitimate, but having a business that handles dead bodies has me seeing Dirk in a different light. But that's probably nonsense brought on by horror stories and my imagination.

It's harder to find anything about Bobbie. After some digging, I unearth an article in the local newspaper that mentions Annie Hart who worked at Knightscourt Funeral Home on Limetree Avenue in Vannersville. It states that Annie is Bobbie's sister, and she was charged with murder. The police alleged Annie shot and killed someone in Vannersville in the early hours of the morning. The police believed the incident to be drug-related. Rival gangs were fighting over territory. The victim was known to police services, and they believed he was part of the Pitbulls Gang. This was eight years ago. Annie's picture reminds me of Bobbie, but her hair and build are different.

After several minutes, I find a follow-up article. Annie was declared innocent. It could not be proved that she belonged to a rival gang or had anything to do with the drug trade. And there was insufficient evidence to prove her guilty of murder. However, she was found guilty of the illegal possession of a firearm and received a one-year sentence. There was no reference to why she carried a gun and what she was doing in Vannersville in the early hours of the morning.

I must ask Dirk about Annie.

I've run out of time to do any digging about Barton or Les Joseph since I'm due to meet with Ada Burkfield and Kenny Linseed at the Animal Equality and Freedom office. I'm pleasantly surprised that they've agreed to see me.

As Kelly, Jake, and I head towards the AEF office, I can't help wondering how Melissa's day's going with the replacement veterinarian at the track. The fact that Melissa is so torn about going to Edinburgh with Edwin has me contemplating whether I've made things more difficult for her. It must be obvious to her how much I love her and would miss her even though I'm not a demonstrative person and am skilled at hiding my emotions—she knows me too well. I want her to be happy, but every time I think of the house being empty again with no hope of her returning and her being so far away, my life loses its colour. Even though the horses, cats, and especially Kelly and Jake, will be good company, Melissa's vanishing would be like a stab into my heart. Interestingly, I didn't feel this way when Frank, Chuck, or even William, left me—and this realization exacerbates my anxiety.

But my determination to find out where Bella is will help me to keep going. Otherwise, I'll be in a deep funk.

I share Dirk's heartfelt concern about his best mare—especially whether she's being cared for. I hope I can find her soon.

The offices of Animal Equality and Freedom are above a café on the main street of Vannersville. I park the pickup on the opposite side of the road and look up at their windows. 'AEF' is painted in large black letters on both windows. Various pawprint and hoofprint stickers encircle each letter.

The street-level door is unlocked. I walk up a dimly lit, gritty set of stairs to the second floor. A dark green door is open, allowing a shaft of fluorescent light to highlight the grubby floorboards on the small landing. Another dark green door is labelled 'washroom'.

I knock on the door and a young woman leaps up from her kneeling position on the floor and almost runs towards me.

"You must be Meg Sheppard." We shake hands. "I'm Ada. Come in. I can offer you black coffee. We've no cream. We're vegans. You would have guessed that." She flicks her long mousey hair over her shoulders. Her grey leggings accentuate the skinniness of her legs.

"I'm fine, thanks," I say. "I've just had some tea."

"And I'm Kenny." His large feet almost appear to precede him. We shake hands and he draws three wooden chairs into a circle.

We all sit. "Thanks for meeting with me."

"You helped a lot of animals when you were with the humane society, so we'd be glad to help you," Ada says. "Oh, Brodie, what a good boy!" An old dog of very mixed breeding wanders over to Ada for a pat.

"I thought animal rights groups were opposed to the ownership of animals," I say. I smile at the dog.

"We are," Kenny says.

"Someone called us about a dog tied up outside a farmhouse. He had a small kennel and was surrounded by bare ground—you know—to the extent of his chain. See his left eye? It had been frozen at one point. He's blind in that eye. His nails were so long they went sideways. He was skin and bone. He'd sort of given up when we found him."

"So, we took him," Kenny says.

"You didn't talk to the owners?" I ask.

"Nope. No point." Kenny almost spits out the words. "Your humane society had been out at least three times, according to the neighbours. Didn't make a difference, did it?"

"Brodie's lucky you're willing to care for him," I say.

"We're caring for an animal those people shouldn't have had in the first place," Kenny says.

"What did you want to ask us?" Ada's piercing blue eyes sparkle as she smiles.

"I understand why you may have concerns about the horse racing industry," I say.

"We sure do," Kenny says.

"Kenny, let Meg ask us her questions."

"I just want to state up front that I do what I do because I'm passionate about horse welfare. I expect you've heard of Frank Sheppard, my late husband. He was instrumental in the introduction of tougher regulations for horse racing. This is my way of continuing his work to help protect racehorses from maltreatment."

"I haven't heard of him, and anyway, it's not enough," Kenny says. "Horse racing is cruel."

"Like any business, there are a few bad actors. And there are a few horses that suffer because of their greed and inhumanity. But most trainers, grooms, hotwalkers, farriers, veterinarians, owners, and so on, are involved in racing because they love horses."

"I can name lots of them who don't give a damn," Kenny says as he folds his arms.

"I'm not here to pick a fight."

"And what about Lasix? That should be banned," Kenny says.

"As I said, I don't want to get into a battle with you. But I will say that, while Lasix has been banned at some tracks in the States, most horse people will say that it helps the horse, rather than hurts it."

"What garbage."

39

"Meg, I'm interested to hear more," Ada says. Kenny sniffs and turns his head to look out the window.

"I'm not an expert, but I can give you a brief overview of my understanding. Under extreme exertion, like running a race, some capillaries in some horses' lungs burst. They say a horse has 'bled' and sometimes you can see blood coming out of the nostrils. This is very disturbing and even worse because horses can't breathe through their mouths. Administering Lasix before a race helps to prevent this—partly because it's a diuretic."

"See. That's my point. These horses shouldn't be raced in the first place."

"We're not going to get anywhere if we just argue," Ada says. "Meg, you'd better just ask us the questions."

"You've been accused of defacing office doors belonging to a few trainers in the backstretch at Vannersville Racetrack. What can you tell me about that?"

"Who says we did that?" Kenny asks. He leans back in the chair.

"That's not relevant. I'm interested to know why you did it, and perhaps more important to me, how you selected which trainers to target."

"We choose trainers we know are abusive," Ada says.

"Ada," Kenny says, "we agreed we wouldn't admit to that stuff."

"I'm not interested in the vandalism as such," I say. "I want to know what criteria you used to select the trainers."

"We looked at their winning percentages compared to the average, and then we checked with Linda Summit. She's your groom, isn't she?"

"She works for Neal Carvey—the trainer I use."

"She seems to have her ear to the ground. She cares about the horses."

"She doesn't care much," Kenny says as he shifts in his chair. "She's in that abominable business, isn't she?"

"Linda's been helpful," Ada says. "She told us about Barton Woking. He stood out. His winning percentage was over twenty-five percent. And two of his horses died on the track. One while training and another just after a race."

"They happened this year," Kenny adds.

"Was Primula Mokka on your list?"

"No. I don't think so."

"Why did you spray-paint her door then?"

"Was she on our list, Kenny?"

"Can't remember. We only had three names, but we should have painted all the doors."

"Well, you defaced her door."

"I don't care," Kenny says. "She shouldn't be making horses run. Why do you want to know about her anyway?"

"I expect Meg is investigating Barton Woking's murder," Ada says.

"No one has specifically asked me to do that."

"So, why are you harassing us?" Kenny asks.

"I'm collecting information. Do you know Dirk Knightscourt?"

"Why?" asks Kenny.

"Barton Woking trained some of his horses," Ada says. "We don't know Mr. Knightscourt, but his winning percentage is over thirty which is crazy. Linda says some of the owners don't know what's going on, so we decided to go after the abusive trainers, at least at first."

"What do you know about Dirk's mare, Bella?"

"A racehorse?" Ada asks.

"No, a broodmare pregnant to the leading Ontario stallion, Magical Black."

"Why are you asking?"

"She's missing."

"Not our problem," Kenny says.

"I just thought you may know something that could help me. I'm concerned for her welfare. And her groom, Orlando, has gone missing as well. Do you know him?"

"Why would we?" asks Kenny.

"If you do hear anything about Barton, Dirk, Bella, or Orlando, please get hold of me." I hand Ada my card. I don't see any point in wasting one on Kenny.

I walk back down the gritty stairs and as I open the door to the street, I hear raised voices resonating down the stairwell. I don't think those two are on the same page. I squint my eyes in the bright sunshine that's in stark contrast to the low lighting in the dingy stairwell I leave behind me.

Kelly and Jake are sitting on the two front seats, looking out for me. They greet me as if they thought I'd disappeared for good. It's a chaotic muddle of ears, tails, and noses as I squeeze into the truck.

"Okay. That's enough greeting. Into the back."

Thinking about disappearance brings something to the front of my thoughts that's been niggling me. Actually, a couple of things—both at Dirk Knightscourt's place.

The security system seemed to be state-of-the-art with excellent coverage. This raises two questions. Dirk said the entire system was down and the alarms didn't alert him to the failure. That's suspicious. The person who deactivated the system must have been familiar with it. Also, Orlando said the cameras had been unplugged. I can't believe that's all that had to be done to have the complete system fail, or that it could be that easy to unplug them. It doesn't make sense. It makes me wonder if Orlando played a role in Bella's abduction, but I can't think of a motive.

We're on our way back to the farm so the dogs can have a run in the field before we head out for the Knightscourt mansion. But, since we're close to the racetrack I decide to check with the security office to find out when Linda entered the backstretch. I hate to see

Linda so stressed. Being interviewed by police services was difficult for her. I'd like to be able to prove she wasn't at the scene when Barton was hit. Besides, my horses are missing her special attention to their needs.

I tell the dogs I won't be long. I hope they believe me. The security officer on duty is keen to help and adds that it's the second time he's been asked for the same information. Vannersville Police Services wanted to know the names of all the people who entered the backstretch between three and four in the morning.

"Do you want the same thing?" he asks. "It's no secret. I can give it to you. I printed the report off for them. I can do it again and quicker this time." He chuckled. I suppose he doesn't recognize the seriousness of the situation.

"That would be great. Thanks."

He is efficient with the mouse and soon has the report printed off. I thank him and scan it as I walk back to the pickup. There are a few names that catch my eye. Les Joseph and Linda Summit arrived at almost the same time and Primula Mokka entered the backstretch at close to four.

The dogs are behind the front seats. They know we're at the racetrack and they need to keep out of sight.

* * *

Neal phones as I'm walking in the back field. The sun's hiding behind a silver cloud and the air has a sudden nip to it. The dogs enjoy the scents as they tear backwards and forwards from one side of the field to the other. The grass has grown quickly this year, and I probably could have got a second cut of hay.

"Hi, Neal. Are the horses okay?"

"They're good. But I expect they miss Linda. I sure do. I don't see why she can't come in."

"I'll have a chat with her."

"I've been thinking about this Barton business. You know what it's like here. Rumours and gossip. Well, I know you like to hear what's going around."

"I do. Sometimes there are grains of truth which can be helpful."

"The barn help has it in for the vet that treated Barton's horses. They even suggest he was more of a problem than the trainer was. I don't believe it, but I thought you'd like to have a chat with him. Dr. Greg Dudley. And someone who's got a lot to say about the whole thing is a farrier, Farley Smead, who cared for Barton's horses. They say he's mouthing off to anyone who'll listen."

"I'll follow up. Thanks for the tips."

"They may go nowhere."

"I'm sure I'll learn something."

During a quick snack, I think of Melissa and hope her day is going well, but I'm sure it won't be easy meeting the vet who's replacing Edwin. And I wonder if Edwin's there too, and if he is, whether she'll have a chat with him or not.

Detective Valeska's face appears on my mobile. I haven't talked to her for a long time.

"Hello, Detective."

"Hi, Meg. I expect you're already on it, but I'm concerned about this Barton Woking business. I'm not convinced he was murdered. I'm keeping an open mind. Based on the evidence to date, my analysis suggests hit-and-run rather than premeditated murder."

"Oh."

"Preliminary autopsy results reveal that his blood-alcohol level was 0.12 percent. In other words, he was drunk. He'd been dropped off by a woman and she says he was staggering. She's a server in a casino. She works behind the bar most of the time. We haven't determined what her relationship was with the deceased or why she was with him at the time of the hit-and-run."

"Why are you telling me all this?"

"Good question. I need your help. I'm sure you know we've seized Linda Summit's car."

"Yes."

"I'm sure you won't like this news, but forensics found DNA on the car around the dent in the passenger door, and it matches Barton Woking's. That car was the one that hit him."

"Oh, no. Oh, goodness. I can't believe it."

"Don't get too upset. At least, not yet. I questioned Linda myself and I don't believe she hit Barton. Her body language, how she answered the questions, and other indicators, just didn't convince me she was behind the wheel."

"So, you want me to see if I can find out who was?"

"Exactly. My instincts tell me she's protecting someone."

"That sounds odd. I can't think who would be driving her car."

"Well, start thinking. I don't like charging innocent people, not even for the stats, and not even to further my career. I'm not that kind of cop."

"I'll do what I can. I appreciate this."

She ends the call, and I hold my head in my hands with my nose nearly touching the table. This isn't an easy assignment. If Linda is willing to face charges for a hit-and-run that she didn't commit, then she must feel passionately about protecting the person who was driving.

And, obviously, Linda lied to me about how her car got dented. And this doesn't bode well for me being able to get to the truth.

Cooper jumps up onto the table and nudges my hand. He snaps me out of my gloom. I pick him up and his fur tickles my nose as his body vibrates with purrs.

"You're not allowed on the table." I stroke him and put him on the floor. The dogs are both looking up at me with flattened ears and slowly wagging tails. "It's okay." But I don't think I've convinced them. They sense my angst.

Linda doesn't answer my call, so I leave a message.

Dirk rings me and says he needs to see me urgently. He won't elaborate.

5

Shot in the Rain

We leave the quiet farm behind us and head towards the Knightscourt mansion. The gates open as we approach. Grey clouds have taken over the sky, so the expansive estate looks more sombre. Even the peacocks are hiding from us, but the deer are grazing on both sides of the long driveway. They don't raise their heads and merely continue to flick their short tails in a rather vain attempt to rid themselves of pesky flies.

Dirk is waiting on the steps and leads me into the room with the ostentatious chandelier.

"Thanks for coming so quick."

"Has something happened?" I'm taken aback that he hasn't interrupted me.

"You could say that. You'll need to sit down."

I sit on a chair that must be an antique. The seat is likely filled with horsehair and the wooden back is straight and unyielding. I can't get comfortable.

"That chair's the worst one in the place but Bobbie likes it. Sit in that one." He points to a wingback that's at least got some soft padding. I change seats. "The cops have been here, asking me questions."

"About…"

"Yeah, about Orlando. Something horrible's happened."

"He's…"

"Been found, yeah. But dead."

"Was…"

"Definite murder."

"Where…"

"This is the most awful part. He was found by our funeral director in the main Vannersville funeral home, the one in town. He called the cops. The right thing to do, of course. He knew it wasn't one of our bodies."

"How…"

"I don't know. The cops will check him out. Our funeral director thought he was shot in the head, but he could be wrong. He hasn't dealt with murder victims before. He's shaken up pretty bad. I said he could have a few days off."

"You're…"

"Yeah. I'm shaken up too."

"Why…"

"I don't know why anyone would want to kill Orlando. And now I'm in the cops' crosshairs. They think I could have done him in. Why would I do that? He was the best stable manager I've ever had. And where's Bella? If he's dead, what are the chances of her being okay?" He bursts into body-wracking sobs as he hunches over. I don't know what to do. I'm saved by the elderly man who turns up carrying a tray with the familiar glistening silver teapot.

Dirk straightens up, blows his nose like a foghorn into a linen handkerchief that appeared like magic, and thanks the man for the tea.

"Tell Bobbie to come in here," Dirk says. The man nods his head and leaves.

"I'm so sorry. What…"

"I want you to find out what happened to Orlando and for god's sake find out where Bella is. Money's no object. This is urgent. I'm desperate. Where's Bobbie?" The elderly man hovers in the doorway and shakes his head. "She's not in the house?" The man shakes his head again and leaves. "She can't have gone missing too. I must have died and gone to hell." He blows his nose again. His face is flushed and the sweat on his forehead sparkles in the glow of the chandelier.

"She could have just…"

"She never goes out."

"Why?"

"I can't talk about it now. I'll tell you another time. Just focus on Bella and find out who did Orlando in. I'll have them skinned alive."

"I wouldn't…"

"I know. It's just my rage speaking. Fury is eating at my insides. Pour some tea. Maybe I'll try to drink some. Put three lumps in mine. Sugar's supposed to help with shock."

I want to ask questions about Bobbie and Annie, but this is not the time. As I pick up my teacup, my hand trembles and tiny ripples disturb the tea. It's delicious but not as satisfying as it would be in more pleasant circumstances.

"Finding Bella is even more urgent now. I'm sure she's in danger. You need to follow up with the people who knew she was here."

"Yes. I was…"

"You were going to ask me. Barton knew because he's been here a few times. I use Greg Dudley, Barton's vet. So, he's been here several times. Les Joseph is, was, one of Barton's grooms. He did some exercise riding for me. And, in the winter months, I've used Farley Smead, Barton's farrier. That way, when the racehorses go back to the track, they've been trimmed the way Barton wants. They're all part of Barton's team. Not good, under the circumstances. And, when I look back, I reckon I made a mistake using them. Anyway, I can't think of anyone else other than friends, and none of them have shown much interest in the horses."

*   *   *

Melissa's car is back at the farm, and I hesitate before I open the backdoor. My hand is cold as it touches the handle, but my heart-beats are rapid. There are conflicting thoughts and hopes dancing in my mind. I want Melissa to be happy, but I'd love her to stay. I want Melissa to marry the right man. Is Edwin the one? I'm not sure anymore. The dogs whine in unison, puzzled as to why I haven't opened the door. I turn the handle, and we all burst into the kitchen together, but Melissa isn't here. Perhaps she's packing.

The dogs lap up water with gusto. I spent too long at the Knightscourt place and didn't have water with me. Melissa runs down the stairs.

"Oh, Meg, I'm so glad you're home." She hugs me. The citrus scent that often surrounds her almost brings tears to my eyes. I will miss everything about her.

"What's the news?"

"It's just terrible."

"You've been crying. Is it about Edwin?" Her eyes look as if they've been outlined with red liner.

"No, I'll get to that later. Russon…"

"Who's Russon?"

"Oh, sorry. Dr. Russon Scully is Edwin's replacement."

"Okay. What's he like?"

"Meg, this is serious. Russon was asked to rush to Primula Mokka's barn. She had two horses in distress."

"Hector!"

"No, not Hector. Let me tell you. Russon asked me to go with him. Primula pointed out nasal discharge and an odd odour. Both horses had trouble breathing. Russon said their lungs were clear. I didn't have much confidence in him. He's younger than Edwin and jokes around. But he checked the horses over thoroughly including shining his mobile phone's flashlight up the nostrils of one of the horses. And then he yelled 'eureka', almost spooking the horse as well as Primula and me. He asked me to hurry to his vehicle and get the forceps. It took me a minute. I'm not familiar with all his stuff, but he's well organized."

"Melissa, please get to the point."

"This is it. He put the forceps up a nostril and pulled out a piece of sponge."

"Someone must have put it there."

"Exactly. Some horrible, cruel person."

"Why?"

"Both horses had the same thing. Primula said that they ran out of steam during their gallop this morning, so the riders backed off. They were out together. She thought they must have been drugged or poisoned. But Russon didn't think so. He said afterwards that he remembered reading a case of sabotage by a rival trainer who inserted a sponge in one nostril before the horse in his rival's barn was to compete against his horse in a stakes race."

"Wow. That's terrible. Are the horses okay?"

"Russon says they'll be fine.

"Does Primula suspect anyone?"

"She's in shock. She can't think who'd have been able to get into the stalls without being seen by someone. It must have happened last night. Honestly, the security at night isn't enough."

"It's lacking, that's for sure. The animal rights people seem to be able to get in without a problem and spray-paint wherever they please."

"Oh, you don't think it's them, do you? That would be really stupid."

"I have no idea."

"Since the only cameras are in the shedrow, Russon suggested Primula install security cameras in the stalls which could be monitored from her mobile. She said she'd think about it. She looked ill."

"You had a difficult day, then."

'Well, I did, and I didn't. I like Russon a lot, which makes it even harder to come to a decision. We should have some food. I bet you haven't eaten all day."

"Have you?"

"I had a yoghurt."

"Let's make something to eat and you can tell me more about Russon."

As she tells me about the vet, who I gather is tall and skinny with dark curly hair and likes to laugh a lot, her eyes sparkle. She tells me he loves to learn and seems to have an endless supply of energy—perhaps that explains his slim build. I didn't ask her about Edwin. I'm sure she'll tell me when she knows what she wants to do.

"You're going to find out who did that awful thing to Primula's horses, aren't you?" she asks, as she stirs tangy spaghetti sauce that's warming in a saucepan.

"I'll add it to my list."

"Meg, I hope you're going to give this top priority. It's horse abuse. It's cruelty to animals." She turns around and looks at me with wide eyes.

"Yes, but I want to find Bella. I'm concerned. She's a pregnant mare and her devoted groom has been murdered."

"What?" her voice is almost a scream, and she drops the spoon she was using to stir the sauce onto the floor.

"I'm sorry. I should have told you earlier. I thought everyone knew. It's been on the news."

"I haven't been listening to the news or checking the app. I've been up to my eyes helping Russon." She picks up the spoon and chucks it into the sink. I get busy clearing up the mess with help from Jake.

"Orlando was found in one of Dirk's funeral homes. The funeral director there reckoned he'd been shot in the head. So, that puts a big hole in my theory that Orlando arranged for Bella to be abducted and left shortly afterwards to take care of her."

"None of this makes sense to me. And where does Barton's murder fit in? This sauce is splashing all over the place."

"It's too hot. Is the pasta done?" I spoon a couple of pieces of penne out of the bubbling water and pronounce it ready. "Let's eat."

As we nibble on our simple meal, I bring Melissa up to date about my meeting with the animal rights people and Detective Valeska's curious call about Linda.

"That's odd that she'd tell you she doesn't believe Linda was driving her own car," Melissa says as she pushes her half-empty plate to one side. "I think it's weird."

"I'm going to chat with Linda and see if I can get more information out of her—the truth this time. I can't believe she lied to me about the dent. I checked with security, and she entered the backstretch at approximately the same time the incident with Barton occurred."

"I heard that some woman, perhaps his girlfriend, often drops Barton off in the road that leads to the security gates. Don't you think you should talk to her?"

"Perhaps. I doubt she would have been able to identify who was driving Linda's car."

"Yeah. She was probably drunk."

"Who knows."

* * *

Linda has texted back, but she has an appointment this morning. I'm beginning to wonder if she's avoiding me. It must be a busy day for everyone because I've not been able to connect with any of the people I hoped to talk with. So, the dogs and I are headed to the Animal Equality and Freedom offices. I chose not to alert them of my pending visit.

The street-level door has a laminated poster stapled to it. It's a black-and-white image of a dead horse with 'Horse Racing Kills' blazoned across it in bold red letters. Another copy of the poster is fastened to the dark green door of their office. The door is ajar. Kenny and Ada are sitting in front of a laptop while The Tragically Hip's music dances around them. Ada smiles and picks up her mobile. The music stops abruptly.

"You've come to complain about the poster," Kenny says. He leans back in his chair and folds his arms. He stares at me.

"No. I've come to ask you about a serious incident that occurred at the racetrack yesterday." Brodie ambles over to me, looking for attention, and enjoys being stroked.

"I didn't go anywhere near the racetrack yesterday," Kenny says.

"Neither did I," Ada says. "What happened?" She puts a chair in front of me. I sit down.

"Are you accusing us of something?" Kenny asks as he peers along his nose at me.

"I hoped you might have seen something. It probably occurred during the night before last in Primula Mokka's barn."

"Were any horses hurt?" asks Ada.

"Yes."

"Don't tell me. More dead horses. See our poster?" Kenny asks.

"I see it." I lock my eyes on Kenny's. "The two horses I'm concerned about could have died if they'd been raced."

"What did I tell you? Racing kills."

"Oh, no," Ada says as she twists strands of her long, mousey hair. Her intense blue eyes seem to be searching mine for answers.

"Do you always work together?"

"What's that to you?" Kenny asks.

"Yeah, we do," Ada says. "And we have members and volunteers who come out to our demonstrations and assist with other stuff, like graphic design and website updates."

"I don't think you can help me, but I'll let you know what happened just in case you hear something or remember seeing someone."

"I told you. We weren't at the track." Kenny's voice is unnecessarily loud. It contrasts with Ada's soft-spoken, squeaky tone.

"I want to know what happened," Ada says.

"Two of Primula Mokka's horses became distressed when they were exercised yesterday morning. Primula called the vet when they got back to the barn. Dr. Russon Scully examined their lungs, and even though they were both having trouble breathing, their lungs were clear. He checked their nostrils and found a piece of sponge shoved up one nostril in each horse."

"Wow. That sounds awful," Ada says.

"It could have been fatal because horses can only breathe through their noses."

"Will they be okay?"

"Dr. Scully believes so, but it's shaken all of us up because it's a blatant case of animal cruelty. I thought you'd want to know but, as I said, I'd like you to tell me anything you think could help me find out who did this inhumane thing."

"We will," Ada says. "That's just awful."

Kenny's body language disturbs me. He lunges forward and puts his hands on his knees, his elbows bent, almost as if he's about to pounce on me.

"Why do you think we would know anything? You don't like us because we're threatening your horse racing business. We're going to shut it down. That's our mission. So, get used to it. The horses will be free." His spit doesn't reach me, thank goodness.

"I can see there's no point in arguing with you." I stand and start walking towards the door and raise my voice. "I just hope you're not harming innocent horses in your attempts to destroy the horse racing industry. There's a tragic irony in that."

It's a relief to leave them, but I can't ignore the possibility that Kenny has become so passionate and determined to put an end to horse racing that he's willing to take any action to make it happen, including abusing the animals he's supposedly wanting to protect. But, if so, I don't believe Ada is on board with Kenny's plan.

As I step over a puddle on the sidewalk my mobile vibrates. Dirk's face pops up.

"Hello, Dirk."

"It's Bobbie, not Dirk. Can I talk with you? It's urgent."

"I could be there in about thirty minutes."

Bobbie tells me to come to the side entrance. I didn't know there was one. It's on an unpaved road that runs at right angles to the one that's adorned with the imposing gates to the Knightscourt estate. But Kelly and Jake need a walk first, so I park by the racetrack, and we follow the trail adjacent to the training track. I have Jake on a leash, but Kelly doesn't need one.

The predicted drizzle starts as we exit the pickup. My light rain jacket has a hood, and I have my head bent down when a bicycle skids to a halt a couple of feet ahead of me and I hear a yelp. Small stones scatter and a couple settle on my shoes.

"Meg, I'm sorry. Is your dog okay?"

Kelly leans against my legs. She stares at the cyclist. Jake has his hackles up as he growls. I check Kelly over and she seems fine, but Jake continues to rumble his disapproval.

"She's okay." I stroke her silky head. "I was hoping to talk with you."

"You were?" Les's voice quivers slightly.

"You were driving Linda's car the morning Barton was killed, right?"

"How come you think that?"

"Because you and Linda went through the security gate at about the same time which was shortly after when Barton was fatally injured. The police have that information. They asked security for it. So, they'll interview the security guy who was on duty, and he'll remember the two of you were in Linda's car and you were driving. The security officers know Linda and her car well. Linda knows everyone. Jake, you can stop growling now." I pat him on the head and he and Kelly sit.

"I'm in deep shit."

"Tell me about it as we walk. I hope you have a few minutes."

"I'm finished for the day. I was in at four."

He wheels his bike—which Kelly keeps well clear of—and Jake and I walk alongside.

"Les, tell me what happened."

"I'm black, so no one's going to believe me, are they? Especially the cops."

"That attitude's not going to get you anywhere. It's best to tell the truth. I'll do what I can to help—assuming you didn't kill Barton. But the car has a dent in it and forensics have evidence that proves Linda's car collided with Barton."

"I know. That's what's killing me. Linda's going through hell 'cause of me."

"What happened?"

"It's dark at four in the morning and that road into the track isn't lit proper. Out of the shadows, I see two people just ahead at the side of the road. It happened quick, but I could make out it was a man near the road. It might have been a woman behind him. He was reeling and staggering, but I didn't see much. Next thing it's like he's jumped into the side of the car. I braked so hard I was expecting the airbags, but they didn't inflate. Linda screamed. She told me she saw the woman push him. She yelled at me to get into the track like yesterday."

"It would have been better if you'd stayed at the scene."

"You would say that. You're white. The cops would have taken me away and beaten me up and charged me with all the shit they can think of. Yeah, I know—it's going to happen anyway."

"Do you have any idea who the woman is?"

"She's got to be his current fling. They go to this private casino and get wasted about three nights a week. If he's bad, he has the sense to shut himself in his office in the morning and have a couple of strong black coffees—you can smell it in the shedrow."

"Does she drive him to the track?"

"They get the bus."

"Do you know anything about their relationship?"

"No. But I guess Barton's farrier, Farley, might."

"Oh. I've been meaning to speak with him. Farley Smedley, right?"

"That's him".

"This is a great help. You're going to be questioned by the police. It's going to happen. Keep calm and don't lie."

"Yeah, right." He flings his leg over the bike and takes off as if his wheels have superpowers.

I'm behind schedule. We jog back to the pickup and arrive at the side entrance to the Knightscourt estate about five minutes late. Ominous black clouds hover overhead as we pull up to the gates which are less imposing than the ostentatious ones across the front entrance, but there is a more obvious presence of security. Cameras point at me and there is one small building on each side of the gateway. But no one's around. The gates remain closed. I get out of the truck in case I've missed a button I should have pressed or can find someone in one of the wooden huts that resemble large sentry boxes. The dogs jump out, barking.

"What are you doing?" The dogs know they should stay in the truck unless I tell them it's okay to get out. But Kelly and Jake couldn't be any clearer—they want us to leave. They're barking at me, not anyone else. The ominous clouds decide this is the time to dump torrents of rain which drench us within seconds. We all scramble back into the pickup. My jacket is soaked. The dogs shake their wet coats at the same time and the spray seems to fill the cab. The windows steam up and I can't see out.

As I message Bobbie, a curious stinging sensation grows. My upper arm begins to hurt, and I have trouble sending Bobbie my note. My wet jacket sleeve has an odd dark streak running down to my wrist. Blood, mixed with rain, appears on the back of my hand. I stare at it in disbelief. Something's obviously wrong. Instead of touching 'send', I call Detective Valeska.

6

Pending New Arrivals

Melissa almost falls through the backdoor. Dripping water onto the mat, she welcomes the damp dogs with pats and rubs. She takes off her soaked jacket and carries it into the laundry room.

"I hope your day's been better than mine," she says as she sits down at the kitchen table. "Meg, what's wrong? What's happened to you?"

"I was shot, but it's just a graze."

"What?" she screams. "Who? Why? Where?"

"At the Knightscourt place. At a side entrance. Bobbie texted me and asked me to meet her, but it couldn't have been her. She says someone must have Dirk's phone."

"Never mind that. Have you been to the hospital?"

"No. An ambulance came at about the same time as Detective Valeska arrived. They cleaned it up and put stuff on it and a dressing. I was surprised the Detective came herself. I think she was concerned. Sort of nice, really."

"You'll need to get it checked. How deep is it?"

"I told you. It's just a graze—my upper arm. Although it's my right, it's not a problem. I can use it fine."

"Well, I think it's a problem—a big one. Why were you shot?"

"I don't know, and I don't care."

"What do you mean?"

"I'm not doing any more of this sleuthing stuff. The dogs could have been killed."

"*You* could have been killed."

"Anyway, I'm not doing this anymore. I've had enough."

"Let's talk about it later."

"Maybe. Tell me about your bad day. Are things not going well with Dr. Scully?"

"Things are going fine with Russon. It's that woman who claims to be my father's granddaughter. I'm not sure she is. She says she went on that ancestry site, but I can't find a match to anyone other than you and our mother. So, where she gets the idea we're related, I don't know."

"Can you make some hot chocolate? I don't feel like food but need something. I'm a bit shaky. I might have forgotten to eat today."

"Honestly, Meg. You need to eat."

"I've fed the dogs."

"The animals come first!"

As I watch Melissa fill the kettle, I can't help wondering how I'll manage without her. I have lived alone for several years in my life, but now we've found each other I don't want her to leave. But I must not interfere. I want her to be happy more than anything, and if that means going to Edinburgh with Edwin, I must accept that.

"So, what's that woman's plans?" I ask.

"I told you before. She's due to arrive the day after tomorrow."

"Oh."

"It's okay. I'll deal with her. She's going to have to come to the track with me. You've probably forgotten her name. Candice Burley. And she sounds stuck up. Awful. I think she's going to be a pain."

"Well, I won't be doing anything, other than looking after our animals and visiting my horses at the track, so I can help out. I don't mind. Really."

"You should rest. You've had an awful shock."

"I didn't realize I'd been shot until I was back in the truck. The dogs and the rain made me jump in. They knew something was wrong. I don't know if it was the rain that got them upset or they knew a bad guy was around."

"They're smart. They could probably sense something. Didn't you hear the gunshot?"

"No, I don't know why, but the dogs were barking, and the rain was torrential."

"Guns make a lot of noise."

"Tell me about your day."

We sip hot chocolate as Melissa tells me about Russon and the horses they treated during a busy, wet day in the backstretch.

* * *

The rain stopped in the early hours and the wet grass sparkles in the sunshine of a new day. I lead Eagle out to the paddock. Kelly and Jake run ahead. They've caught the scent of something exciting and send droplets into the air around them that shimmer like jewels. Eagle puts his head down as soon as I release the clasp on the lead-rein. He tears at the grass with gusto, and I can't help but smile inside. I turn to fetch Bullet. My mobile rings. I ignore it.

Bullet does the same thing as Eagle. They munch side by side and the noise of their ripping and chewing drowns out nearly all the other sounds around me. My mobile rings again. I pull it out of my back pocket. It's Detective Valeska. I suppose I should let her know my investigating days are over. For good.

"Meg, I need your help."

"But."

"No buts. This is serious. We got a warrant to search the Knightscourt place. As we've suspected for a while, we found evidence of an illegal casino in the basement of the south wing. We're onto that, but I'm more concerned about Dirk and Bobbie Knightscourt. No sign of them. All we found was an ancient male staff person in the house and one frightened barn worker. We think there's a link to the missing horse and Orlando's murder."

"Oh."

"I want the staff to leave and the horses to be moved to another property."

"Oh."

"The staff are so upset they're not much help. Can you organize for the horses to go somewhere, like yesterday?"

"How many?"

"Five. They're young. I think the barn worker said they're yearlings, whatever that means."

"What about the peacocks and the deer?"

"They'll just have to cope. Let me know when you've found somewhere for the horses."

"By the way," but she ends the call before I can tell her my decision.

I watch my two horses graze, and it comes to me that there could be a silver lining to the Detective's request. I phone Linda and leave a message. I know she'll return the call.

"Melissa! I thought you'd left for the track ages ago."

"That woman comes tomorrow, so I thought I should get some groceries and do a bit of cleaning even though she's not staying here. I've got to fetch her from the airport tomorrow evening. What are you doing today? You're still in your barn clothes."

"I haven't decided."

"You should talk to Barton's vet and farrier, you know—Greg Dudley and Farley Smead."

"Mm."

"Seriously, what are you doing today? I don't like thinking there could be a murderer working at the track. What's your plan? Do you need my help?"

"I don't have a plan. I told you—I'm not doing this sleuthing stuff anymore."

"I thought you were joking. You could at least find Bella. That poor mare could be suffering."

"I've been shot and now Dirk and Bobbie are missing. The old butler, or whatever he is, and a barn help were still there when the police searched the place. They found an illegal casino which they had had strong suspicions about, but no clue as to who shot me. Detective Valeska says the security system was offline—cameras not working. Again."

"What about the horses? We saw some horses there. Are they gone too?"

"I was coming to that. Detective Valeska has asked me to find somewhere for Dirk's five yearlings."

"They could come here."

"Maybe. I have a call into Linda. I'm hoping she'll help look after them, and that way I'll get more information out of her."

"I thought you'd hung up your badge, figuratively speaking of course."

"I have, but I don't want Linda to be wrongly accused. I owe her a lot. She's so good to my horses. And I want her back at the track. I've got four horses there that will be missing her terribly. And Neal needs her."

"I don't understand why you're quitting."

"I got shot. Honestly, Melissa. I don't like being shot at, and I don't like the dogs being put at so much risk."

"That hasn't stopped you before. I only sort of understand. It's not like you to quit."

"Stop using that word. It makes me feel like a loser."

"By the way, talking of losers, I had dinner with William yesterday evening."

"So, that's where you went off to."

"I didn't want to tell you because I wasn't sure how you'd feel, and I didn't know how it would go. Well, it was pathetic."

"What do you mean?"

"I mean William was pathetic."

"Oh."

"Anyway, he invited me, and I nearly didn't accept. But I suppose my curiosity got the better of me."

"So, how was it?"

"Bad. He's split up with Ramona. He said he was miserable from the start. And because it got awkward, he had to dismiss her and pay her a big settlement to avoid a lawsuit. I don't know how these things work."

"Who's his new assistant?"

"He says he's searching."

"Where's he living? He's rented out his apartment above his office, right?"

"He can't get in there for a few weeks. He's in the Vannersville Inn and not happy about what it's costing. Do you miss him?"

"Of course I do, but if you're going to ask me if I want him back here, I realize I don't."

"I'm surprised, I think."

"Well, don't be."

"He wants Jake, by the way."

"In a hotel room?"

"No, when he's back in his apartment."

"The answer is no. That would not be fair to Jake, or Kelly. She'd miss her BFF."

"I thought you'd say that, and I told him you would. He's so miserable. Can't he stay here for a bit?"

"No."

"I hope you change your mind, but I've got to get going. I have a lot to do before this woman arrives tomorrow." She looks straight into my eyes with an imploring gaze. "I wish you'd find Bella as well as looking after those horses."

Melissa pats both dogs who wag their tails, picks up her small bag and leaves. Cooper leaps up onto the table and I can't be bothered to put him back onto the floor. He's been taking liberties recently. He weaves under my arms—which are helping to hold my heavy head up. The dogs sit on either side of my chair, and I can feel their eyes staring at me. I sigh and lay my head on my crossed arms. I suppose this is what it's like to feel sorry for oneself. Fortunately, I'm saved from further self-pity because my mobile rings and Linda's round face looks at me.

"Linda. Thanks for calling back."

"You want help with some horses?"

"I do. It's a long story. I'll explain later. There are five yearlings at the Knightscourt place that need somewhere to go and to be looked after until some things are sorted out. Do you know of somewhere?"

"Don't you have space at your place?"

"Yes, but I don't have the help I'd need to look after a total of seven horses."

"I'll help. I'm going crazy. I need like something to do."

"Okay. Let's arrange transportation." This worked even better than I'd hoped. I didn't have to do any convincing.

Despite the good news, I still can't mobilize my body. It's as if I have lead weights scattered throughout my arms and legs. My neck refuses to hold my head up—gravity must have doubled its effect.

Kelly whines. I can't remember the last time she whined. Jake sits next to my chair and pushes against me as if to tell me I should do something. Cooper is up on the table again, licking my hair. The three of them convince me, and perhaps shame me, into getting a grip and making a move.

"Okay. We'll go for a hike." Kelly knows that word and runs to the backdoor wagging her tail. Jake looks a bit confused but trusts that whatever I said means good news. Cooper jumps down from the table and tears out of the kitchen as if catapulted. He's acting silly.

A few minutes later the three of us are in the pickup making our way to the trail that's nearest to us. It's where Kelly and I were attacked by a vicious dog but that was a long time ago. Walking helps me to think, and being out in nature has a calming effect. Orange and red-tinted leaves rustle overhead, and pine needles float down to join others that cushion the path. Chickadees chirp their cheerful songs as they flit among the scrubby undergrowth.

Kelly and Jake run and sniff and run and sniff. Their joy and vivacity send tingles down my spine. It gives me so much pleasure to see their happiness and love of life.

As we reach the end of the trail and turn to head back to the truck, my mind is clearer and lighter. Melissa is right. I need to find Bella. But I also want to prove Linda's innocence. This is going to be tough and could put me in danger because Barton's murder must be linked to what's going on with Dirk and Bobbie, and probably to Orlando's murder as well.

I meant to leave my mobile in the truck. It's ringing and I can't ignore it in case it's Linda. It's Neal.

"You haven't forgotten that Speed's racing this afternoon, have you?"

"Oh dear. I had. I'm sorry. I just have too much going on. I'll be there. What time is the race?"

Neal gives me the details. It's a mile and a quarter, which is long, but Speed is an older racehorse and he's not a fan of sprints. This could be his last year at the racetrack. He's one of two racehorses Frank owned. The other is Rose.

I need to smarten up. I don't know what's the matter with me. Well, I do know really. Gabriel left, William is out of my life, and Melissa will likely be going to Edinburgh soon. My world is falling apart. And then someone shot me. But surely I can summon some of my usual resilience. No one else is going to prove Linda's innocence and no one is trying to find Bella, as far as I know.

My mobile rings again. Melissa.

"Meg, I'm not happy."

"Oh dear."

"This Candice woman. There's something not right."

"What do you mean?"

"I don't think she's related to me at all. Can you do some more digging? I haven't got time. And if you could come to the airport with me tomorrow, that would be great."

"Okay."

"Thanks. I'll pick up something for us to eat before we have to leave to meet her."

"Dogs, we have work to do." They look up at me and wag their tails.

* * *

I didn't want to leave the dogs at home, so they're in the truck in the parking lot. I'm walking towards the guardrail by the race-track. I arrive just in time. The post parade is starting. I lean on the rail and listen to the announcer. Scarfin is Speed's racing

69

name. It's an anagram of Francis, Frank's name, and Rose's racing name is Alusio, an anagram of Louisa—the name of Frank's late, beloved first wife. Speed looks beautiful, but I suppose I believe all horses are beautiful. Although he's not happy about being ponied.

Someone taps on my shoulder.

"Sorry I made you jump. It's me, Dirk. I knew you'd be here to see Scarfin's race, but it's taken me a while to find you." He's wearing sunglasses that I can see my frowning face reflected in, and a brown cowboy hat.

"Are you and…"

"We're okay. We're shaken up and out of our minds with worry about the horses. Have you found Bella yet?"

"No, but…"

"You will. I sure hope you do. I don't know if anyone's still at that place—that estate, I mean. What about the yearlings? Do you know?"

"They're…"

"Going to your place? That would be the best. Find Bella."

"Where…"

"Don't tell a soul. We're at the Vannersville Inn under the name of Collingwood. Bobbie doesn't know I've come here. I'd better get back. Oh, and here's my new number. My phone's gone missing." He hands me a business card with a handwritten number on the back, pats me on the shoulder again, and walks away. If he's trying to go unnoticed, he's not going the right way about it. Everyone else is making their way towards the track, not away from it.

Neal appears beside me and lifts his enormous binoculars to watch the horses being loaded into the gate. Speed is a pro, and he walks in with no issues. The sky is cloudy, so he won't have to face a dazzling sun as he turns for home. The gates open and the horses spring into action. But Speed is trailing.

"I think he got bumped," Neal says. "He didn't get a good start."

Speed is one length behind the pack and doesn't appear to be making much of an effort to catch up. But perhaps the jockey is biding his time. It's a long race.

"Is something wrong?" I ask. The jockey doesn't seem to be asking Speed to pick up the pace.

"I don't know. The jockey hasn't pulled him up, so he can't be injured. We'll be able to see better when we watch the replay, especially the head-on view of the start."

Speed finishes last. Neal walks out onto the track to meet the jockey as he dismounts. They walk back towards the grandstand and then the jockey dashes off to prepare for the next race.

"He says that Speed got squeezed by the horses on either side of him as he came out of the gate, and it took the wind out of him. It shook him up. It's a surprising thing to happen with older horses. They usually know how to break from the gate without veering off to one side."

"And both of them from either side."

"I know. Let's watch the replay."

The head-on view is sickening. The horses on both sides of Speed ram into him and my horse loses momentum. His head flies up and then I can't see him for a second or two as the horses that bumped him almost collide in front of him.

"Could that have been deliberate?"

"I don't think so, Meg. I know you have a suspicious mind, especially when you're in the middle of investigating, but I can't see anyone doing that deliberately. It would be too risky. Someone, including the horses, could have been badly hurt. It's horse racing, what can I say? And we've been lucky—when I gave Speed a quick look just now, he seemed okay."

"That's the main thing. I can't come to the backstretch to see him. Please let me know how he is. I'll visit another time."

"Will do. See you later."

Neal's right. I do have a suspicious mind. His comment had me thinking about Melissa. She wants me to find out who Candice truly is. Somehow. I should do that before we meet her at the airport.

7

Poison

Melissa left me a handwritten note telling me she's sent me an email with links that may help me find out more about Candice. I open my laptop, and the landline phone rings at the same time.

"Is that Meg Sheppard?" The voice is husky, almost breathless.

"Yes. Who are you?"

"Suzie. I was with Barton when he got hit."

"Barton's girlfriend."

"No way. I worked at that casino the cops shut down. Barton went there three or four nights a week. He'd get wasted and 'cause I got the bus to where the track is, I'd make sure he got there okay. I live near there. I could do with your help."

"Why?"

"Because the cops say I'm responsible, and somebody told me you're investigating his death."

"I don't understand."

"I thought you knew all this stuff. Sorry. The cops say his alcohol level was nuts. They say I'm responsible because I served him drinks."

"I'm not on Barton's case anymore, for personal reasons."

"Oh, my god. I was counting on you. What the hell am I going to do? Can't you help me?"

"You need a lawyer."

"I don't want no lawyer. The cops say the casino was illegal. How was I supposed to know? I did my job, that's it. I didn't get no profits or anything."

"As I said, I'm not on this case."

"But don't you care what happened? I know stuff like who was in the car that hit him. Bet you'd like me to tell you."

"I know who was in the car."

"There's other stuff. Look, I'll buy you a coffee. Meet me at Trixie's Café in town tomorrow at ten. I'll be there." She ends the call. Perhaps I'll go. It depends on how things evolve between now and then.

I'm having a tough time making decisions. It's as if my mind is made of putty that's changing shape as I'm pulled in many different directions.

There's one thing I must do—find out about Candice Burley. Melissa said something's not right. I wish I'd asked her why she thinks this. Candice told her she's Melissa's father's granddaughter. I have access to Melissa's ancestry report and her adoption information. It was thanks to the adoption reunite site that I was able to connect with Melissa. Our mother gave my baby half-sister to an adoption agency and didn't tell me. I didn't know Melissa existed until relatively recently. My life has been enriched by her smile, her compassion, and her spirit. I'll start wallowing in self-pity again if I'm not careful. The thought of her leaving this house, our home, threatens to eat a hole in my heart.

It doesn't take me long to find nothing about Candice. Neither the ancestry nor the adoption reunite sites include her name in the records or the data linked to Melissa's. I put the kettle on and listen to it hiss as I watch the two dogs dreaming. They're stretched out on the floor. Kelly is paddling with her paws and Jake is making soft 'woofs'. I'd love to know what they're up to in their dreams. Cooper laps up small scoops of water with his tongue and then swipes the liquid with his paw, sending droplets onto the floor. He trots away with his tail straight up like a flagpole. He's pleased with himself—as usual.

What to do next? Because I can't think of anything better, I 'Google' Candice's name, and that of her grandfather, Melissa's father. My tea cools as I dig into a few leads. I get lucky. I discover an obituary for the grandfather, and it has a detailed list of all those in his family who he predeceased. It doesn't include Melissa— that must be because he either didn't know or didn't want it to be known that she was his daughter. Candice is included in the list: 'and Candice Burley, stepdaughter of Malcolm Woodsmith'. Malcolm is the grandfather's son, who would be a half-brother to Melissa. This makes it clear that Candice is not a blood relative of Melissa which is what Melissa suspects.

I slam the computer shut with more vigour than I meant to and both dogs lift their heads. The cold tea is condemned to the sink drain while I vacillate about what to do next.

My mobile makes some noises, and I pick it up without enthusiasm. I'm sliding back down into a slump. Two texts from Les Joseph, Barton's groom. I remember the delicious tea I had in his home and think of the unpleasant tea I've just poured down the drain. Perhaps I'll get a decent cuppa. But he's asked me to meet him outside the security office at the track early tomorrow morning. So, I'll have to settle for tea in a Styrofoam cup in the cafeteria.

* * *

The early morning sun dazzles me as I drive towards the track. When I stop at a red light, I realize my mistake. I'm only looking into Bella's disappearance and attempting to prove Linda's innocence. I should have asked Les why he wants to meet.

Detective Valeska calls as I'm driving, so I pull over. I find it hard to concentrate on driving while talking to someone on the phone, so I don't have a hands-free setup. The dogs are confused but that's replaced by enthusiasm when they see a field containing woolly sheep grazing close to the fence.

"Hi, Meg. I have some news."

"You're at work early."

"Lots to do. I've just seen the toxicology report. Barton Woking had a high alcohol content in his blood, as expected, but they also found arsenic. Hair analysis revealed that he'd been exposed to arsenic over several weeks."

"Oh. Wow."

"Yes. But it gets more interesting. The pathologist's report states Barton was dead before he was hit by the car."

"Wow. I don't understand. How could that be true? Didn't they say he died in the hospital?"

"All I can say is the pathologist is adamant. I asked him myself. He said he could tell the body was hit with considerable force, but the bruising is much less than it would have been if Barton had been alive at the time. Bruising is smaller but clearer when the blood can't spread. He told me Barton was dead moments before the impact of the car."

"How weird. How did he get hit by the car, then? I can't quite imagine what happened."

"Les Joseph came forward. He says you advised him to. He left police services without a mark on his body, for the record."

I'm not sure if I'm supposed to laugh or not, so I merely sigh.

"I was joking. Never mind. He told us he was driving Linda's car, and Linda saw a woman push Barton into them. We're having another word with that woman, Suzie, I think her name is."

"What about Orlando?"

"The funeral director was right. He was shot through the head. How's your wound, by the way?"

"I'm fine."

"No leads on any of that business so far. You might be interested to know that the so-called fancy security system at the Knightscourt estate is just a sham, so no help there. Keep in touch."

She ends the call as I'm about to let her know I'm restricting my investigation to Bella since now I don't have to be worried about Linda. I wonder if they've told Linda about the pathologist's findings.

The dogs have lost interest in the sheep since they've wandered away to greener grass at the farther end of the field. I can see them both in the rearview mirror. It's as if they're wondering why we aren't going somewhere.

"It's okay. We're going."

* * *

Les is waiting outside the security office near the gate into the backstretch. I park the pickup in the lot, show my pass, and shake Les' proffered hand.

"Thanks for coming," he says.

"Sorry I'm a couple of minutes late."

"No problem. I'll buy you a terrible tea in the cafeteria." His white teeth gleam as he smiles. He must be relieved.

"I'm glad you talked to Detective Valeska."

"As cops go, she's okay. I didn't get treated bad, but I was kinda nervous."

It doesn't take long to get teabags, hot water, and milk.

"I'm paying. I think it's my turn."

"It was my brother who paid last time." He smiles as we sit down at a table in a far corner.

"So, is this just a celebratory drink or do you have something you want to tell me."

"This don't count as a celebratory drink." He sips and winces. I'm not sure if it's too hot or tastes like pond water or both.

"So, what do you want to tell me?"

"It's about Barton. I feel a load off me, so I can talk. And, for some weird reason, I want to know who killed him and what for. And how come he died just before he hit the car? And poisoning? Crazy shit, that's what I call it."

"You could say that."

"I didn't even like the guy."

"He wasn't well-liked here."

"I can't drink this stuff." He pushes the Styrofoam cup to one side. "Barton has some history. I know because of my connections. I used to work on the street helping homeless people. I was employed by an agency. But I left. Too many overdoses and other bad stuff going on. I couldn't take it no more. Anyway, Barton was part of the Blackbirds Gang in his past. And one of the gang members shot a member of a rival gang called the Pitbulls Gang. It hit the press. You probably read about it."

"I didn't, but I read a bit about it online just recently. A person called Annie Hart, who had previously worked at one of the Knightscourt Funeral Homes, was charged with murder, but then acquitted."

"Annie was Barton's girlfriend. But word on the street was that she didn't have anything to do with it."

"Who do they think did it?"

"I don't have anything on that."

"I can't recall reading who was killed?"

"His name was Pablo. Not sure if that was his real name or his gang name."

"That's interesting. It could be a coincidence, but that's a Spanish name, similar to Orlando possibly. I wonder if there's a connection between Pablo and Orlando."

"Could be a link. Well done, Hercule!"

"Don't be silly. And I'm not interested in the murders anymore. I'm leaving it to the police. I'm focussing on finding Bella."

"Dirk's favourite horse?"

"Yes."

"Come on, you need to do your thing and find out who Barton's murderer is. I'd feel better if you were on the case. Gotta get that guy. You know people are scared around here because they think there's a murderer running amok in the backstretch. Come on. Say you're still in the game."

"I can't."

"You could save someone's life."

"I want to focus on Bella."

"I know women can multitask."

"Ha!"

"Think about it." He stretches and yawns. "Sorry, but gotta go. That was one bad cup of tea."

"I'll get you a better cup of tea next time we meet—if we do."

"Get the bad guys." He smiles and leaves.

Since I'm in the backstretch I decide to check on my horses and see if I can track the farrier down who worked for Barton and Dirk. Fortunately, I remember his name is Farley Smedley.

Neal whistles as he strides down the shedrow carrying a pile of clean saddle sheets. The washing machines in the backstretch work overtime churning bandages, towels, saddle pads of all kinds, fluffy girth straps, and all sorts of other horse paraphernalia. And I can often hear the dryers whirring and thumping as they thrash their loads around, and smell their sweet, floral aroma.

"Linda must be coming back. You're smiling."

"Hi, Meg. Yes. I got the good news just now. Linda's coming back tomorrow. She said she can't come until late morning because she wants to be at your place when some horses arrive. She didn't explain."

"I'd almost forgotten. Dirk Knightscourt's five yearlings are coming to my farm and Linda said she'd help me look after them. This was while the police still considered her a person of interest. I hope we can work something out, Neal, because I could do with an extra pair of hands."

"And we all want you to find out who killed Barton. I heard he was poisoned which makes it even more sinister."

"If Linda helps me for a couple of hours in the mornings, would you be able to manage?"

"As it happens, I was a bit short-staffed anyway, even before Linda took time off. And Les Joseph turned up this morning saying he was looking for some hours, so I'm getting him on board. I know he worked for Barton, but he's explained all that and why he was fired, and I'm fine with it."

"I don't know whether he's a good worker, but he seems a decent person."

"I like him. And I'll soon find out. And Linda will let me know if he sets a foot wrong."

"That's for sure. Is Speed okay after his bad experience coming out of the gate?"

"Come and see. He's full of himself. We'll take him to the gate in the mornings a few times just to make sure he hasn't been scarred by the squeeze he got. But I reckon he'll be fine given a bit of time and patience. He has a good head."

Speed whinnies as I approach. I rummage in my pocket for

mints, and he crunches with relish. I stroke his long nose, and he gently brushes his muzzle and lips on my other hand to retrieve a couple more mints.

"He looks good. I don't think Linda will be able to criticize the care he's been getting."

"I should hope not. I've been doing most of the work myself on the horses assigned to her. And that's another reason I'm relieved she's coming back tomorrow."

"Would you happen to know where I can find Farley Smedley?"

"The farrier? No. He could be anywhere. I'll text you later with his number. I think I have it."

"Thanks, and thanks for everything, Neal. I must get going. I have to meet someone soon."

"Good luck in finding out who killed Barton. We want to know. It's making people edgy around here."

Both dogs stare at me as I walk towards my truck. Kelly seems to know she can show her face if the truck has not gone through the security gate. Sometimes I think she's smarter than I am, but I don't think the bar is all that high.

We park near the trail that runs around the outside of the fenced training track. The dogs can't be cooped up in the truck all morning. I clip a leash to Jake's collar. I have a feeling it won't be long before I'll be able to trust Jake off-leash along with Kelly. He's a quick learner—although he'll never come up to Kelly's exemplary standards.

A pickup stops beside us, and we all stand and watch as the man rolls his window down. I tell the dogs to sit.

"Are you Meg Sheppard by any chance? I heard you have a border collie, and I just thought you might be her."

"Who are you?"

"Sorry. I'm Farley Smedley, farrier. I think you want to chat with me. Neal let me know. You are Meg Sheppard, then?"

"Yes. And yes, I do want to talk to you." Why am I doing this? However much I try, I seem to be sucked back into this case whether I like it or not.

"I can see you're exercising your lovely dogs. I could walk with you. I've got a few minutes."

"That would be good."

He jumps out of his truck and lands lightly on his feet. He must be about fifty, but he's strong and fit, with broad shoulders. A farrier's work is gruelling. Horses, especially high-performing racehorses, can be difficult to handle. They don't like having one foot lifted off the ground since they feel vulnerable—they can't flee danger. They are powerful animals weighing about one thousand pounds and are capable of giving a deadly kick. So, it takes a special person to trim their feet and shoe them.

He shakes my hand, and I can feel the callouses on his large palm. He pats the dogs, and they seem to like him, which I take as a good sign.

"You worked for Barton, right?"

"Don't hold that against me, but yes, I worked in his barn. I'm sure you realize I wasn't employed by him. I sent him the bills and he got them paid by the owners."

"I didn't mean you were on his staff."

"Since we don't have much time, how can I help?"

"Tell me what you know about Barton. You also went to the Knightscourt place, so anything you can tell me about Orlando, Dirk, and Bobbie would be good."

"Orlando's death sure shook me up. He was good with the horses. I never had any trouble, even with the yearlings. He handled them a lot and had them leading nicely and they were good with their feet being touched. Decent man, I thought. He got shot in the head, didn't he? Almost sounds like a gang killing. So bizarre in somewhere like Vannersville. I know we're in a city, but this is a bit much for Ontario. I mean, we don't expect that sort of thing here, do we? Who's looking after the horses now? There was a stable boy there, but I'm not convinced he'd know how to handle yearlings or even what to feed them. Worrying."

"That's under control or will be very soon. How well do you know Dirk and Bobbie?"

"I met Dirk several times, but I never met Bobbie, his wife. She doesn't have any interest in horses as far as I know. But I heard they've disappeared."

"Yes. Do you have any theories about who could want Barton dead?"

"I heard he was poisoned. That's sort of creepy. Perhaps the Russians had something to do with it?" He turns towards me and smiles. "No, you're right, this is serious. What can I tell you? Well, Barton wasn't much liked by anyone. He went to the casino quite often. He talked about it sometimes and some mornings he seemed hungover. He'd be absent from the rail at the training track and drinking black coffee in his office. I could smell it. And the staff sort of resented him leaving everything to them. He'd have worked out the training schedule and riders the day before, but he wasn't observing the horses, or talking to the riders, or watching how the horses came back—you know, if they were puffing, or even bleeding, or lame or anything. His staff were always stretched. He was a skinflint. He didn't always pay his bills and didn't always pay his staff on time. It was a difficult barn with some unhappy campers. Then he fired Les. That was a mistake. He was the best worker there. But I think Les got tired of Barton's cheating. However, I'm not sure if it was Barton who was the cheat."

"You think it could have been the vet Barton used? Dr. Greg Dudley? Did Greg have part ownership in some of the horses perhaps?"

"Don't know, sorry. Have you talked to Les? Les was working

there every day. He'd know better than anyone what was going on. He might have an idea who Barton's enemies were. Someone poisoned him for a reason. Now, Orlando. I don't know what to think about that guy and how he got himself shot. Putting him in a casket in one of Knightscourt's funeral places was like a sick joke. Nasty stuff. Orlando is one of a big family, I know that much, and he was sending money back to Guatemala. He told me his mother and sisters weren't well off. He wouldn't have had much to send because I can't imagine his wages at Knightscourt's place would be too good. He told me about the casino there. He thought it was illegal. I hear it's been shut down. There'll be people out of work. Not sure if it's a good thing to mothball it, but I suppose it was competing with wagering at our horse races. I don't know. I don't think I've told you anything useful. Here's my card. Call me any time if you think I can be of help."

"Thanks. I haven't got a card on me, so I'll text you my contact info."

"See you around. Have a great day."

"You too."

We've arrived back at his truck, and I only have a few minutes to get to Trixie's Café to meet with Suzie.

"Come on dogs, we must trot to the pickup."

8

Hot Horse

It must be Suzie who's standing outside the café. Her large, white-rimmed sunglasses almost fill her face. I was lucky to find a parking spot just across the road, and she guesses it's me.

"Hi, I'm Suzie. You've got to be Meg, right?"

"Hello, Suzie."

"I like sitting on their patio. It's a nice day. Do you mind?"

"No. I think this is great." The café has set up an improvised patio on the wide sidewalk with square tables each with a small, green umbrella tilted at a different angle than its cousins. The feel of the place holds the promise of a decent cup of tea.

"We have to order inside, but they'll bring it out. I'm so glad you've come." She takes her sunglasses off as we walk inside and I almost gasp. Her false eyelashes dominate her face almost as much as the sunglasses did. It's hard to ignore them. And her dark purple nails are long and have what looks like Christmas glitter glued to them. "I don't like them either."

"Sorry?"

"The fake lashes. They bother my eyes, and I've had trouble removing them. I'm off to buy some different glue-dissolving stuff after this. They liked this sort of thing at the casino." She spreads her fingers out so I can see her dazzling nails.

We order our drinks, and I pay, although Suzie wanted to pay for hers.

We sit down outside but Suzie has trouble sitting still.

"I so want to talk to you. I hate what's happened to Barton. And I hate that the cops think I had something to do with it."

Just as my hot water arrives with the teabag separate in its paper envelope which means I won't have a decent cup of tea, my mobile rings. It's Melissa, so I don't answer. I catch the eye of the server.

"The teabag should be in the mug when the hot water is poured."

"We're not permitted to handle the teabag for health reasons." She scurries away, holding four empty mugs in one hand.

I mutter under my breath how ridiculous that is when my mobile rings. It's Melissa again.

"Melissa. Are you okay?"

"I'm home because I have a migraine."

"Oh, no. I'm so sorry."

"That's not why I'm calling. When I got back just now, I found the padlock had been cut and it looked like a heavy vehicle had been in here. Then I saw a horse charging around the back field. You ought to hear the racket. Looks like a mare. Tail high in the air, snorting, whinnying and sending Eagle and Bullet ballistic. I don't know what to do. I don't feel well enough to deal with it."

"I'm coming. I'll be right there. I'm in town but it won't take me long." I end the call. "Suzie, can we do this tomorrow? There seems to be an emergency at my farm. So sorry."

"I suppose so."

"I'm very sorry."

She looks dejected. It's hard to leave her but easy to walk away from the lukewarm water and the sad-looking teabag.

* * *

The gate is open and a large vehicle, probably a horse trailer, has not cleanly negotiated the corner into the driveway. Wheels have dipped partway into the ditch. It must have been a lurchy ride for the horse if it happened on the way in.

The gravel in front of the barn has been churned up and the grass beside the barn has deep ruts. It's clear that the driver didn't bother to take much care.

Whinnies and hooves pounding the ground drown out other sounds as I and the dogs jump out of the truck.

"Leave the horse," I tell the dogs, just in case they get caught up in the excitement and give chase which could result in injuries for horses and dogs. Bullet and Eagle are cantering up and down the fence line, but they don't appear to be frantic. They've probably settled down a bit since Melissa called. But the mare is on the other side galloping backwards and forwards with her tail in the air, snorting and calling out. She spins around in each corner of the field, digs her hooves in, and charges back the way she came. She wants to be with Eagle and Bullet and is stressed.

The mare must be Bella. I can't think of any other alternative. Whatever the thief thought he was going to gain from stealing her couldn't have worked out, or plans have changed.

First things first. I get a small bucket of water and put it in the field. She doesn't pay any attention. I talk to her, but it doesn't help. Okay. They'll all have to go into the barn.

It doesn't take long to open a couple of bags of wood shavings, throw two flakes of hay into the corner, and fill a bucket of water and hang it. I check Bullet and Eagle's stalls are okay, and then grab a lead-rein. I lead Bullet in first, and then Eagle. Of course, the mare is even more frantic now, but she lets me clip a lead-rein onto her dirty halter. She's steaming. Her coat is soaked with sweat because she's hot from charging around. And she's filthy. She smells of wet manure and grimy sweat. I'll have to cool her off before leading her into the stall. I can't risk her succumbing to colic—which could be life-threatening.

I talk to her. The dogs walk calmly ahead which I think is helping. She dances on her toes, but she has good manners and doesn't pull me around even though she's stressed and agitated. Farley must be right. Orlando knew how to handle horses. I walk her up and down the aisle in the barn. I grab a sponge off the shelf by the sink, lead her into her stall, and use the water in her bucket to dampen the sponge and wipe her as she walks around in circles. She puts up with my weird maneuvers as I keep hold of the lead-rein. I empty the bucket down the drain by the tap and fill it up. I let her drink for about ten seconds, then I walk her again. Too much water too quickly could cause problems for this hot horse. Leading Bella— she must be Bella—up and down the aisle gives me an even greater appreciation for the work of the hotwalkers. who take such excellent care of our racehorses after their workouts and races. They lead their charges around and around the shedrow as they cool off and regulate the amount each horse can drink out of a bucket hanging outside their stall door.

She's more settled now. The calling out to Bullet and Eagle stopped as soon as we entered the barn because she could see their heads hanging over the stall doors. They are interested in her, but not excited anymore. The dogs are dutifully walking up and down with us, but I wish they could tell me what they smelled outside. Perhaps they know who drove the truck, or at least some of their characteristics. I'm going to find out. I must.

After another fifteen minutes of walking, I think it's safe to put her in the stall with water and hay. She's drunk about two gallons in small amounts. Her coat is cleaner, damp but not wet, and smells less acrid. The air is warm, so I don't think she'll get a chill. It would help if she rolled and let the wood shavings help to dry her off.

I lead her into the stall, turn her around, undo the clip on the lead-rein, and fasten the door. She looks out, sees the other two and nuzzles the hay. I think she'll be okay. I take a couple of photos when she lifts her head. She's dark bay with a distinctive white blaze on her face which looks like an inverted white triangle.

I must check on Melissa.

The dogs dash out of the barn and run around with their noses almost touching the ground. I wish they could tell me what they're discovering. Kelly looks up at me and barks as if to say something went on that she doesn't approve of. Someone strange was here without us.

"Kelly, you're right. But we must go and see Melissa. Come on dogs."

Melissa is lying on a recliner with a throw and curled-up Cooper on her lap, and what looks like a damp washcloth over her forehead and eyes.

"Hi," she mumbles.

"Oh, Melissa, I'm so sorry you're ill."

"It's just a migraine. I'll get over it. I've taken something. It's all the stress of not knowing what's happening in my life."

"I get it. So, no decision yet as to what you're doing?" I regret asking. I'm putting more pressure on her.

"Is the horse okay? She was thundering around the field. It was awful. I could barely see what was happening because the sun was too bright. It made my eyes sting and my headache unbearable. I had to come in. But it looked like a mare. It wouldn't be Bella, would it?"

"Could be. She's fine. She took a bit of cooling down, though.

I can't be sure it's Bella, and I can't tell if she's in foal. I guess she would be less than halfway through the eleven months. I'll get you some water and would you like me to refresh your washcloth?"

"No. I'll manage. You have enough on your plate. I'll be okay now that I'm in the peace and quiet of home and can rest." Kelly licks her hand and Jake sits, leaning against the recliner. Cooper hasn't even opened an eye.

"Okay, I'm going to connect with Dirk. And there's no need for you to come with me to pick up Candice. I'm going to leave in about an hour."

"That's kind. Thanks."

"That's what sisters are for."

* * *

Dirk replies to my text almost instantly and is ecstatic that Bella has shown up. He's sure she's his mare from the photos I took and can't wait to see her. I text him to ask what feed she was on, and he doesn't know. I suppose it's irrelevant because she wouldn't have been kept on the same feed unless the thief stole some when he took the horse from Knightscourt's place. I also ask if he knows her vaccination status. He has no clue. I've come to the conclusion that Dirk doesn't know much about horse care. He relied on Orlando, Barton, and Les for horse management, as well as Farley Smedley and Dr. Greg Dudley. I wonder how many horses he had in training with Barton and who's training them now.

I text Dr. Dudley to ask about Bella's vaccinations and to request a check-up as soon as he can make it. He's coming tomorrow.

Dirk and Bobbie will visit after his five yearlings have arrived and settled in. I suggested late tomorrow morning.

It's going to be a busy place. I hope Melissa will be well enough to cope with all the commotion.

While Melissa rests, I try to figure out who was most likely to have delivered Bella. Dirk doesn't seem to care. He's simply relieved she's arrived at my farm where he says he's sure she'll be well cared for. It sounds as if he expects me to look after her indefinitely.

My starting point is shippers who I know have been here before. And the one I zero in on is a driver who is not as skilled as others I've had experience with. I'm thinking of the trailer dipping into the ditch and of the marks in front of the barn. I suppose those could be the result of haste, but I've got to start somewhere.

"Hugh Bracknell?"

"Yeah. Who's calling?"

"Meg Sheppard."

"Oh, yeah. You were out. I had to cut the padlock."

"Why didn't you call me? And how come you carry cutters?"

"I've been caught out before, haven't I? A horse on the trailer and no one at home."

"You could have called."

"And waited how long for you to show up? You've got to be kidding. That damn mare was kickin' and squealin' like she was being tortured. Had to let her off before she trashed my trailer. Do you know how much these damn things cost? I'll get you a new padlock if that's what you're bitching about."

"I don't care about that. I want to know who paid you to ship the mare. I wasn't expecting her and need to find out."

"That's weird. Never heard that one before. Let me think. It was a farm. Run down. I was surprised you were getting a horse from a place like that. But I reckoned perhaps she was a rescue. She looked a bit scraggy although with a decent belly on her. I forget the person's name, but the place is called Three Willows Farm. It's by the river at the other end of town."

"I dealt with them when I was at the Humane Society. Thanks for the info. I'll follow up."

"I have a nasty feeling I'm not going to get paid for my work if you didn't ask her to be shipped."

"Send your invoice here. I'll make sure it's paid."

"That's decent of you. Thanks. I'll deduct the price of a padlock."

"Haha. Thanks for your help."

*   *   *

Kelly, Jake, and Cooper are keeping Melissa company while I drive to the airport. The last thing we need to deal with is this mysterious person who falsely claims to be a blood relative of Melissa's and whose motives for visiting are unclear. I'm concerned that Candice will add to Melissa's stress. In fact, she already has.

I find a spot in the dingy parking garage that's a bit of a hike from the terminal, but ever since they rebuilt, the distances have at least quadrupled.

The arrivals section is busy with a colourful variety of people of different ages and ethnicities, all apparently excited to be greeting their families and friends. I hold up my sign whenever the large, frosted glass sliding doors open and wonder what she's like.

"Where's Melissa?"

I must have missed her in all the chaos of people and bags. She stops pulling her small suitcase and is about to take a bag off her shoulder.

"I don't think we should stop here. My truck's in the parking lot."

"Truck?" Her hazel eyes widen despite the weary look on her face.

"Pickup. Melissa's recovering from a migraine. She'll see you tomorrow I expect."

"Aren't I staying with her?"

"No. I thought that was arranged between you. There's a room booked at the Vannersville Inn."

"I see."

"I'll drive you there and we can have a quick meal in their restaurant. I can't be away from the farm for long."

"You have cows or something?"

I wonder how much Melissa has told her.

"Horses. I have five more arriving tomorrow morning. And I expect Melissa will have to go to work at the track."

"An athletics place then?"

"A horse racetrack. She works as a veterinary technician."

"I see."

"I don't want to appear rude or unwelcoming, but why have you come?"

"To see Melissa of course. I think she's the only relative I haven't met."

"Candice, you must know you're not a blood relative, so we're curious as to why you'd make such an expensive trip to see someone you don't know who's not a relation. Just wondering."

"You'd rather I turned round and went back." I've been too blunt. Her pale face has flushed pink, and her eyes are watery. But I can't help thinking she's got a nerve showing up like this, expecting our hospitality.

"Melissa has a lot of stress in her life right now. I'm her half-sister, and care about her a lot, and want to protect her from further unnecessary pressure. We've had people show up just because they think we have lots of money. I want to be sure that's not your reason for coming. I'm being blunt, I know, but sometimes it's best to have these things out on the table to avoid misunderstanding and disappointment."

"I see." She struggles to climb into the truck. Her short skirt and high heels hinder her maneuverability.

"I'll take you to the Inn. We can talk while we have a meal."

"I'm starving. The airplane food was ghastly, and we were packed like sardines. I could barely move for the whole eight hours and got no sleep. Beastly."

Once Candice is registered and her small suitcase is in her room, we take the elevator to the restaurant. Her short stature and cropped brown hair bear no resemblance to Melissa's looks—and that's no surprise.

Her hands tremble as she accepts a menu from the server.

"How did you discover Melissa? I couldn't find you on the websites I checked out."

"I'll make a long story short. I don't want to waste your time. I don't have a return ticket, but I'll arrange it as soon as I can." Pools of tears form in each of her red eyes, and she looks down at the menu and sniffs. "Sorry, I'm not usually this emotional about things. I promise I'll get my act together."

"Let's order and then we'll talk."

Despite voicing how hungry she is, Candice doesn't eat much of her vegetable curry and I eat even less of my lasagne. But the tea is decent and we both sip on our drinks as we talk.

"I don't want this to be a sob story, but it'll probably sound like it to you."

"I'm listening."

"I found out my step-grandad, Benjamin Woodsmith, is Melissa's father—was, I suppose, since he's gone. Malcolm Woodsmith, my stepfather, is his son. I don't know who my father is, and I wonder if my mother knew—not nice to admit." She folds her napkin into a tight square and pats it.

"How did you find out that Benjamin Woodsmith was Melissa's father?"

"I've been desperately unhappy. My stepfather nor his family want me. My mother was treated like dirt, and I reckon that's what eventually caused her to get cancer. She died last year."

"I'm sorry to hear that, but it doesn't explain how you found out…"

"Getting to that. I wanted so much to know who my father was. I thought I could start a new life with him. After my mother died life became unbearable for me. So, as I was putting my stuff together and trying to come up with an idea of where to go, I went through Mum's papers hoping to find out something about my father. It was awful because she kept records in shoeboxes under her bed. There was nothing helpful. I was so desperate that I wondered if there'd be something in my stepfather's papers. I was nervous about going through them. It took a while, but I found a lawyer's letter that mentioned someone called Miriam—I don't remember her surname—it was about Melissa and a DNA analysis report was attached. The letter stated something along these lines—that even though the DNA results confirm Miriam's assertion that Melissa's father is Benjamin Woodsmith, they advised their client, my father, not to accept the results of the analysis and therefore, not to offer a financial settlement. It was dated around the time Melissa was born, I expect. I suppose they gambled on Miriam not having the funds to take them to court or do whatever it would take to get a settlement, which I think is outrageous, don't you?"

"Miriam is my mother, as you know, but this is the first I've heard of it."

"I didn't discover any follow-up. And I didn't find out anything about my father. But what I clung onto was Melissa—to the fact there's a connection. It wasn't hard to find her—and you—and I immediately made plans to escape my misery. I don't ask for your sympathy or charity; I just need some time to breathe in some kindness. I can't take any more hurt and humiliation. But the irony is, you don't want me here. Sorry, I shouldn't have said that. I do get it. You have no reason to welcome me or have anything to do with me."

"I appreciate your honesty, and I can understand, at least to some extent, how you feel and your need to escape. I was sexually abused by my stepfather while I grew up in England. I escaped as soon as

I could. I emigrated here and started a new life."

"Oh, you understand! Oh, but I'm so sorry you had such a horrible childhood. I wasn't sexually abused—I suppose it was neglect and I was made to feel worthless or worse. But I know it's not the same."

"We're not in competition over who had the worst childhood." I smile at her and her lips tremble. She hangs her head.

"I'll go as soon as I can buy a return ticket." Her voice is muffled as she gazes down into her lap.

"Let's leave it like this—I'll talk with Melissa."

"If I could meet Melissa and see your farm, I'd like that." She lifts her head. The bottom lids of her red, puffy eyes barely hold back the tears.

*   *   *

Melissa's in the kitchen heating tomato soup. The dogs greet me with an over-abundance of enthusiasm as if I've been away for a week.

"What's she like?"

"She's fleeing a horrible family situation."

"Abuse?"

"In a way, yes. Unwanted and neglected. Her stepfather, who's the son of your father as you know, doesn't want her in his life, it seems. Perhaps I was rather tough on her. I now wonder if I should have been. But we don't want her here, do we?"

"I know what it's like to be unwanted."

"Mm."

"Did you ask her why she's come here—why she's seeking me out? Is it about money?"

"It could be, but I think it's more about escape. My direct approach seemed to deflate her."

"You can be very blunt." Melissa raises her eyebrows with a trace of a smile on her lips.

"Okay, I probably was a bit too tough on her, but I'm tired of people coming here for the sole purpose of extracting money."

"But it sounds like you don't think she's one of those?"

"I'm not entirely sure. She doesn't seem to know anything about us. She asked if we have cows and didn't know where you work."

"Cows? Ha. I didn't tell her much. We've barely communicated. As you know, her email came out of the blue, and all she talked about was coming here. She didn't ask and I didn't share. I suppose I've had too many things on my mind." She hands me a mug of tomato soup and sits across the table from me.

"You'd think she'd have done some research. But perhaps she was desperate for somewhere to go—a long way away from her troubled life in England—and money isn't what it's all about."

"We've both been there." Melissa sighs and moves so Cooper can jump up onto her lap.

"You know, I don't mind her staying at the Vannersville Inn for a few days while we get to know her a bit."

"I'm fine with that. But what do we do when the few days is up?"

"Let's not worry about that until then. I gambled on you agreeing, and I hope you don't mind, but I said she could come here late tomorrow afternoon. She asked how she'd get here, and I told her to get a taxi. She was concerned about the expense, so even though she may not be here in the hopes of getting rich, I'm certain she has very little money."

"She's young, so I'm not all that surprised."

"But unless you want me to, I'm not inclined to give her any. I could help with her hotel bills, but that's about it."

"I don't think you should even do that. But we'll see how things go. I agree we should find out what she's like and show some compassion if her story is true."

"It'll be a busy day here tomorrow."

"I've been able to arrange for a day off, so I can help."

"Thanks."

"That's what sisters are for, after all. You said so yourself."

"I'm relieved to see you looking much better."

*　*　*

The drizzle is a disappointment. I'd hoped for another sunny day to make all the comings and goings easier. Today is going to be hectic. There's a knock on the backdoor before I've even had a chance to get back out to the barn to clean the stalls.

"Hi, Linda. So nice to see you." The smile on her face, and her rosy cheeks, say it all.

"All's good but I hope I never have to deal with cops again."

"So glad that's over for you. But you should have told me the truth. I thought we trusted one another." I pull on my boots and grab a jacket. We start walking to the barn. Kelly and Jake trot ahead.

"Sorry, but I was uptight about Les being black—if they knew he was driving, that would be it for him."

"But you also lied about the dent—something about a parking lot—that didn't ring true with me."

"I panicked. I wasn't thinking."

"But if you'd told me, I'm sure we could have cleared it all up with the police. You're lucky they haven't charged you with obstruction of justice or something like that."

"Well, they didn't, and Les is okay. Sorry, that came out rude." She picks up a fork and walks into a stall.

"Why was Les driving?"

"I said I'd give him a lift sometimes, but that morning I had a funny cramp in my foot. It wouldn't go away. So, he said he'd drive."

"You should have told me."

"Yeah, well."

"Linda, I've been trying to help you."

"I know. I'm sorry. I'm not good with this stuff."

"Okay, let's move on." I pick up a bag of wood shavings and put it in a stall.

"I hope you find out about Barton. I didn't like the guy, but I really want to know who poisoned him and what for. It's sort of scary."

"It's an odd case. Anyway, I'm glad you're here. Did you go to the Knightscourt place first?"

"Yeah. The horses'll arrive soon. I helped load. I got there early because young ones can be hard to get on a trailer. It took a while, but not bad."

"You got here in good time. Did the stable guy help?"

"Yeah. The poor guy. He's been sleeping in the barn with a loaded shotgun beside him. He's been like scared shitless."

"Do the horses look okay?"

"Not bad. They need their feet trimmed, and their coats don't gleam."

"Not up to your high standards then."

"They soon will be." She empties a bag of wood shavings into a stall and spreads the sweet-smelling bedding.

"They'll have to go into the large field. Bella is in the paddock and Eagle and Bullet are in the small field behind. But we should separate the fillies from the colts when we've got organized."

"How's Bella?"

"She looks okay. She's settled in quickly considering the state she was in yesterday when I first saw her. The vet's coming today to check her over."

"Not Greg Dudley? Meg, please don't use him."

"Why?"

"Ask Les."

"I'm not convinced there's an issue with Dr. Dudley."

"Can you cancel and ask that new vet to come? You know—Dr. Scully, Russon, who Melissa works for."

"They're not my horses."

"Dirk doesn't know one end of a horse from the other. Please."

"I suppose I can do that. I'll ask Melissa to get Russon here and I'll cancel Dr. Dudley. I'll do it right now."

We agree it makes sense to put the horses back in their stalls to avert pandemonium when the young ones arrive. We've now got five stalls set up for them, complete with buckets of water, flakes of hay, and new bedding. Linda leads Bella into the barn, and I follow with Eagle and Bullet. Despite the drizzle, they were all grazing calmly, and as we walk them into their stalls, I can almost see puzzled looks on their faces. After all, they've been out for less than an hour. But the three of them decide to accept the situation, and snatch up some hay and start munching.

"I'll pick up some broodmare feed as soon as the young ones have settled in and all the visitors have left," I say.

"I can pick up a couple of bags after the yearlings get here if everything's okay."

"That would be a great help, Linda. I've got several people coming today, including Dirk and Bobbie, a visitor from England, and the vet."

"The farrier should come. All of them need a trim, except Eagle and Bullet."

"I'll ask him to come tomorrow. They'll be calmer and there won't be so much coming and going."

9

Bullet Holes

The dogs rush out of the barn, wagging their tails. "Melissa!"

"I'm here to help and Russon's coming. He says he's going to perform an ultrasonographic examination on Bella to confirm pregnancy, and I can't wait to see the images."

"Ultrasound, great," I say. "When's he coming?"

"As soon as he's finished at the track—probably about noon he thinks."

"Has Edwin gone to Scotland then?" Linda asks.

"Yes," Melissa says and then turns away from us to pat Bella. "I hope you still have your foal, Bella. I can see her ribs. She needs your TLC, Linda."

"Linda's picking up broodmare food later and we have lots of good pasture. She'll be okay."

"Who was looking after her?" Melissa asks.

"The shipper picked her up from a rundown farm called Three

Willows."

"I've heard about it," Linda says. "Nothing good."

"Do you know who stole her and why?" asks Melissa.

"No. But I'd like to know," I say. "It's odd that Dirk didn't seem to be anxious to find out what happened but, to be fair, we only communicated by text."

Kelly barks, looks at me, and then both dogs tear off down the driveway. The horse trailer has arrived. I'm glad of all the help available to unload five yearlings. Fortunately, I have plenty of lead-reins, so each of us has one. I suggest we take three yearlings off the trailer to start and then go back for the other two.

The shipper takes off his cap and scratches his head.

"They didn't load too bad, so I reckon they'll come off okay. My ramp isn't steep."

"Thanks."

"Who do I give the invoice to? I'm Norm."

The trailer is bouncing as its passengers fidget—wondering what's happening. I feel for them. They don't know where they are, if they're safe or not, or if they'll be fed—I'm sure they're anxious.

"You can send the bill to me."

"Meg Sheppard, right? I did some shipping for your husband, Frank. I was here several years ago. Nice place. Sorry to hear about Frank. I thought he was a decent guy."

"I think we should unload the horses."

"Sure. I'll lower the ramp. They're in standing stalls. Should be easy to unclip each one, attach a lead-rein, and lead it straight out. Nice horses."

The three of us watch as he lowers the huge ramp covered in textured black rubber that has bits of hay and straw stuck to it. The inside of the trailer smells of fresh horse manure and sweat. One of the colts is edgy. I lead him out first. He looks around, stops on the ramp, whinnies—making his whole body vibrate—and then steps off the ramp. I talk to him as we walk towards the barn. I can hear Bella calling out, so he knows there's another horse where he's going. He points his ears forwards and starts a contracted, bouncy trot as we enter the barn. I turn him around in the stall nearest Eagle and unclip him making sure the door is almost closed behind me. He tries to barge past me in an attempt to escape, but I slip out of the stall and latch the door (before the horse has bolted).

Melissa has learned a lot about leading horses since she arrived at the farm. She and Linda do an excellent job of bringing two more in. Linda and I go back to fetch the remaining two while Melissa keeps an eye on things in the barn.

The filly I lead down the ramp is agitated and sweaty. She probably should have been led off the trailer first, but I hadn't realized how upset she was. Steam rises from her back. She looks terrified. As she scrutinizes the unfamiliar environment, the whites of her eyes are visible. She has her ears pricked and they're moving this way and that—almost in circles. Her nostrils are flared as if she's doing her best to take in every possible whiff of danger. She's trembling with fear. This is going to take time.

Linda walks down the ramp with the last yearling.

"Why don't you go ahead?" I suggest. "This filly may prefer to follow one of her mates."

"I'll try, but he doesn't want to move."

"Hey!" the shipper calls out. A loud crack sets the dogs howling and barking and scares both horses. They each rear but we manage to hold on. The long lead-reins help. We let out extra length rather than risk being lifted off the ground—or worse—having to let go. Melissa trots towards us wearing a deep frown.

"Get them in the barn. Something weird's going on," says Norm.

Another loud crack. The dogs run down the driveway.

"Kelly and Jake, come!" Melissa screams at them. They stop, look around, and then streak back to us. Meanwhile, both young horses are whirling around making Linda and I spin on the spot. I gently yank on the lead-rein a couple of times, pat the frightened filly's sweaty neck, and continue talking to her. Finally, she relents and moves forward. She hears horses calling from inside the barn which makes all the difference to her attitude. But Linda can't get her colt to follow.

"Kelly, time to get the horses in!" I don't know if this is going to work in these circumstances, but when I say that in the evening, Kelly will play at rounding up Eagle and Bullet, as if they're sheep, encouraging the horses to come to the gate, making it easier for me to bring them in.

She trots backwards and forwards behind the colt. I'm so proud of her. She understands what I mean! The colt puts his ears back but isn't terrified of her, thank goodness. He decides the best thing to do is to move forward. So, he and Linda follow me and the filly into the barn.

I'm shaking with exertion and stress.

The drizzle has been persistent. But I haven't noticed it until now and only because I'm damp. But I'm not chilled. I don't think any of us are. The effort of getting the horses into the barn has generated heat, and the soft rain has helped to cool the sweaty horses. We'll give them sponge baths and dry them a bit later. I'm relieved to have them all safely in the barn.

Kelly and Jake join us.

"What on earth made those bangs?" I ask as my legs tremble. I must have expended more energy than I realized.

"I have two holes in my trailer and if I didn't know any better, I'd say they're goddam bullet holes."

"What?" I say. "That can't be true."

"You've been shot at before, remember?" Melissa says. "You were at the Knightscourt place. I suppose whoever it is wants you to stop investigating. You always seem to get threats when you're doing your sleuthing stuff, and the dogs often get hurt too."

"Something tells me this isn't the same. I think the target is the Knightscourts."

"Why shoot at the trailer?" asks Linda.

"Another warning or threat," I say. "Perhaps they're not such a good shot and were aiming at the horses. I don't know."

"But it was you they shot at when you were at the Knightscourt place."

"I've been thinking about that. I want to talk to Dirk, but I think they thought it was someone else. The visibility was poor. For some reason, I can't think that it's about me."

"Jake's limping," Melissa says. "I can't see anything though."

Linda and I check him over and can't find visible evidence of trauma. But his thick black coat which is damp with drizzle could be hiding things.

"I wish he could tell us what's wrong," Melissa says.

"Probably twisted something," Linda says. "He sure dashed down the driveway."

"What about the damage to my trailer?"

We all leave the barn and walk towards the vehicle.

"There's no one in the road, is there?" Melissa asks. "Did you see anyone or a truck or anything?"

"Nope," Norm says. "I didn't. I was focused on the horses and then I put my ramp up. That's when I heard the racket. I suppose I was lucky not to be hit. The bullets must be in the trailer. I'll find them when I clean it out."

"Wow. They do look like bullet holes," I say. "I'll call the police."

"I've got another horse to pick up. I can't wait for the cops to arrive."

"The police won't like it if you leave."

"I'll lose a packet."

"Can't you reschedule?"

"That puts my whole timetable out. I'm darned near booked up."

"How about I reimburse you for the extra time? You must have a connection with someone else in the shipping business who could fill in for you today?"

"I don't like it. It's not good for my reputation."

He grumbles to himself as he pulls out his mobile and walks away. He probably realizes he has no choice. Meanwhile, I've texted Detective Valeska and she's sending some of her troops. Linda doesn't want any more interaction with the police and doesn't want to stay. But I tell her she shouldn't leave before they arrive because that may cause her problems later. She reluctantly agrees to hang around.

So, she and I check the horses over and sponge down the two more settled ones. We agree they should be let out once the vet has finished his work here. Melissa is in the house with Jake, but he has already shown improvement. Kelly wants to be where the action is. She stands in the wide barn doorway and barks. Two police cars. Fortunately, they're taking their time and not making enough noise to disturb the welcome peace in the barn. Eagle thinks he should be outside, so he's whinnied a couple of times, but the others didn't join in.

Despite being disgruntled about the time he's spending here, Norm cooperates with the police and I believe he tells them all he knows. There isn't much. The young police officers ask Linda and me for our accounts. I don't mention Melissa. She's in the house and wouldn't be able to add anything. Two officers ask Norm if they can check the inside of his large trailer, and he shows them around. The ramp is on the side, the bullet holes are in the back. Norm dismantles a couple of the standing stalls by removing the partitions, and the officers take an interest. They've not had experience with large horse trailers. They sift through the straw with their gloved hands and find a bullet. They can't find another, so it's not clear where that one ended up. One of them grabs a bag out of his pocket, turns it inside out, seals the bag and writes information on the label.

"You're not going to take my trailer, are you?" I can see that this horrible thought has suddenly struck Norm. His face has turned a pale greenish colour as if he's about to throw up.

"I don't think that will be necessary since no one was injured. But we need to take photos. We won't be long."

"That's good. This is my livelihood."

"Sorry to keep you waiting. But I'm sure you understand that this is a serious matter."

"Yeah. I get it. I've never been shot at before."

"If you need counselling, we have a list of agencies here." The officer hands over a card and then gives one to each of Linda and me.

I'm about to thank him when Kelly barks again.

"I wonder who that is?"

A large black SUV with blackened windows crawls up the driveway and stops in front of the barn, blocking most of the entrance and making it impossible for the truck and trailer to turn around.

"Can…" I begin to ask Dirk, whose head is leaning out of his open window.

"Where do you want me to park? I reckon right in front of the barn doorway isn't right."

I point over to the side of the house. It takes him about five minutes of complicated turns and reversals to get the SUV over there. I walk towards him as he climbs out. Bobbie doesn't move.

"Hi, Bobbie. How are you?" She doesn't look at me. She's dressed in black and almost invisible.

"She's not feeling good. She won't get out. What are the cops here for?"

Surprisingly, he lets me tell him without cutting me off. He shuffles from one foot to the other and fiddles with the gold medallion nestled in his curly ginger hair on his bared chest. His hair is getting damp, and the shoulders of his jacket have darkened in the relentless drizzle.

"Are my horses okay?"

"This way," I say. We move towards the barn. I should have thought to usher him in earlier, but I'm discombobulated. Linda sneaks past us and walks towards her small, and still-dented car. I shout out my thanks. She waves. Neal will be glad to see her. I turn my attention back to Dirk.

"As soon as…"

"You'll put them in the field."

"Dirk, you…" I let my exasperation show in my voice.

"I have a feeling you have questions about me and Bobbie."

"I do."

"You were shot at and now this trailer's been hit. You're reckoning it's not you they're after, but me and Bobbie."

"Yes."

"I reckon you're right. Bobbie can fill you in, but she won't get out of the car when there's cops around."

"They'll…"

"Be gone soon. But other people are coming, right?"

"Yes."

"Ah, Bella. Oh, you look great. Is Greg coming to check her out?"

"Dr. Russon…"

"Scully. That's good. I'm happy with that. You do what you think is best. You must have guessed by now I know zilch about horses. I think they're majestic and beautiful and I love looking at them and watching them. Owning some is a dream come true."

"Do you have others…?"

"No. I don't have any others. I used to have three racehorses with Barton, but two were claimed earlier this season and the third went to that retirement place just before Barton got himself killed. And before that, I had a couple with that Primula woman, but I sold them." Dirk strokes Bella's nose, but he appears to be slightly nervous. I grab a couple of carrots and break them in half.

"Does she…?"

"I don't know." I hand him a piece of carrot. "Are you supposed to hold it out on your flat hand? I've never done this."

"Just hold it…"

I show him how to hold it with his fingers with most of the carrot showing. Bella takes it from him gently with her soft lips and makes loud crunching noises.

"She likes it!" He turns with a grin on his face like a little child's.

"Haven't you…?"

"I didn't want to let on I know nothing about horses, so I've always played the big boss and kept my distance. But I've spent hours watching them in the fields and went into the barn sometimes just to hear them munching on hay and see them sucking up water from their buckets. I loved that barn."

"You'll be…"

"No, Bobbie will explain. We can't go back. Thanks for taking care of the horses. I will pay you, but it might be a while. I'm having challenges. Can we come back tomorrow to chat? Bobbie's not doing great. Tomorrow will be a better day. What time?"

"The afternoon…"

"We'll come about two then?"

"Sure."

"What about carrots for the yearlings?"

"They aren't…"

"They're not used to having them. Okay."

"Mints."

"Ah, I'll pick up some mints. See you tomorrow. Bye, Bella, bye guys." He waves and leaves the barn with a couple of backwards glances towards the horses who politely keep their heads out over their stall doors so he can see them.

I watch him drive cautiously down the driveway and as they reach the open gate, a taxi stops. My heart sinks. Melissa and I will have to deal with Candice on top of everything else. She gets out, flings a small bag onto her shoulder, puts up an umbrella, and the taxi creeps forward a short distance and stops.

Candice wobbles on her heels as she navigates the gravel driveway. She's wearing a skirt but not as short as the one she had on yesterday. Her appearance wouldn't turn heads in the Vannersville Mall, but she looks incongruously out of place at my farm. I text Melissa to let her know Candice has arrived and suggest we should let the horses out as soon as the police and the trailer have left.

An officer approaches me and says he believes they have everything they need, and Detective Valeska will be in contact with me. Norm can't wait to get out of here. As soon as the police vehicles get moving, he waves and with an expertise I admire, turns his rig around without driving on the lawn or over garden beds, and his truck rumbles down the driveway.

"Hi, Candice. Can you wait in the barn for a minute while I shut the gate?"

"Okay." She sounds hesitant. I suppose she doesn't know what she's going to encounter in there. Kelly ignores her. She must sense Candice isn't an animal lover.

"And please put your umbrella down before you go in because it could spook the horses. Thanks."

"Okay." She totters on her heels towards the barn door.

Kelly and I trot down to the gate. The taxi is still here, at the side of the road just past the gateway, with its engine idling.

"Oy!" The driver beckons to me. I tell Kelly to stay in the driveway. "Yes?"

"That woman hasn't paid."

"Here's my card. Send me your bill. I don't have anything on me right now."

"Uh. I won't come out here again." He slams his foot on the accelerator. His tires churn up stones and damp sand as they create ruts in the dirt road.

I turn around and shut the gate. I don't fasten the new padlock because Dr. Scully will be coming soon. But I want to deter other visitors.

10

Forced Off the Road

My face is wet from the drizzle and Kelly looks as if she's had a dip in a pond. We must appear bedraggled and careworn as we trudge back up the driveway. As I enter the barn, I message Melissa again and suggest she join me and Candice out here.

"Sorry, just texted Melissa. How's your room at the Inn?"

"Fine," Candice says.

"Before we go into the house, I thought you'd like to see the horses. We've had some new arrivals."

"That explains the ginormous trailer, but why were the police here?"

"Just part of an investigation I'm involved in. This is Bella. The vet's coming soon to do an ultrasound examination. We're hoping to see a live foal inside her."

"My shoes got dirty." She gazes down at her large feet encased in red shoes now decorated with tiny bits and pieces of sand and miscellaneous dirt, with a couple of flakes of wood shavings for good measure.

"Haven't you brought any boots with you?"

"Wellies? I don't have any."

"What about jeans or pants?"

"I do have underwear, but no jeans." She looks at me with wide hazel eyes.

"Trousers or jeans."

"Just skirts."

"You may be a bit shorter than Melissa, but perhaps we can lend you some clothes. I don't think we'll have any boots that fit. Come to think of it, I think William left some behind. They could be about right."

"Who's William? I'm not sure I should wear someone else's footwear."

"Up to you. Let's meet the other horses. Here's Melissa."

"Hi, Candice. Nice to meet you. Aren't the horses beautiful?"

"Oh!" Candice exclaims as Jake nudges her leg.

"This is Jake," Melissa says, as she rubs his ears. "He was limping, but he seems to be okay now."

"I'm not used to animals."

"That's a shame," Melissa says.

Kelly and Jake yap and tear out of the barn. This is becoming a regular occurrence today.

"What's the matter with them?" Candice asks.

"They've heard Russon's truck, that's all," Melissa says. "I'm looking forward to introducing him. He's the vet, Candice, Dr. Russon Scully. I work with him at the track."

We wander out into the drizzle. Candice opens her umbrella part way but then closes it. Russon drives slowly up the driveway and parks his large pickup in front of the barn.

"Well, hello everyone. So nice to meet you, Meg." Russon extends his hand. His handshake is warm and firm. His eyes sparkle as if he's amused. "Hi, Melissa. How are you doing?"

"Much better, thanks. This is Candice. She's visiting from England."

"Hi, Candice. Pleased to meet you." He walks to the back of his truck. "So, we have a patient that dropped in, do we?"

"That's about it," I say. "She was stolen, we don't know why, and ultimately dumped here. I'm looking into who and why. Meanwhile, the rightful owner, Dirk Knightscourt, has confirmed that she's his mare, Bella, believed to be in foal to Magical Black."

"Nice. Let's hope all is well."

"She has been through an ordeal."

"Is she staying here or going back to wherever Dirk had arranged for her care?"

"I get the feeling he wants me to look after her. We also have his five yearlings, and it would be great if you could give them a quick examination while you're here."

"Sure. I can do that. What a lovely place you have. It looks beautiful even in the drizzle. Candice, you must feel at home in this weather."

Candice allows a brief, weak smile to show itself and then looks down at her feet again.

Russon's tall, lean body walks to the back of the pickup and retrieves what looks like a suitcase and a stand.

"This aisle is fine," Russon says as he strides back into the barn. "I don't need power. This has a good battery. It's the latest in ultra-sonographic equipment. I always get excited to use it. The images are excellent. It's like taking a trip inside!" He laughs. Melissa and I chuckle, but Candice is still staring at her shoes. He sets up the stand so he can look at the screen without crouching down. "Let's see what we've got." He puts disposable gloves on and selects a probe while Melissa extricates Bella from her stall where she was contentedly munching on hay.

"She could do with a bit more weight on her, but just looking at her belly I'd say there's a high likelihood there's a foal in there. Melissa, turn around and hold her about here, please."

"Her coat looks a bit dull to me," I say.

"I don't think that's anything to worry about. If I had to guess I'd say she's been in a stall rather than out on pasture. I notice you have great grazing here. That'll put things right. And I know you'll feed her the good stuff, so she'll look like a million dollars in no time. Name of the horse? I mean the racing name."

"Oh. I don't know," I say.

"Never mind. I'll enter Bella Knightscourt. Do I send the bill to him by the way?"

"No. Send it to me." No one seems to be paying their bills. But I'm thankful I'm fortunate enough that I can step up.

"You're taking on a lot for Dirk."

"Yes, I suppose I am. I want the horses to be well cared for— that's the main reason."

"Here we go. Meg, you'll see better from this side. Bella's being a good patient which is due to Melissa's skill at keeping horses calm and still while I do my stuff."

Candice has stepped back. It's as if she's overwhelmed.

"Candice, are you okay?" I ask.

"Fine."

It takes a minute or perhaps two for Russon to find the right area with his probe. "See here. Her foal. Let me look around to check things are as they should be."

It's an incredible image. It's like a miracle to see a tiny horse inside Bella. There are tears in my eyes even though she's not my horse. Candice inches forward and peers past Russon's elbow— whispers "Ooh"—and then shuffles backwards to where she's been standing.

"Amazing, isn't it Candice?" Russon says. "A new life—very exciting." He turns to Melissa. "I've recorded it all, so you'll get to see it." The screen isn't visible from where Melissa is despite the equipment being mounted on a stand. She's close to Bella's head, reassuring her and keeping her still.

"I can hold Bella," I say. "She's being so quiet I think she'll behave for me." We switch places.

"That's awesome," Melissa says. "I don't think I've seen anything like this before. It's wonderful. We must take good care of Bella, Meg. So many things can go wrong with pregnant mares."

"It doesn't help to think like that," Russon says. "Yes, things can go wrong, and we can't control everything, and we vets can't fix everything, but she's a strong mare, she's in good hands, and she's survived some ordeals, so I think she'll be fine. She couldn't be at a more caring farm." He looks at Melissa and grins. Melissa smiles back. She hasn't smiled much recently. A shiver of delight tingles my spine. But then I start thinking the worst—from my selfish point of view—that she's probably decided to go to Edinburgh after all. I shut down my thoughts and lead Bella back into her stall. I thank Russon for coming at short notice and remind him I'd like him to look at the five yearlings before he goes.

Russon, Melissa and I wander into each stall. A couple of the yearlings are a bit skittish—three people at once is a bit much, but I don't want to miss anything Russon says about them because it's likely we'll be looking after them for a while.

* * *

Candice peers into her mug of tea as if she's expecting something to emerge from the steaming liquid. I wonder what she's thinking—perhaps she regrets coming. I'm not sure what she was expecting, but I don't think this is it. At least she's stopped shivering—Melissa

117

has lent her a fleece sweater because Candice's lightweight jacket absorbed a lot of drizzle.

Melissa asked her to take her shoes off as we came through the backdoor—Candice thought she was joking. I forgot that, in England, people usually just wipe their shoes on the mat as they enter a house. Candice hasn't said a word since.

Melissa thought ahead, as usual, and bought groceries. She's busy making sandwiches. I've made tea and coffee. There's a strained silence wrapped around us broken by the occasional tapping and tinkling as Melissa prepares lunch.

Cooper jumps up onto the table and wakes Candice out of her daydream.

"Ooh. Is he allowed on the table?"

"No. But he's a cat and he breaks the rules," I say.

She raises her head and glances towards Melissa.

"I thought you'd have staff—a maid or something."

"I don't know why you'd think that," I say.

"Only rich people have racehorses. And they have large houses with staff."

"It's not the same here as in England. People of more modest means can own racehorses. And some join partnerships. And not all people with money live in big houses and employ staff."

Not much else is said during lunch. Candice appears deflated and her face is pale.

*　*　*

Linda shows up early, just as I'm leaving the house to feed the horses. Yesterday's drizzle has stopped and, as the sun peeks over the horizon, reds and oranges are reflected off a few scattered clouds. The horses will have a lovely day for grazing.

"Thanks, Linda."

"Sorry I couldn't get the feed yesterday, but my mother wasn't good."

"That's a shame. I hope she's feeling better today."

"Sort of. She liked me being at home when the cops had my car."

"Ah." She opens her trunk. "Your car can hold more than I expected. This will keep us going until I can arrange for delivery." We bring the bags of feed in from her trunk and pile them in the barn. "Thanks so much. They had some of Eagle and Bullet's fat and fibre yesterday evening but now I can give them the right nutrition. You're in time for the morning feed. So, let's get them fed and then have a cup of tea. After that, we can lead them out."

"Nice day for a change," Linda says as she and I scoop up sweet-smelling grain and dish it out to expectant horses.

All of them tuck into their breakfast, which is great to see. I'm sure they'll settle in quickly. We walk to the house, and I make tea and coffee. Linda drinks half a mug of coffee and says she wants to clean the yearlings' halters.

"I noticed Bella's is a nylon one," I say. "I'm sure Orlando wouldn't have had a nylon one on her. It's also caked with dirt. I have a couple of spare leather ones in the feed room."

"I like cleaning tack. I'll do that when they're out in the field. I don't have to be at the track early. Les is working out real well."

"That's good. Neal must be pleased."

"He's hoping he'll go full-time". She stands, ready to leave the kitchen. "I'll find the cleaning stuff."

"It's all together in a cupboard in the feed room. But before you go, tell me exactly what you saw before your car hit Barton. I know it's difficult for you, but you weren't driving, and it wasn't your fault. The only thing you should have done was report it right away."

"That woman was there. She must have called the ambulance."

"Let's not go over that. Tell me what you saw exactly." My mobile rings just at the wrong moment and it's Detective Valeska. "We'll

119

talk later, Linda." She waddles out of the door. "Hello."

"Hi. I assume you've heard the news."

"What news?"

"Dirk and Bobbie Knightscourt have reported that their vehicle was forced off the road. They're in hospital, but the airbags protected them, and they're expected to make a full recovery."

"Where? Do they know who did this?"

"They say they don't. That's where you come in. They might tell you more than they're willing to report to us. Meanwhile, I've assigned officers on security duty outside their rooms. Eating a hole in my budget, I'll add. The sooner we get to the bottom of this, the better."

"Bobbie was accused of murder in a gang incident several years ago."

"I think you mean her sister, Annie. She was acquitted. That's all I know right now. We're reviewing the files because of what's happened—in case there's a link."

"I'll visit them today."

"Good."

She ends the call just as Melissa appears in the kitchen.

"I thought you were going to work today."

"I was, but Russon had a last-minute opportunity to attend a workshop at the University of Guelph. He asked one of the partners to cover for him and left it up to me if I wanted to go in or not. I decided not, given all that's going on. And I need to talk with you."

My stomach immediately turns effervescent, and not in a pleasant way. It's so unsettled that I fold my arms over it in a futile attempt to quell its unrest.

"Is it about Edwin?"

"No, it's about William."

"Oh." Fortunately, I'm rather good at hiding my emotions, so I'm reasonably sure Melissa didn't detect the tsunami of relief that washed over me from head to foot. However, I remind myself that I still face the prospect of her leaving. No final decision has been made for her to stay. I want the best for Melissa, but there's a selfishness on my part that raises its ugly head quite often—my strong desire to continue my enjoyment at having my half-sister in my life.

"I like William. I think you overreacted about the whole Gabriel thing." She sits down.

"But I don't." I unfold my arms but stay standing. "He was the one who left. And he went to live with his assistant, Ramona."

"He's not with her anymore. You know that."

"What are you getting at?"

"I think you should give him another chance."

"It's none of your business."

"It is, when you mope around, being grumpy and hardly eating anything." Melissa stands and moves towards the coffee machine.

"I do eat. And I'm not grumpy."

"Yes, you are." Melissa raises her voice. "You think you're good at hiding your emotions. But I can see through you. You've not been happy since William left." She puts the kettle on instead of the coffee maker and reaches for a couple of mugs.

"I don't tell you what to do in your relationship with Edwin. But he's behaved just as badly as William. I don't tell you to put your engagement ring back on. I could say that you've not been in the greatest of moods either."

"Touché, I suppose." She flops down on a chair and rests her head on her folded arms as they lie on the table. "By the way, I'm not going to Edinburgh," her voice is muffled. "But that's nothing to do with William and you."

"Oh, Melissa. Are you sure you don't want to join him?"

She lifts her head, tears in her eyes. "I am sure. He's been much worse than William. He's not thought of my feelings one bit as he's made a life-changing decision."

"Neither did William think of mine when he arranged for Gabriel to live with Maddy and her family in Saskatchewan. That would have been life-changing too—having a child living with us."

"It's not the same. I'd be leaving so much behind. Not only you, this farm and all the wonderful animals, but my job, my friends, and this country that's been good to me. I know it's Scotland and not England, but I have some weird and disturbing association with being on that island and my profound unhappiness."

"I understand what you mean, but things haven't always gone well for you here."

"I know. But it's not the same somehow. I have your consistent love regardless of what happens to me. And I have this stable home, whatever I'm doing. And I'm forgiven when I do stupid things, like register for courses with the goal of becoming a veterinarian."

"That wasn't stupid. You'd make a great vet."

"Well, it was stupid to let Candice visit. I'm the one who complains when people come, and especially if they want to stay here. She does. She can't afford the hotel."

"Don't worry. I'll pay her bill. Anyway, that's beside the point. Are you sure you don't want to go? What does Edwin say?"

"I haven't had much contact with him since he left to find somewhere to live in Edinburgh—at least I assume that's what he's doing. You'd think he'd be sending me pics of places or something. Nothing. I honestly don't think he cares enough about me."

"But you still care about him."

"I'm a bit confused about my feelings. I didn't have any doubts until this Edinburgh thing came up, and now I'm not sure."

"I hope you're not staying because of me."

"To some extent I am. We're sisters. And they say blood is thicker than water, and I sort of get it."

"Don't miss out on life because of me. Having a family and children is not something I'm going to experience, but you're younger and have your future ahead of you."

"I loved the idea of living in Milkweed Farm, just a couple of doors down. That was such a wonderful wedding present. But the fiancé left so that bubble burst."

"It's sitting empty. I must do something about that."

"Now we're on that subject, I have a favour to ask."

"Mm."

"William is…"

"No."

"Meg! Please listen. He's willing to pay rent and says he won't ever come here unless he's invited. He's got nowhere to go. He's left Ramona, and the tenants are still in his flat. He says once they leave there'll be all sorts of redecoration to do. He's lost some clients. He's in a bit of a mess and I'm worried about him. What if he goes back on drugs?"

"Why is this my problem?"

"Meg! I've not known you to be so hard. The man did a lot for you."

"He didn't treat me with respect."

"Oh, for goodness's sake get off your high horse. We're none of us perfect all the time. Can't you forgive him enough to let him rent Milkweed?" She looks at me as if waiting for a response. "He said he misses helping you on your investigations. He said he doesn't have to come here, but he'd like to be part of that again. He misses you a lot—you know that don't you?"

My body starts to shake, and tears roll down my cheeks. I can't stop them. I hold my head in my hands. Melissa shoves a tissue in front of me and I grab it. I can't understand why I don't have my emotions in check. I'm sobbing. My ribs are heaving, my nose is running, and the tears keep coming. Kelly whines and puts her paw on my lap, and I can see concern in her eyes through my fuzzy tears. I stroke her paw but can't stop crying. It's almost as if that action makes the tears come faster.

Melissa puts her arm around me awkwardly because I'm still sitting in my chair.

"Meg, I'm so sorry. I didn't know this would upset you so much. I didn't know how strongly you feel about William. I won't mention him again."

But she's wrong. It's about her decision to stay here. It's the enormous relief that I'm not losing her. But I can't say that. I sit upright and strap an imaginary corset around my body to stop it from convulsing into sobs again.

"Melissa." I blow my nose. "It's okay. It's an accumulation of stress about things. I'm just feeling a bit low."

"That doesn't make sense, Meg. Tell me the truth."

"Part of it is William, I admit. But not the way you think. While he messed up badly and I'll never be able to forgive him entirely, he obviously still wants to be in our lives. So, I'll relent and let him rent Milkweed Farm. And I welcome his help with my investigations. I miss his contacts and his suggestions and thoughts. But I don't want him thinking he can move in here."

"Meg, that's fantastic. I'm so happy. I like him a lot and it'll be great to have him as a neighbour and a friend."

"Don't get too carried away."

"What's the other part?"

"What do you mean?" I look at her with puffy eyes and red cheeks.

"Don't play games with me, Meg."

Kelly nudges me with her nose. "It's okay, Kelly." I stroke her silky head slowly.

"Meg." Melissa walks around the kitchen as if searching for something while the kettle emits clouds of steam but is ignored. "Oh, no. I know. But I didn't think of what it would mean to you— me going to live in Edinburgh, leaving here, leaving you. And I bet

FORCED OFF THE ROAD

you thought I wouldn't come back—that me and Edwin would settle there. That's the other part, isn't it? You can admit it now because I'm not going."

"Melissa, I'm sorry. I shouldn't be so selfish."

"We could have an argument about who's been the most selfish if you like. I'm good at starting arguments." She sits down opposite me and grabs my hand. Her fingers feel warm and supple. "I'm so glad you want me here. I can't say how much it means to me. This is the only home I've ever had and I'm not going to leave it on a whim and that's how it feels with Edwin. He's not committed. He's got excited about this opportunity in Edinburgh, and I've been left in the dust. I know that's exaggerating, but only a bit."

Melissa makes scrambled eggs. I don't like to say I'm not hungry. She spoons a small portion of the steaming yellow stuff onto toast. I surprise myself by eating it hastily, but it's partly because I remember Farley Smedley is coming and is due in about thirty minutes. I need to have the horses back in their stalls. I gulp down the rest of a mug of tea—which I managed to make once I pulled myself together—and get ready to go to the barn.

"I could stay and help if you like," Melissa says.

"Thanks, but don't you have to work today?"

"I told you, Russon is at a workshop."

My mobile tells me there's a text. Linda has been called in by Neal. Les didn't turn up. "It seems Linda can't stay, so I'll take you up on your offer. Can you help me bring the horses in? Farley's due soon."

11

Gangs

The horses behave well as we lead them into their stalls. A couple of the yearlings are pawing at their rubber mats. They would rather be out in the pasture and probably feel that we tricked them into being brought in much too early. Farley arrives on time and assembles his tools. He puts his chaps on, and we begin the lengthy process of bringing each horse out into the aisle to allow him to clean, trim, and rasp their hooves. Kelly and Jake lie in wait for the trimmings which they know they can pinch once each horse is back in a stall.

"Since you're investigating what went on," Farley says, "I'd like to add a couple of things to what I told you the other day when we were walking by the training track."

"I'm not sure where I stand with the investigation," I say.

"Well, whatever. I'll tell you anyway." He pulls up one of the horse's hind feet and grabs it between his thighs. The young colt surprises me with his acceptance of being immobilized. However, if he wanted to send Farley tumbling, he could. Melissa talks to the horse and strokes his nose which helps the colt to stay calm. Farley's bent over and working hard, but I can hear his strong voice. "For all the show, Dirk isn't all that well-off, you know." He looks up as if to emphasize the point. He resumes rasping the hoof and white flakes fall like a snow shower onto the dark rubber flooring of the aisle. The smell reminds me of filing my nails. I suppose they're made of the same stuff.

"He lives in an opulent place," I say.

"He has peacocks," adds Melissa.

"He doesn't," Farley says as he releases the colt's leg. The horse stamps his foot in mild protest to the goings on but otherwise stands quietly. "You know he rents that awful place, don't you?"

"No. I assumed his business was successful and he owned that estate."

"Nope." There isn't a bead of sweat on his forehead. He must be incredibly fit. Farley picks up the other hind foot and starts trimming. "Nope, he rents. I reckon his business is doing sort of okay otherwise he wouldn't be able to afford it—he has half the first floor."

"He has servants or whatever you're supposed to call them these days."

"The old man comes with the house. And there's a housekeeper."

"So, they don't have anything to do with the casino?"

"You know about the casino? Well, of course you do. I reckon Barton was addicted to gambling. It seemed to me he went there most nights. That probably has something to do with his death. I bet he owed a lot of money. But, nope, the Knightscourts had nothing to do with the casino as far as I know. It operated out of the basement and was illegal of course. I never went there. I wouldn't consider doing something stupid like that. I have my reputation to think of and I don't want to squander my hard-earned dollars. I don't even bet on the horses although trainers are happy to share their tips with me." He chuckles. "They always think their horse is going to beat all the rest."

"Optimism is the name of the game. But tell me more about Dirk and Bobbie."

"I don't have much else, except that Dirk did pay his bills, so he's not hard up, just not rich. When I think about it, I'd say he's not as well off as you'd expect from owning those funeral homes. He's the biggest player in that business in Vannersville and we all die eventually. But back to where they live. Bobbie is the one, I've been told, who wants to live the high life. But she hardly ever goes out. I wonder if she has agoraphobia or some form of it. My theory is she needs to make her home her castle, surrounding herself with opulence and extravagance, or at least as much as they can afford. I could have it all wrong, though."

* * *

Farley wouldn't accept offers of food and drink even though he worked hard and long to get all the hooves in shape. Bella's were the worst, and she was the most difficult. Despite his obvious fitness and strength, Farley took a breather a couple of times. She was the last one and he showed signs of tiring.

As Farley gets into his truck to leave, Candice shows up. She's transformed herself into a reasonable human being for a visit to the farm. She's wearing jeans and a fleece top which looks familiar, so it could be another one of Melissa's. Her large feet look more comfortable in a pair of simple running shoes.

"Hello," she says. Melissa walks out of the barn and suggests they go into the house for coffee. I've just received a text from Dirk telling me they're out of the hospital and staying at a farm just up the road from us—could I go there this afternoon? Since it's afternoon already, I say I'll come now. I plan to drive on to Three Willows Farm after I visit with them.

*　　*　　*

Kelly, Jake, and I get into the pickup and turn its nose towards the farm where Dirk and Bobbie are staying.

It's not far along the dirt road and has a clear entrance but the gate is closed. Goldenrod is thriving along the front of the property, although only in partial bloom, and wild grapevines have a strangle-hold on the wire fencing. A stony track, with many potholes, leads to the old farmhouse. The long grasses on either side of us shiver in the breeze and sparkle in the sunshine. There are no vehicles in sight. I park in front of the house and let the dogs out for a run. They immediately become fascinated by the various scents and keep their noses close to the ground.

"Meg, thanks for coming." Dirk stands in the doorway twiddling with his gold medallion.

"How..."

"I have some minor burns from the airbag. I didn't know they have nasty chemicals in them, and I thought they'd caused a fire—it smelled so smoky. Terrifying things they are."

"I'm sorry to hear this."

"The hospital treated my blisters and had us in for observation. Bobbie and I have a few bruises. It wasn't as bad as it could have been though. I suppose those frightening airbags saved us. Otherwise, we could be in a couple of my coffins lying in one of the Knightscourt funeral homes."

"Don't..."

"I know, I shouldn't say that. Bobbie's inside. Come on in."

"Can..."

"The dogs are welcome."

"Why..."

"Why are we here? Because this is safer right now."

"Meg!" Bobbie greets me as if I'm a long-lost friend. "Thanks for coming so quickly. This isn't the greatest place, but we feel safe here." She pats Kelly and Jake.

"Someone died in this house," Dirk says, "that's how I knew it was available and the person who inherited it owes me one or two favours."

"Dirk, don't remind me," Bobbie says. "I'll be listening for ghosts. I hope it wasn't murder. If it was, I won't be able to sleep."

"Bobbie, for goodness' sake. Anyway, we agreed to tell Meg all we know."

"I expect you'd like tea. I found some Irish Breakfast. I'll make it. We even have milk."

"Thanks, Bobbie," I say, hoping I'm not revealing my surprise at her effusive friendliness. Up to this point, I've thought of her as cool and aloof.

She disappears into the adjacent large kitchen. I imagine it was the centre of family life years ago. Kelly and Jake lie down at my feet. I'm proud of how well-behaved they are.

"Meg, we haven't been straight with you. Bobbie didn't know if you could be trusted. There's stuff that's sort of hanging over us and we've been threatened. It's not a nice place to be, I'll tell you that." He leans back in a roomy armchair that must have provided many years of comfort and still looks serviceable. I've sunk into its companion sofa which hasn't stood up to the rigours of farmhouse life nearly as well.

"Don't start without me," shouts Bobbie. "I'm almost ready."

I'm hesitant to even try speaking to Dirk because he always anticipates what I'm going to say. But I decide to give it a go.

"Your yearlings," I hesitate.

"Go on, what about our yearlings?"

"They were great with Farley today. Their feet look good."

"What about Bella?"

"She gave…"

131

"Farley a tough time. She always does. That's Bella, but I love her like crazy. I'm sure glad she's with you."

"Aren't you…"

"No, I'm not worried about them being at your farm. They want us, not them."

"But…"

"Yeah, someone stole Bella, but I'm not even sure it's related to what's going on with us. You're going to find out, aren't you?"

"I'm going…"

"Good."

I wanted to say I was going to Three Willows Farm to discover who delivered Bella there and who paid the bills for her board. But Dirk is back to his usual trick of cutting me off.

Bobbie brings a tray complete with a teapot and three cups and saucers.

"Quite civilized," she says, with a smile.

"Wonderful," I say.

"Bobbie likes things to be civilized," Dirk says.

We finally have our tea, and I hope they'll talk.

"I'm going to do the talking," Bobbie says. "Then you can ask questions without being rudely interrupted." She stares at Dirk for one or two seconds.

"Okay, okay. You go ahead."

"I'll get straight to it. I have a sister, Annie. We both worked in Dirk's first funeral home. That's how Dirk and I met. But there's a story behind Annie. She was the rebel."

"She sure was. She wasn't a good worker. Not reliable."

"Dirk, I'm doing the talking. Anyway, I tried to be a good sister, but I wasn't really. I couldn't understand her behaviour. To me, she was following a dangerous path. She was in with some tough characters and got involved in drug trafficking. It scared me to death. She joined a gang, would you believe, and was dating Barton, yes, the guy who was killed in the hit and run recently. She acted as if she'd won the lottery, being his girlfriend, so he must have been an important gang member. But alarm bells were going off like crazy in my head. It was around that time that Dirk fired her because she didn't show up for work for days at a time. I've told Dirk I was worried he would fire me too, so I worked extra hard. Dirk and I weren't a couple then."

"I wouldn't have let you go. Her behaviour had nothing to do with you."

"Well, anyhow, Annie was out of control. She must have been taking drugs, but I was rather clueless about those things. I still am. I lived in a different world, and I didn't want anything to do with hers. So, as I said, I wasn't the greatest of sisters."

"We did try to find her."

"That's after she hadn't shown her face for a month, and I hadn't been able to get hold of her. But we weren't successful. And the next we heard of her was in the papers and on social media. She'd been arrested and charged with murder in the shooting of a member of a rival gang, called Pablo."

"But how is this connected to someone shooting at me," I ask, "and the shots fired at the horse trailer, and you being forced off the road?"

"We think there's a connection with the murder of Orlando."

"But..."

"How are these things related, you're asking," Dirk says.

"Dirk. Meg and I are doing the talking. You'll just have to curb that impatience of yours for once."

Dirk grunts and slumps back into the large armchair as if he's been swallowed by a giant Venus Flytrap. His cup of tea is untouched. I'm enjoying mine.

"Orlando was a member of Barton's gang like Annie was."

"Where's Annie now?"

"We don't know. I should feel terrible about that, but I don't. I gave up on her and my gut told me I'd lost her, and I couldn't think of any way of bringing her back into my life. Have you got a sister?"

"Melissa, who works for Dr. Russon Scully. She's my half-sister."

"I can tell by the way you said it, that she's special to you. I wish I hadn't lost Annie, and the worst is that I'm almost sure she's dead."

"Oh no."

Dirk grunts.

"That's what I believe. Anyway, what I'm worried about is that someone is out there picking off the members of Barton's gang one by one, including Barton, Orlando and probably Annie. But why target us? And why use terrorism tactics rather than kill us outright like they did with Barton and Orlando?"

"They didn't kill Barton outright. According to the toxicology report, he had been poisoned with arsenic over a period of time. His would have been a slow death and it might have simulated heart disease or bad indigestion. He likely had abdominal pain along with diarrhea and other horrible symptoms."

"That helps to explain his irritability, poor guy," Dirk says. "Could his weird skin have been caused by the arsenic?"

"Probably," I say.

"Orlando was shot," Bobbie says.

"But wasn't he missing for at least a couple of days?"

"Can you find out if they tortured him or something awful?" Dirk sits up and rubs his fingers on his forehead. "He was such a good guy. I couldn't care less about Barton, but Orlando was so good with the horses, such a pleasant person."

"One of the reasons you liked him so much was that he hardly said a word and you could talk non-stop."

Dirk sinks back into the chair again as if he's been stung.

"The couple of times I saw him, Orlando was polite—I'll give you that. I can't comment on his horsemanship because I don't have any horse sense."

"I'm cut up about Orlando," Dirk says. "I relied on him to run the barn and had no complaints. I can't bear to think of someone hurting him. Being shot outright is one thing, but—it makes me feel sick."

Bobbie gives Dirk a sideways glance, but he pays no attention.

"Bobbie," I say. "Who would be doing this? Members of the gang Pablo was in?"

"Gotta be," Dirk says. "But we don't know who they are."

"So, it's probably all about revenge. But it's been about seven years since Pablo was killed, right?'

"Nearly eight," Bobbie says. "And we don't know who the members were."

"I want you to find out who killed Orlando," Dirk says. "I can't stop thinking about what he must have gone through."

"My plan is to find out who stole Bella. After being shot at I decided I wasn't going to continue with murder investigations."

"Whoever it was, thought they were shooting at us," Bobbie says, "because we use that side entrance sometimes. It was a case of mistaken identity. I'm sure when you got out of the truck, they thought it was me."

"Why would anyone want to kill either of you?"

"As I said, it's like terrorism," Bobbie says as she shakes her full head of curly mahogany brown hair. "And it's working because we're running and hiding."

"But why wait nearly eight years to get revenge? And why target you? Neither of you were involved in gangs, right?"

"We weren't. I don't know the answers to your questions."

Dirk shakes his head in apparent agreement.

"But you believe you're in danger."

"We do."

"That's another reason to find out who killed Orlando," Dirk says as he leans forward again. "Whoever shot Orlando is the man we need. We're next. We've got Bella back and my gut tells me her theft has nothing to do with the murders. I'll pay you well. Just find him. The cops aren't doing an effing thing."

"I'm sure they are."

"Meg," Dirk says. "We don't have confidence in the cops. They haven't got a suspect for Barton's murder, and they're doing damn all to find Orlando's killer. I'm sure you won't get shot at again. They're not after you."

"I'll think about it."

"Don't take long."

"Dirk, you can't order Meg about. She's not one of your staff. I'm sure she's got better things to do."

"I have a lot on my plate," I say. "But I can see you're under a lot of stress. I'll think about it."

*   *   *

My energy level is low, partly because I haven't eaten and partly because I'm not enthused about this case. But it's as if someone has attached a rope to me and is winching me into the middle of this rotten business. One problem is I'm concerned for Dirk and Bobbie's safety. I don't think they'd be difficult to find. Whoever the murderer is, was able to find my farm and knows I'm involved. Could they have followed me this afternoon?

Three Willows Farm appears on my right. It looks even more decrepit than I remember from my humane society days. We visited at least twice because we received complaints from neighbours about lack of hay and water, and long, untrimmed hooves. Weeds and tall grass surround the barn and other outbuildings. Fences are chewed and repairs are makeshift. The gates sag and the 'pasture' is nothing but dirt due to overgrazing—which isn't uncommon, but the good farms make sure the horses have lots of hay. The horses here have dark-coloured round bales in battered bale feeders. But at least they have something to eat. The name of the owner comes back to me as I see her walking towards my truck. I open the door and hop down from the running board.

"What do you want?"

"Hi, Glenda."

"I remember you. You can get out."

"I'm not with the humane society. I'm here on another matter. I need your help."

"Huh. Why should I help you?"

"I'm an amateur sleuth now, and I'm investigating two murders."

"The goddam cops should do their jobs instead of ticketing for speeding."

There's probably a story there, but I'm not here to talk about speeding or police services.

"I'll get straight to the point. I'm sure you're busy."

"You got that right. You can't let your dogs out."

I look behind me and they're sitting on the two front seats as if they're about to drive off.

"Glenda, a mare was delivered here a few days ago and then was picked up by Hugh Bracknell and brought to my farm although I wasn't expecting her."

"I don't want her back here."

"That's not what I'm saying. I'd like to know who brought her here and who paid her boarding fees."

"Huh. That's funny. I didn't get paid, did I? So, when Hugh came to pick her up, I did a happy dance."

"Who brought her here?"

"I can't remember who the shipper was, but the guy who said he was the owner had a name like Denny or Kenny. He said he'd visit the day after she arrived and give me all his info, but he never did. And he hasn't answered texts or voicemails. I gave up after two days of tearing my hair out and I was wondering what the hell to do with the horse. I was about to send her to auction when Hugh showed up and said he was picking her up. Queer business—the whole thing—and I'm poorer for it."

"Here's my card. You can send me the invoice." It seems I'm paying everyone's bills. I'd better keep track of it all—otherwise I could end up in financial difficulty myself.

Her deep frown disappears and her lips quiver as if undecided whether to smile or not.

"Oh. That's nice. Is she your mare?"

"No. Someone has asked me to take care of her."

"Why did he have her sent here and not to your place then?"

"She'd been stolen. The person who connected with you to arrange shipment here is not the owner."

"Geez. Fancy that. I've never had a stolen horse here before."

"Hopefully you won't again. I promise to pay the invoice. And thanks for your help."

"You're welcome. Is the guy who stole the horse the murderer? You said you were investigating murders. Gives me the creeps to think I could have had a killer on my property if he'd showed up. Is this Kenny or Denny character the guy you're after?"

"I'm after him for stealing the mare, that's all."

"Bad enough," she sighs. "I'll send you the invoice then."

"Okay."

"I'd better get on with things."

* * *

Candice looks more relaxed. Cooper has used his feline charm to gain a spot on her lap as she and Melissa sit at the kitchen table. I feed the dogs and replenish their large water bowl.

"Have you eaten since breakfast?" Melissa asks.

"I don't think so, but I had a nice cup of tea with Dirk and Bobbie."

"So, you are investigating the murders?"

"I'm still not committed, but I am concerned for Dirk and Bobbie's safety and that's making it tough for me to turn my back on them."

"Did you find out anything at Three Willows Farm? You said you might go there after."

"It seems that Kenny, from Animal Equality and Freedom, probably stole Bella and had her sent to Three Willows. Glenda, the owner, said the person who called her to arrange shipment to her farm had a name like 'Kenny'."

"And then he must have arranged to have her shipped here? Why?"

"I don't know. Perhaps he had second thoughts about the theft or perhaps he found out more about Three Willows. He's an odd character. He professes to be an animal rights activist, but then he goes about harming horses and putting them at risk. I don't trust the guy or pretend to understand his actions."

"He could be a fanatic," Candice says. "There are a couple of animal rights groups in England that are OTT. Members chain themselves to cattle lorries, spray-paint butchers' shop windows, things like that."

"That doesn't explain why he stole Bella, if he did. What was his motive?"

"You'll just have to ask him," Melissa says as she fills a saucepan with water. "We're having pasta. No complaints—it's all we've got."

"It was so nice to meet William," Candice says.

"Meg, he's moving into Milkweed Farm tomorrow. I said you'd invoice him because I don't know what you're charging or if you want first and last month's rent, or what. He really didn't have any questions about it, though. He's so pleased to be moving in and

Candice has agreed to help him get organized."

"He's such a nice man," Candice says as she strokes a purring Cooper. "He's brilliant."

"He wanted me to let you know, Meg, that he has some information on the murder of Pablo, and on the post-mortem results for both Orlando and Barton. He said you can call him. He really wants to help."

"I think that's so nice," Candice says.

I roll my eyes at Melissa. It's as if Candice has fallen for William. Melissa laughs.

12

Collapse

Candice and Melissa are getting along better than I expected. Perhaps Candice is a helpful distraction from Melissa's thoughts of Edwin and her broken engagement.

Melissa picked Candice up from Vannersville Inn in the early hours of this morning so that Candice could shadow her at work.

Having cleaned the barn with Linda's help, I'm staring into a mug of tea. I don't know why I need to summon up courage to call William. The last time we saw each other we had a blazing row about his unilateral decisions on his young nephew's—Gabriel's—move to Saskatchewan without even saying goodbye. It still stings. But I admit I miss William. He was a partner in my life and in my investigations.

The tea is lukewarm and bitter. Kelly and Jake sit either side of my chair and look at me with shiny eyes as if they're wondering why I'm not doing anything.

"You'll have to wait. I'm going to call William." Saying it aloud motivates me to pick up my mobile and call.

"Meg! How nice."

"Hi. Melissa said you have some info."

"I cannot thank you enough for the use of Milkweed Farm. It's an idyllic spot. I will take diligent care of it, I promise. I don't think I will ever want to leave. I don't know what the rent is. Would you send me an invoice? And are there any rules I need to be aware of?"

"Not really. I'll make sure the septic tank is pumped. The well hasn't run dry yet so you shouldn't have to worry about that. The heat pump is nearly new. You shouldn't have any issues other than the usual challenges of living in the country, and you know all about those."

"Yes, I do. What should I do about the barn?"

"Nothing. I'll check it now and then. I'll let you know when I'm coming."

"There's no need. Is there a lease agreement I should sign?"

"No."

"Would you like me to draw one up? It would protect you as well as me. I wish to avoid misunderstandings. I want to get off on the right foot here."

"I have no objection—if you would prefer something in writing."

"Now, back to the reason you called. I have been asking a few questions of a couple of my contacts and have some information that could be helpful to you in your investigation."

"I'm not sure what I'm investigating. I'm not keen on continuing with the murder investigations—the deaths of Barton and Orlando—because someone shot at me when I was entering the side entrance to the Knightscourt property. Bobbie Knightscourt has assured me that it must have been a case of mistaken identity, but I admit I'm literally gun shy."

"That's disturbing, to say the least. Were you badly hurt?"

"Just a graze."

"But that's serious, Meg. I understand why you would not want to continue. But, let me tell you what I unearthed anyway. Are you sure you're alright?"

"Sure."

"The post-mortem results first. The cause of death in Orlando's case was a gunshot wound to the head. But there's more to it. It's not pleasant, Meg. He was tortured, to be blunt. There were several signs of this, apparently, including cigarette burns, but he was also dehydrated—this type of violent behaviour is often found to be gang-related. But I'm unaware of any evidence to support that it was a Blackbirds Gang member who shot Pablo."

"But that doesn't mean it can be ruled out."

"No. That's correct. I do know that Annie Hart was acquitted because her defence counsel was able to provide evidence that she was not a member of the Blackbirds Gang. She was a member of the rival gang to which Pablo belonged."

"That's extremely interesting. Bobbie Knightscourt told me her sister Annie was a member of the Blackbirds Gang."

"It's curious that Bobbie would tell you that. Anyway, the Crown was unable to prove Annie had fired a gun. For instance, there was no evidence on Annie's hands or clothes to substantiate the allegation that she'd used a firearm. She remained at the scene whereas all other gang members were able to escape before the police arrived. Furthermore, my source said that part of Annie's defence was that, in her written statement, she included an assertion that she and Pablo were in a relationship."

"If Annie was telling the truth—and it could explain why she was found at the scene with Pablo—could Annie be the one seeking revenge since both Barton and Orlando were members of the Blackbirds Gang?"

"From what you tell me, there is concern for the safety of Dirk and Bobbie Knightscourt. If your suggestion of revenge is correct, surely Annie is unlikely to attack her own family members? There's no reason to believe that either Dirk or Bobbie had anything to do with these gangs is there?"

"No, you're right. Annie wouldn't have forced Dirk and Bobbie off the road. I wish I knew where Annie was. I'd really like to talk with her."

"So would police services."

"Thanks for this, William."

"You're more than welcome. Perhaps we could have a coffee, I mean tea, later?"

"Perhaps."

"Thank you again for the use of Milkweed Farm. I feel like I've come home."

*　　*　　*

Suzie looks different without her false eyelashes. And her long nails are painted a muted red—rather than dark purple with something resembling Christmas glitter embedded in them. We walk into the café to order our drinks. This time I hope we won't have any interruptions.

"Have you found another job?" I ask once we're seated on the patio. My tea, with the bag on the side, arrives. I sigh as I put the bag into the tepid water and know I'm not going to drink it. I should have ordered hot chocolate.

"I thought I was going to have a bunch of trouble finding something 'cause I worked in that illegal casino, but the illegal bit doesn't seem to matter. I'm starting at the new casino next to the racetrack. It's bartending, which I know a lot about, and I don't mind working late. I guess it must be difficult to find people."

"They don't expect you to wear false eyelashes then."

She giggles. "No, they expect workers to look classy. I'm not classy, but I'm trying."

"That's good. Suzie, you want to talk to me."

"I sure do. The cops had me in for questioning again. That's three times. I got a rash and sick to my stomach every time. It takes me a day to get over it. They make me feel like some sort of criminal. I've done nothing wrong."

"What questions did they ask?"

"Did I push Barton? Did I serve him drinks? How many? Was I qualified? All sorts of questions. They had my head spinning. Yeah, I actually got dizzy."

"And what did you say?"

"The second time I went in to be grilled by the cops I took my Smart Serve certificate with me to prove I'd taken the course. Even though that casino wasn't legit, the owners still wanted bartenders to take it. I'm sure glad I did."

"Tell me what happened."

"I hate going back over this. It's like a nightmare in my head. I haven't been able to sleep properly."

"I need to know everything you can tell me if I'm going to be able to help you."

"Yeah, sorry. Feeling a bit low and edgy today." She takes a couple of gulps of coffee and puts the mug down with a shaky hand. "Barton had been acting funny for a while. I've been thinking about it a lot and I reckon I missed stuff I should've picked up on, you know? He wasn't my boyfriend, but perhaps I told you already. He used to chat with me when he came to sit at the bar now and then, but that was it. But I sort of got worried about him, you know, because it seemed like he was sick. I asked him if he was alright. He said he thought he had a stomach ulcer or something, but he couldn't take time off work to have it checked out. I kept on at him a bit and then he said he'd go see his doctor soon. I reminded him whenever I saw him. His skin was going funny. I could see it even in the awful lighting they had by the bar. He said he was tired, too."

"But he kept going to the casino."

"Yeah. He wasn't exactly addicted to gambling—but getting close. He didn't come every night 'cause there were a few times when I worked and he wasn't there. But I reckon he must have lost quite a bit of dough, and he didn't seem rich. You could say it was none of my business, but I did get worried about the guys who drank too much and gambled more than it looked like they could afford, you know?"

"Did he meet anyone there? Or was there anyone he had contact with?"

"The cops asked me the same thing. I can't say I noticed anyone. Why did they want to know that?"

"Oh, I bet you don't know the circumstances of Barton's death."

"What do you mean? He was hit by that car. He sort of fell into it, though. I tried to hold him back, you know, not push him like the cops wanted me to say."

"He was suffering from chronic arsenic poisoning. He was dead before the car hit him."

"What the? Why are the cops on my case, then?"

"They haven't questioned you recently, have they?"

"When I think about it, the last time I was there they asked more about Barton in the casino than about me."

"They're trying to find out who poisoned him. They probably think someone put arsenic in his drinks at the casino."

"I would've noticed that."

"Are you sure?"

"Yeah. I'm sure. I was the bartender. I knew what I was doing, and I would've noticed someone sneaking up and dropping something in his drink."

"And this would have been repeated over a period of time. His hair contained traces of arsenic, so it was not an acute poisoning. It was chronic or long term."

"It didn't happen on my watch."

"Okay. It could have happened somewhere else."

"At the track."

"I suppose so."

"Got to be. He lives on his own. At least, that's what he told me. So, it has to be someone who's got it in for him for some reason."

"He wasn't well-liked. Anyway, I'm sure the police don't suspect you of having anything to do with his death."

"But they said he was drunk."

"That didn't cause his death. And you were trying to help him. But I wouldn't be surprised if the combination of arsenic and alcohol made matters worse for him."

"I just assumed he couldn't hold his drink. He didn't have all that much."

"The arsenic was doing much more harm to him than the alcohol."

"Yeah, well." Her bottom lip trembles a little. "I hope you find the creep who did this. Barton was always polite to me. He didn't deserve to suffer like that."

*　*　*

Kelly, Jake and I make tracks through the long grass in the large field. I keep a watchful eye out for the three male yearlings. They're in a tight group close to the fence that's farthest away from us. From where we are, it seems as if they're all eating the same blade of grass. This pasture must agree with them—they already have gleaming coats and bright eyes.

This field is usually cut for hay but I'm glad I didn't organize a second cut this year—the yearlings have made a noticeable impact on the grazing in a relatively short time.

The three males are not reacting to me or the dogs, but I'm staying close to the fence in case I need to make a hasty retreat should they gallop over hoping to have fun with us. Even though these colts have been gelded recently (and should be called 'geldings' but I'm stuck on 'colts'!) they are still rambunctious. They play with each other's halters, rear up, buck, squeal, and canter around. The two fillies are in a separate paddock and are more sedate, although they occasionally kick up their back legs and charge from one side of the field to another.

My mobile tells me Detective Valeska is calling.

"Hello, Detective."

"Meg, I haven't heard from you recently. I'm sure you have information to share with me."

"I was about to give you a call." This is a little white lie. I planned to call her tomorrow morning. "There's not much to report except that I think there's a link between the murders."

"Of Barton and Orlando, you mean?"

"Yes."

"Not the same method."

"No, but they weren't killed quickly. They were each made to suffer."

"Oh, how did you find out? It's okay, you don't have to tell me. I can guess. I agree with you, as a matter of fact. Anything else?"

"I don't think Suzie—the woman who was with Barton before he was hit by the car—did anything wrong. She swears that no one could have put anything in Barton's drinks when he was at the casino."

"That doesn't stand up. She could not have been monitoring his drink all the time."

"Perhaps not. Do you have anything you can tell me?"

"I've been reviewing Annie's case file, and it seems she was a member of the rival gang, not of the Blackbirds Gang. Her defence counsel was able to convince the court of this and it assisted in obtaining an acquittal."

"Do you think this is true?"

"I don't find the evidence to be compelling, but it created doubt and was enough for the jury. In Annie's written statement she claims to have had a relationship with Pablo—the gang member who was shot—and that helped as well. The court believed her."

"She must have had a good lawyer."

"That, and there was insufficient evidence to prove she shot Pablo. I'd go as far as to say there was none. I can't understand why prosecutors agreed to move forward on the case. They are pressed for time and have scarce resources, so they are selective about which cases they're willing to take to court."

"Do you know who forced Dirk and Bobbie's vehicle off the road?"

"No witnesses have come forward and none were at the scene when our officers arrived. Got to run. Keep in touch."

"Okay."

*   *   *

Kelly and Jake are lying down behind the front seats in the pickup. I parked by Neal's barn and visited with my horses before my walk towards the cafeteria. I have another meeting with Les Joseph who was Barton's groom. I thought he was working for Neal now, but Linda says he hasn't shown up for a couple of days which has made her and my life difficult—Linda must work her usual hours at the track which means I have little help with the yearlings.

Les is hunched over a bottle of water at a table by a window. I order a hot chocolate. I don't have the stomach for another bad cup of tea today.

"Les, are you okay?"

"I'm not at my best." His white teeth barely show as he gives me half a smile.

"What's wrong?"

"Stomach stuff. Weird things. I'll get over it."

"Have you been checked out?"

"I'm fine."

"Les, I don't like the sound of this. You'll probably think I'm overreacting, but you know Barton was poisoned. It wasn't acute poisoning. It was chronic because they found traces of arsenic in his hair."

"I get it."

"I'm concerned. Did you have anything to do with the Blackbirds Gang?"

"Maybe."

"And, while I'm on this subject, according to the case file, Annie was not Barton's girlfriend as you told me, but Pablo's. You know, the guy who got shot."

"I'm no liar." He bangs his water bottle on the table. Fortunately, the lid is on.

"I'm not saying you are. I just want to understand."

"My bad."

"Help me here."

Before he can answer, he topples off his chair and lands on the gritty tiled floor with a frightening thud. I yell into the room for someone to call an ambulance. I check his breathing and roll up my fleece jacket to put under his head. I ask a man sitting nearby if I can have his jacket to put over Les. He readily gives it up but apologizes that it could do with a wash. It has a pungent horse odour, but it'll help to keep Les warm as he lies on the cold floor.

The paramedics finally arrive. It seems like it's been an eternity, but it has probably only been a matter of minutes.

"Please check for arsenic. It's very important. I believe he could have been poisoned. I'm calling Detective Valeska right now."

"Okay, lady. We'll let them know."

I'm not convinced they've taken what I said seriously.

"Detective?"

"Meg, you must have something."

"Les Joseph, who was Barton's groom, has just passed out and is off to hospital in an ambulance. From what he told me I suspect arsenic poisoning."

"Thanks. I'll follow up."

"His life is in danger."

"You mean he needs police protection."

"Yes."

"My budget is going out the window. But that's my concern, not yours. I'll get on it."

My next call is to Dr. Milton. He's my go-to person at the hospital.

"Meg, how nice to hear from you. When are you and Kelly going to visit?"

"Almost immediately, if you have time to chat for a few minutes."

"I'm taking an almost unheard-of coffee break in about ten. How about we meet in the conference room on level four. I think you know where it is. I'll get you a tea."

"That sounds great. Thank you very much."

I dash back to the truck and am horrified to see swirls of fluorescent orange paint defacing the sides and tailgate of my pickup. The dogs are on the back seat, barking.

"Meg. I've only just noticed this," Neal says. "I'll ask everyone around if they saw anything."

"Thanks. I can't stop. Les Joseph is in hospital. He won't be at work for a while. I'll tell you about it later."

"What's going on? Staff are scared enough as it is."

"I know. Sorry, I really must go. I'll call you."

He turns around with his cap in his hand. I leave him standing and scratching his head—literally and figuratively.

13

Attempted Murder

Kelly has her therapy dog vest on. Jake looks forlorn as he stares out of the truck window, his nose dabbing at the glass. I need to enrol him in the training program so that he can participate too. Kelly's tail rises a few inches when she has her vest and badge on.

We find the conference room and reach the door at the same time as Dr. Milton.

"I was afraid I'd kept you waiting," he says, as he places two tall paper cups on the round table.

"It took longer than I thought to get out of the racetrack and make my way here."

"How's Kelly?" He rubs her ears and lifts her head. She wags her tail. "You should come more often."

"I know. Anyway, I want to ask a favour."

"I'll do my best."

"Les Joseph, a groom at the racetrack, has just been brought here by ambulance. He collapsed when he was with me. I can't go into a lot of details, but he likely has arsenic poisoning."

"That's unusual these days: there is a much-reduced risk of exposure to arsenic through inhalation in the workplace or through drinking contaminated water. So, what makes you think this man is suffering from arsenic poisoning?"

"Because Barton Woking, the trainer Les used to work for, was murdered, and the post-mortem result revealed that he died of chronic arsenic poisoning."

"A forensic pathologist must have tested his hair."

"That's what I understand."

"Your suspicion is well-founded then. And the police must suspect deliberate poisoning in that case."

"I'm sure they do."

"Unfortunately, if the person, Les, collapsed, then it could be too late for treatment."

"I hope they'll try, though. That's where you come in. They'll listen to you if you suggest they consider arsenic poisoning."

"I'll follow up."

"I'm hoping he collapsed because he was low on blood sugar—it happened to me once when I was here if you remember. He was complaining of stomach issues, and I wouldn't be surprised if he hadn't eaten for some time."

"I'll go and find out what's happening. I'll let you know."

"Thank you. I do appreciate it."

"This is what I'm here for. To make a difference. If I can help this man, it'll make me feel good too. I'll track him down right now. I hope Kelly will do some visiting."

"We will."

* * *

Detective Valeska was not happy to hear that my truck had been spray-painted. And I'm not happy that I need to go to the car rental place again. My insurance payments will go up another notch—that's for certain.

Neal texted me to let me know that no one saw anyone spray-painting my truck or carrying a can. So, I can only make wild guesses as to who would do such a thing. If I don't know who or why, I don't see the point, and that's another piece of the puzzle.

As I drive home in my shiny dark grey pickup, I know I'm right back in the middle of the murder investigations whether I like it or not. I can't pull back. I'm being tugged in by strings of all sorts. My mind is in perpetual turmoil, and I can't stop my thoughts from going over all that I've seen and heard, trying to make sense of it all—or at least some of it.

Melissa and Candice have gone to bed. Melissa surprised me and relented—Candice is in the room decorated with dinosaur stickers for Gabriel when he was here.

Linda put all the horses in for the night including feeding them. She's had an exceptionally long day.

*   *   *

The early morning sun is dissipating the mist that shrouded the farm when I woke up. The barn appeared to be floating in clouds when I opened the backdoor. The motion-sensitive lighting was diluted and hazy as Kelly, Jake and I approached ready to give the horses their breakfast.

It has taken longer than I hoped to feed the horses, lead them out to their respective fields and clean the stalls. But the three of us are now sitting in the pickup ready to visit Animal Equity and Freedom.

I find a convenient parking space in front of the AEF office. The air is fresh and cool, and the mist has vanished. Bright sunshine reflects off vehicles' windows—almost dazzling at times. Nevertheless, the street-level door leading to the AEF office stands out. But the large 'Horse Racing Kills' poster isn't stapled to it anymore. Kenny was proud of it, so I wonder what prompted its disappearance. Perhaps someone ripped it down.

Ada kneels on the floor surrounded by boxes and piles of paper. The office looks as if it's been ransacked.

"Ada, what happened?"

"Hi, Meg. I'm packing up. Kenny and I had one too many disagreements". Her blue eyes sparkle, but she's frowning.

"I wondered if you were on the same page."

"He's become fanatical. He's obsessed with attacking some people for reasons I don't get. And he's so terribly angry all the time." She pushes herself up onto her feet and sits on a chair. Her skinny legs look too feeble to support her. "If I tell you something, please don't tell the police, at least don't let on how you know."

"I can do that." I find a chair and bring it over next to hers.

"Kenny told me he spray-painted your truck."

"I wondered if it was him. Did he say why?"

"Because you have racehorses."

"I don't think that's the whole story. There must be more to it because it's a significant risk to take—to get into the backstretch without a security pass and in daylight hours when there are lots of people about. I suppose he knew which truck was mine from my having parked in the street below your office, but he'd have to know where to find it and when I was there."

"Kenny's good at finding out things."

"But there's got to be a more compelling reason than just because I own racehorses."

"I told you, Kenny's fanatical."

"When did you last see him?"

"I haven't seen him for a couple of days. I told him I was leaving

AEF, so he took his things and left me to clear up this chaos."

"Where's your dog?"

"Brodie? He's at my mom's."

"What are you going to do?"

"I've got a second interview with Greenpeace. They like the fact that I've been part of peaceful protests and have office admin experience and a science degree. My mom suggested some time ago that I should try Greenpeace—when I told her I didn't get along with Kenny."

"I wish you luck. By the way, do you know anything about Kenny's background?"

"No. I met him at a web design seminar. While I thought he was a bit raw when we chatted about animal rights—not sure how we got onto that—we agreed on the basic principles. But he's become an irrational zealot."

"Do you know where he is now?"

"No, but I'd guess he's at home. He sounded incredibly angry when I called to ask him about some of the things he's left behind. I suppose he's upset about the collapse of AEF, but he should have behaved better."

"He couldn't run it without you?"

"He hasn't got the admin skills. He's just a hot-headed bully. I shouldn't have said that, but that's what I believe."

"You sound pretty upset."

"You could say that. And I had another arrogant S.O.B. in here this morning."

"Who was that?"

"He was looking for Kenny. He was red in the face and kept asking where Kenny was. Well, it was more than asking, it was more like demanding. I wasn't going to give him Kenny's address. He looked like he wanted to strangle him with his bare hands."

"He sounds intimidating."

"He frightened me. I'm shaken up. That's why I've been kneeling on the floor to pack these boxes—my knees turned to jelly."

"What was his name?"

"He left his card." She reaches over to a table covered in leaflets, posters, and miscellaneous office supplies. "Here it is."

"Dr. Greg Dudley. Interesting."

"Why do you think he wanted to see Kenny?"

"I can only guess that Kenny has spray-painted his office trailer in the backstretch, or Kenny threatened him. I've been meaning to have a chat with Dr. Dudley."

"If he's a crooked vet and harming horses and Kenny got to know, Kenny will be doing more than spray-painting his trailer."

"I don't have any evidence whatsoever to support that. But I want to chat with Dr. Dudley since he was the vet for Barton Woking's horses."

"I must get back to work. I want to get out of here tomorrow."

I leave Ada to deal with the mess in the office and head back home. I miss Linda's help, but Neal would be short-staffed without her now that Les is in hospital. I've cleaned the barn, but I have water buckets to scrub, hay to put in the stalls, feed to scoop, and wood shavings to spread around for bedding.

It had promised to be a fine day, but the weather has suddenly changed course. The sky has become dark and threatening. Kelly senses a storm is coming, while Jake is oblivious to the signals or doesn't care. Kelly stays in the barn close to me while Jake chases leaves being tossed around by the wind gusts.

I'm humming along with an ancient Beatles song playing on the radio when furious barking erupts. Despite the pending storm, Kelly dashes out to see what Jake is so agitated about and starts a frantic burst of yapping. I down my pitchfork and walk outside as large raindrops hit my face. The rain appears to be horizontal. A man pulls his rain jacket up around his ears and trots towards me.

I must have forgotten to fasten the padlock. He's left the gate open and parked his large SUV—I didn't know they came that big—close to the house. I hope he hasn't been inside. I should lock it when I'm in the barn, especially when I'm the only one around.

"Greg Dudley," he says with a gruff voice. He walks into the barn as if he owns it. The dogs continue to bark because I haven't told them it's okay.

"Can't you shut your dogs up?"

"They have a right to bark. You've come here without an invitation, and I don't know what you want."

He grunts.

"Kelly, Jake, come, sit." They obey and stop barking. We are about eight feet away from Dr. Dudley. I planned to talk with him, but I wouldn't have invited him here. "So, why have you come to my home?"

"You're part of that animal rights group."

"No, I'm not, although I don't know why it's any of your business."

"I saw you go into their offices this morning."

"That doesn't mean anything."

"I think it does. What were you there for? It seems to me you're a hypocrite. You own racehorses and profess to be continuing some of the work your husband, Frank, was doing for racehorse welfare, but then you join a radical organization that's determined to destroy the horse racing industry."

"I don't see why I have to answer to you, but you're wrong."

"Am I? Who spray-painted my office trailer and threw a stink bomb through the window?"

"It wasn't me. Why would someone want to do that? Why did you assume it was someone belonging to Animal Equality and Freedom?"

"Oh, is that what they're called?"

Our voices are raised because the rain is pounding on the metal barn roof, and the wind is rocking the trees and shaking the bushes.

"I must check on the horses. I may have to bring them in if they're not in the run-in sheds."

"You're avoiding my questions."

"No. I've told you I'm not part of an animal rights group, and I resent being accused of spray-painting your trailer, and I've never thrown a stink bomb in my life. I happen to know they're illegal in Canada. Here's a lead-rein. You can help me bring the yearlings in—they're standing in the rain. They belong to Dirk Knightscourt."

He snatches the lead-rein out of my hand, but I sense that some of his hostility has dissipated as if it's been diluted by the raindrops. The dogs stay close to me probably because they're not sure what to make of this man. Kelly has her eyes half-shut against the rain. Jake is sloshing through the fast-growing puddles. Kelly walks around each one with her ears flat on her head and her tail almost between her legs.

All of us are soaked by the time we have the five yearlings settled in their stalls. With great reluctance, I invite Dr. Dudley into the kitchen. Even Jake appears to be glad to be inside. I rub them down with old towels, and it takes four of them to get the worst of the rain off. I give each of the dogs a biscuit.

"By the way, if I was an animal rights fanatic, I wouldn't own dogs or have a horse farm. You must realize that."

He grunts again, takes his jacket off and sits on a kitchen chair looking like a sulking schoolboy.

"I'm making hot chocolate. Would you like some?"

He nods.

"I've been wanting to talk to you, so I'm glad of this chance. From what I've been told, Les Joseph, who was a groom for Barton Woking, asked you about a tub labelled 'Equine Top Performance'—I hope I've remembered the name correctly—and Barton said it came from the vet—you. Les asked you about it, and Barton fired him the following day. If you supply performance-enhancing drugs, and the animal rights group has discovered that, then you're going to be in their crosshairs."

"My turn to deny."

I put a mug of hot chocolate in front of him and he clutches it with both hands. His fingers are short and chubby, and his hands look strong.

"Your turn to explain." I sit down opposite him and take a sip from my steaming mug. The smell of wet dog isn't obliterated by the aroma of hot chocolate—unfortunately.

"Barton and I go back a long way."

"Oh."

"We met at college."

"University, you mean?"

"Yes. We were part of the same social circle, but he chose a path I wasn't willing to travel. Eventually, he dropped out. I went on to qualify as a veterinarian, but he ended up on the streets and in trouble."

"What sort of trouble?"

"All I know is that he was involved in drugs. Les can tell you more because he helped Barton get out of the mess he got himself into. Les worked for an agency that provided services for homeless people, I guess. And, once Barton was straightened around, more or less, I helped him get a job as a hotwalker at the track. To give him his due, Barton seized the opportunity, worked hard, and eventually met the criteria to qualify as a licensed trainer. Les and I felt good about it."

"Sounds great. So, why did he fire Les?"

"It had nothing to do with that tub of whatever it was. I forget exactly what was in it, but it would have been a compound supplement that made Barton feel like he was doing something extra for the horses. I'm sure he made a decent profit from it—he would have billed the owners at about one hundred percent markup."

"But Les was fired after he talked with you."

"You'll have to follow up with Les."

"You know he's in hospital, right?"

"Who, Les? No, I didn't know. What happened?"

"He's been poisoned with arsenic, just as Barton was."

"I didn't know any of this. My god. Who would want to poison either one of them, let alone both? Blows my mind." He rubs a hand across his forehead. Three or four long seconds of silence follow which is peppered with a couple of Jakes puffs as he lies asleep stretched out on his side. "I don't like to speak ill of the dead, but Barton was paranoid that someone was trying to kill him. I told him he should report it to the police, but he was paranoid about them too. He didn't look well to me, but I assumed it was stress and anxiety getting the better of him. It took me aback at the time, but he thought Les was scheming against him. He mentioned it to me a couple of days before he let Les go. I chatted to Les about it, and he appeared to be genuinely shocked."

"So, why would Les say he was fired because he asked you about that supplement?"

"Les is the only one who can explain that."

He finishes his hot chocolate, puts on his wet jacket and leaves. I ask him to close and lock the gate.

As I put the mugs in the dishwasher my gut tells me he was telling the truth. But that means that Les lied which disturbs me—a lot. I want to trust him. Liars trap the truth in their tangled web of tales. All I try to do as an amateur sleuth—usually reluctantly—is to separate the truth from the lies. But it seems it's never easy.

I let out a shuddery sigh as Melissa stumbles into the kitchen. Strands of wet hair cling to her pink cheeks and she has a raindrop hanging onto the end of her nose.

"It's raining cats and dogs out there."

"That's a weird saying, isn't it? Close the door, Melissa, that wind wants to blast its way in. And where's Candice?"

"It's so funny. I'm just going to change and put my clothes in the wash. I'll be back in a minute. Any chance of a hot chocolate?" she asks as she leaps up the stairs two steps at a time. Jake follows her, but Kelly can't be bothered.

I look out of the kitchen window to check that Bella is still in her run-in shed. She has her head out but the rest of her is under cover. I'll lead her into the barn soon if the rain doesn't stop pelting down. I make a mug of hot chocolate and as I place it on the table Melissa and Jake trot into the kitchen.

"Aren't you having any?"

"I've just had some with Dr. Greg Dudley."

"You invited him here? Meg! Really!"

"I did not. He showed up. He accused me of being part of AEF. He'd seen me go into their offices, He thought I'd spray-painted his office trailer and thrown a stink bomb through the window."

"What the hell? What a nerve. Did you set the dogs on him?"

"No, I didn't. Honestly, Melissa, you know I wouldn't do that unless I was in danger." I give her an account of how our conversation went.

"I love how you got him to help you lead the horses in." She smiles.

"I think it helped to melt the ice a bit. Animals are amazing for that."

"And how on earth could you be an animal rights activist if you own horses, dogs, and cats?"

"I pointed that out to him. But where's Candice?"

"That's the funny thing I want to tell you about. She's at Milkweed Farm talking to William. He needs an admin person to replace Ramona and Candice wants to live in Canada. Because her stepfather was Canadian, she hopes she can get a work permit and be William's assistant. She might even be able to apply for Canadian citizenship—William's looking into it."

"Is she qualified?"

"She hasn't got legal training, but William's desperate. Honestly, it makes me laugh. She idolizes William. I think he's a replacement father figure or something."

"Why's William so desperate? What do you mean? There must be lots of qualified legal assistants out there."

"Ramona's been bad-mouthing him, and with his previous bad record, he's lost some business, and he's concerned he won't find someone willing to work for him. He likes Candice. She looks the part when she's wearing her smart clothes. She's more at home in an office environment than she is among the animals. She's been making an effort, and she's better than she was, but she's not a true country person—yet. She's had some experience, by the way. She worked in a local government office of some kind. Anyway, she's so excited. You're not jealous, are you?" Melissa laughs and tosses her long blond hair back over her shoulders.

"Haha."

"You must be itching to talk to Les."

"I am. Oh, Detective Valeska is calling. Hello, Detective."

"Meg, do you know Primula Mokka? A trainer at the racetrack."

"Yes." It's hard to hear the Detective because of the background noise of voices, sirens, and horses whinnying. Rain must be coming down in a deluge on a metal roof somewhere. "What's wrong? I can't hear you very well. Are you at the track?"

"Yes, and I'm treating this as attempted murder," she says with a raised voice. "Primula was still alive when the ambulance got here. It left about ten minutes ago. I happened to be in the area. I'd like you to come. Wear rubber boots. Must end this call."

"Melissa, Primula Mokka has been hurt. Detective Valeska says it's attempted murder."

"Oh no! That's just terrible. Who on earth would want to hurt her?"

"No clue."

"Where?"

"In the backstretch. Her barn I assume. The Detective wants me to go."

"How badly hurt is she? What happened?"

"I don't know the answer to those questions."

"The world's gone insane. What's going on?"

"Melissa, getting this upset isn't going to help. Do me a favour and look after the dogs. And would you put Bella in her stall? The weather has turned nasty again."

"I want to come with you."

"Come when you've put Bella in. I must leave. Bring the dogs and park in the security parking lot. Thanks."

"Okay. Sure. I'll see you later then."

I'm glad Melissa is coming to the track because she can take the dogs home if I'm tied up in the backstretch for hours since I don't know what to expect. Although I miss Kelly and Jake's company in my still-shiny grey pickup, they'll help Melissa put Bella in her stall. Bella has fallen in love with Kelly and follows her willingly. It makes me smile to see their relationship blossom. But there's no smile on my face now as I drive to the track.

14

Water, Water, Everywhere

There's no one I can think of who would want to hurt Primula. But there have been some strange and disturbing events—her office was spray-painted, and two of her horses each had sponges inserted in one of their nostrils. So, someone doesn't like her. But I don't see any reason for her to be targeted by AEF, and harming her horses doesn't make sense. Kenny has shown signs of being irrational and more fanatical than Ada. But why would he want to kill Primula? I'm no further ahead with my jumbled thoughts by the time I park near Primula's barn. There are police vehicles, a fire engine, a black police vehicle, and officers dressed in what look like spacesuits as well as regular police officers and two track security personnel who appear to be watching. The torrential rain has eased off but the churned-up mud around the entrance to the barn looks as if a monsoon hit.

As an officer approaches me, Detective Valeska waves me in at the same time as shouting to the officer to allow me to pass.

I'm thankful for my rubber boots. Water is spewing in rivulets out of the wide barn door. The mud is slimy and sticky in the shedrow.

"What happened to Primula?"

"First things first. I need your help. Some of the horses are standing in a foot of water and some are obviously stressed. I don't know anything about horses, but I'd say they should be moved."

"I'm on it." I text Melissa and ask her to get hold of Russon and have him come, if he can, to check the horses out. I text Neal and ask if he knows how to find out where there are empty stalls and who I need to get permission from to move the horses.

My next thought is Hector. I must check on him. But I wonder if I'm going to lose a boot as I pull each foot out of the mire with each squelchy step. As I get closer to Hector's stall, the mud thins because there's more water about. His stall is across from one of the taps. Someone must have turned it on, and probably the two other taps in the shedrow to make such a disastrous mess.

An officer stands outside Hector's stall door. This must be where Primula was found.

"Hang on!" Detective Valeska is behind me, waddling from side to side. She isn't wearing boots. I hate to think what she's got on her feet and what it feels like to wade in this muck without the proper footwear. "We can't go into that stall. This is where Primula was found."

"Oh, no. This is unbelievable."

"She was lying face-down in the water. Her head showed signs of trauma."

"You don't think Hector kicked her?" I can't imagine Hector lashing out at anyone, but I can't be certain something couldn't have gone wrong. He may have been frightened or hurt and overreacted— as horses are prone to do.

"No. The preliminary info I've been given is that it was something like a metal rod or pipe, or even a crowbar to the side of the head."

"Hold on, I've just got a reply from the vet, and he says he can come right away. He's in the backstretch, so he won't be long. This horse was mine and was claimed."

"What do you mean claimed? Claimed back or something?"

"It'll take too long to explain, but Primula claimed him on behalf of another owner. Fortunately, he's got a good head on him."

"What do you mean by a 'good head'? Talk in plain English."

"Some horses would have gone berserk and may have trampled Primula. While Hector is upset, he's not freaking out. He's not hurting himself and I don't think he would have done anything to add to Primula's injuries." I get as close as I can to the stall door and talk to Hector. He won't move from the back wall and holds his head high. Trembling, he turns to look at me with wide, frightened eyes. He's standing in over a foot of water which covers all the rubber matting in his stall. A mixture of straw and hay combined with balls of manure floats around him. The odour of his sweat adds to the smell of wet bedding. Mucky water trickles under his stall door, but there's so much water everywhere it hasn't got an effective escape route. "If Primula was face-down, wouldn't she have drowned?"

"I'm sure she has water in her lungs, but they were able to do the magic that paramedics do and get her breathing. I don't know the details."

Melissa, Russon, and Neal show up almost simultaneously, with a police officer in tow. The officer looks as if he might topple into the mud since he's rather top-heavy. He has grime up to the knees of his smart uniform pants.

"Meg, are you alright?" asks Melissa, somewhat out of breath.

"Fine". I make brief introductions. "Melissa, look at Hector. Detective, can we lead him out? You said we couldn't go into the stall."

"I'll chat with my officers and find out." She turns away from us with some difficulty. It's as if she has suckers on her feet.

"I can't examine the horses in these conditions," Russon says. "The sales barns are empty. Let's take them there. It's not far. I'll deal with any flack from the Stable Office. We'll start with the other horses and move Hector last, once we have the go-ahead from the Detective."

"Okay. Let's find some lead-reins," I say.

"I'll get some," Neal says.

"Some of the horses won't like walking in this stuff," I say. "The water must have been running for a long time."

"It was a clever tactic," Detective Valeska says, "because it has destroyed footprints and other evidence, and likely was intended to ensure Primula died."

"How horrible," Melissa says.

"Ah, just got a reply," Detective Valeska says. "You can move the horses. The Scenes of Crimes Officers have finished in this stall."

"Meg, hold Hector while I inject a small dose of Xylazine," Russon says. "But I need to go back to my vehicle to prepare. I'll bring enough for a few horses. It could take a while. If I don't show up in about ten, send out a rescue party." He smiles, but none of us reciprocate.

"How many horses do we need to move?" asks Neal as he struggles back with four leather lead-reins.

"What's he injecting them with?" asks Detective Valeska.

"A sedative," Melissa says. "It'll be a small dose because they have to walk to the sales barns."

"Who'll look after the horses, Neal?" I ask.

"Primula has a competent assistant trainer. I'll ask security to get hold of him."

Detective Valeska shivers. Her light grey pants are splashed with globs of mud. I can't see what she's wearing on her feet because they're buried in sludge.

"I've got to get out of here," she says. "Good luck with the horses. Meg, give me a call tomorrow. We'll need your help on this one."

"Okay."

"You sound reluctant," Melissa says. "I can't understand you sometimes. Surely you want to help find out who tried to kill Primula? Honestly, Meg, what's the problem?"

"This isn't the time or place to discuss it, Melissa. We'll have a chat when we get home. Russon's coming and we must get these horses to safety."

Neal pretends not to hear our exchange. He grabs Hector's halter that hangs just outside the stall door, sloshes up to the wide-eyed horse, gently pulls it over his head, and clips the lead-rein on. His jeans are soaked up to his knees. Russon injects Hector and the horse barely notices but radiates tension. It seems to take an eternity for Russon to sedate Primula's twenty-three horses, but Melissa says he's working as fast as he can.

The water reached all their stalls, and it will take days for the barn to dry out. Fortunately, the feed room is separate, and the hay and straw are housed outside in metal storage units. I can't see anything in the shedrow except stall cleaning tools and garbage pails, so I don't think there's material damage. But I'm not sure how the trauma has affected the horses. I'm particularly concerned about Hector, of course.

By the time Russon has finished and put his supplies away, Hector has dropped his head a little. Not much. And he still doesn't want to move.

"Meg, see if you can encourage him."

"He probably saw the water coming in under his stall door, so he's wary about leaving." I wade over to Hector and talk to him. He sniffs my face, and I stroke his velvety muzzle. He's standing perpendicular to the exit, so I turn his head and ask him to 'walk on'. He doesn't respond. I've left the door open, and he looks in that direction, but it's as if his feet are set in concrete even though the rubber matting in his stall means there's no mud—just a cocktail of water, bedding, hay, and manure. Neal trudges past leading a large chestnut who's picking his feet up like a fancy dressage horse. He doesn't like the footing but he's moving forward. Hector shows some interest. I stroke his neck and gently fondle one of his soft ears. I walk towards the door, letting out the lead-rein as I continue to talk to him. He lifts his front right foot and puts it down again. It splashes which causes him to throw his head up. I need help.

As Neal passes the door again returning to collect another horse, I call out to him and ask for assistance. He nods. It seems like a long time before he shows up with Russon. They go to Hector's rear. Neal squeezes between the back wall and Hector's hind. He and Russon hold hands behind Hector's back legs, creating a kind of sling or cradle, and push. He takes two steps. I keep talking, stroking, encouraging, praising, whatever I can think of to get him out of here. I don't like him standing in these terrible conditions for this length of time. I wonder if his feet could become infected or damaged because they'll be softened. And the whole experience could shake his confidence.

Neal and Russon take a breather and then try again. This time Hector takes four steps, so his head is poking into the shedrow. Melissa walks past leading a grey horse, and Hector agrees to follow her. Perhaps he's friendly with that horse, or remembers Melissa, or both. It's a tedious trip as Hector and I trudge after Melissa and the grey along the shedrow, but I'm relieved no one's in a hurry since my boots are in danger of being sucked off if I try to walk any faster. Once we arrive at the sales barn it's no surprise that Hector is keen to walk into a dry stall.

The dogs need to be fed, so Melissa leaves and says she'll give them a run in the large field. I tell her I'll be back home to put Eagle and Bullet in the barn, and I'll feed the horses.

It takes nearly two hours to get all the horses into the sales barn. Primula's assistant trainer, Yuki, arrives to help us gather straw, hay, and water and feed buckets, to make the horses comfortable. They settle in their new surroundings surprisingly quickly and all of them are soon munching on hay that hangs in nets just outside their stall doors.

Two police vehicles remain. I'm not sure what they're doing. The place looks like a tidal wave has hit and I can't imagine there's a trace of evidence of any kind to be found in the quagmire. I take off my boots—they're wet inside. I had the sense to tuck my stretchy jeans into them—they got splashed with muck, but they didn't get caked in mud. I roll them up to prevent spreading the dirt and chuck my boots into a dumpster that's outside the barn where I parked. My socks are wet and slightly muddy—I'm not sure how that happened—but not enough to make a significant mess in the sparkling clean rental pickup.

*   *   *

Back at the farm, my knees are wobbly and my head aches. My legs seem to have lost their strength. I wonder how I'm going to do the barn chores. I stumble into the kitchen and almost fall into a chair.

"Meg, you're exhausted!"

"I've got to feed the horses."

"No, you don't. I called Linda. Haven't you noticed she's here? I'm getting you a brandy and running a hot bath with Epsom salts while I finish getting dinner."

She pours me a brandy and hovers over me to make sure I take some sips before she dashes upstairs to run a bath.

"Thank you, Linda."

"No problem. Sorry I've not been able to help much. Les being off has put Neal in a spot."

"I know." I can't help but fold my arms on the table and rest my head on them.

"Drink the brandy," Melissa says. I didn't notice her reappear. Kelly has her head on my lap and I'm stroking her silky head. It makes me feel a bit better, so I take a few more sips. "I've put out some clothes for you. Too bad if I've not chosen the right ones. Don't stay long in the bath, you must eat. But you need to get those filthy, smelly clothes off first, and warm up."

I lift my head again and glance at my clothes. Melissa's right. They're bad. It's as if I've had a roll in a muddy puddle like Jake loves to do. And I'm shivering. I down a gulp of brandy and Linda helps me up the stairs. I feel a bit better by the time I'm stepping into the deep, warm bath water.

"You didn't take long," Melissa says as I shuffle into the kitchen wearing an eclectic outfit of old jeans, a red sparkly sweater, and green socks. I look ready for Christmas. "Don't get too excited about dinner. It's more like a lunch."

"I don't care. Thanks for getting something."

"You forget to eat. Have you had anything since this morning?"

"I can't remember."

"That means you haven't." Melissa serves cauliflower soup in large bowls and puts a platter of cheese and a bowl of fresh rolls on the table.

"Did you make the soup?" Linda asks.

"Yes," says Melissa.

"It's great."

"Thanks, Melissa for everything you've done," I say. "And yes, this soup is delicious."

"That's what sisters are for." She smiles. "Linda, do you have a sister?"

"No, I'm the only one."

"You're missing out," Melissa says. "Meg, is it because you were shot at that you aren't keen?"

"Keen? Keen about what?" The sudden change of subject throws me for a second.

"Meg don't be funny. You know what I mean. Keen to find out who killed Barton, who shot at you, who shot at the horse trailer—when it was here which makes it worse—and who poisoned Les, and who drove Dirk and Bobbie off the road, and who tried to murder Primula. Don't you want to find out? Even Detective Valeska has asked for your help. I can't understand you, sometimes."

"Les called me," Linda says. "He like, feels real bad about not being at work."

"How's he doing?" I ask.

"He's at his brother's house. He said he'd call you."

"Okay."

"He didn't tell you everything about Barton."

"Oh."

"He doesn't, like, want to go to the cops."

"See," says Melissa.

*   *   *

Melissa must have thrown out the clothes I wore in the quagmire yesterday. I can't find any trace of them.

Linda's coming in a few minutes. Apparently, Neal's found a groom and a hotwalker looking for extra hours, so he's not short-staffed for now at least. Linda will go to the track after she's helped here.

Kelly, Jake, and I breathe in the crisp air in semi-darkness as we follow the well-beaten path to the barn. My legs are stiff but otherwise I've recovered well from the muddy experience of yesterday. It promises to be a fine day, and I'm relieved I won't be at risk of getting dirty, wet, and cold.

A couple of the yearlings whinny. They've heard the backdoor close. I can tell it's them because their voices are more high-pitched than their elders. Bella sounds like a baritone—she has a large, deep, chest which encases superior lung capacity. She adds her voice to the chorus. The sounds lift my spirits but they're making it clear they want their breakfast.

Linda arrives just as we walk into the barn.

"Hi, Linda. Thanks for coming."

"Here you go." She hands me a coveted carrot muffin and a tea. She walks ahead of me into the barn, holding her coffee, and switches the lights on. There are many blinking eyes looking towards us—adjusting to the bright lights—and increased whinnying. I can't remember hearing this much noise in my barn ever before.

Linda has amazing stamina and strength. Her rotund appearance is deceiving. She works steadily serving the horses their feed and topping up their water buckets.

Meanwhile, my mobile rings.

"Hello, Les. Linda said you'd call."

"I knew you'd be up early and wanted to catch you."

"How are you doing?"

"A lot better. Can you visit?"

We arrange for me to go to his brother's house once Linda and I finish the barn chores. He says he's not going anywhere.

"That was Les. I'm going to see him later."

"Good." Linda looks at me as if she's plucking up the courage to say something. "It's not my business but, I hope you find out who hurt Primula. She's a good person."

"I haven't made up my mind what I'm going to do yet, but it doesn't seem to matter anyway because I keep getting dragged back into it. I should give this investigation stuff up—I've said that several times—but my reputation, albeit imperfect, comes back to bite me and there's no escape."

"But you must feel good about what you do?"

"I suppose I must because I keep on getting myself into trouble."

"You help the racing business and the horses. And you, like, get the bad guys."

"Thanks, Linda."

15

Threat

On our way to see Les we take a detour via the racetrack because I want to know how Primula's horses are doing—Hector in particular. I take the opportunity to give the dogs a walk along the trail that runs beside the training track. I love hearing the footfalls of the horses and their rhythmic breathing as they breeze past on the other side of the chain-link fence. The hazy sunshine and still air make this a beautiful morning. I let Jake off his leash, and he stays with Kelly.

After a leisurely stroll for me and a run for the dogs, we drive through the security checkpoint and park by the sales barns. Primula's assistant trainer—I've forgotten his name, Yuki I think—is pushing a wheelbarrow mounded with soiled bedding.

"Meg. Nice to see you. They're all fine but we're not training today. Just walking."

"Makes sense. I'll just say hello to Hector and get out of your hair."

"Stay as long as you like. He's doing fine. He ate all his breakfast with gusto, that's always a good sign. Sorry, have lots to do."

"How's Primula?"

"I haven't heard any news today." He parks his wheelbarrow and strides briskly back into the barn. I make a mental note to follow up.

Hector enjoys the mints I brought him. He's had a bath and looks great. His bright eyes and pricked ears are good to see. I talk to him, and he stays calm as I stroke his neck. Much relieved, I walk back to the truck.

The dogs poke their heads up from behind the front seats as I drive off.

* * *

I park my pickup under a stunted tree on the street and negotiate the concrete steps to the front door of the townhouse that looks as if it's been squashed by its neighbours. Les isn't waiting for me this time. I press the doorbell and am told to come in.

Les is lying on a sofa in the front room. Beams of sunlight land on the floor as if they're acting as spotlights to draw attention to the swirls of blues and greens in the area rug.

"How are you?"

"Much better. I was sick, man."

"You look brighter."

"You've got it wrong. I'm not smarter, but I promise not to fall off this sofa." He grins. It's nice to see his white teeth and a twinkle in his eyes. "Cup of tea?"

"I'll make it. You want one too, I expect."

"I enjoy my tea. Could only face water for a while. Still drink lots of that too."

"Perhaps you're lucky you got such severe digestive issues. That might have saved you."

"Just glad to be alive. Feels like I'm in an Agatha Christie story, but for real. It sure makes you think."

"Nearly ready." I raise my voice as I boil the water, find mugs and the tea strainer, and warm the pot—I hope I'm going to produce tea that's up to the exemplary standard set by Les during my previous visit.

"Here you go."

"Looks the right colour." He smiles.

"Good."

"There's stuff I need to tell you."

"The truth would be helpful."

"Yeah. Can't argue. My bad. Tea's okay."

"Good." I don't think it's quite as delicious as the last time I was here, but I'm enjoying it.

"To get right to it, Barton didn't fire me because of that tub I mentioned."

"The vet, Greg Dudley, said as much. He told me the tub contained a supplement, not performance-enhancing drugs, and that you wouldn't have been fired for talking to him about it."

"Yeah, well."

"Tell me what really happened."

"A bit of background. I told you I used to work for an agency that helped street people."

"Yes."

"I worked with all sorts. Most were in deep shit—drugs or gangs or prostitution or all of the above."

"And Barton?"

"He was in a dark hole. But he showed signs of wanting out, so I got him referrals, got him into a support group, and other stuff."

"You said Annie was Barton's girlfriend."

"She was. I didn't lie. Annie broke it off. That's what sunk him into that hole."

181

"But it sounds as if it also made him think, and eventually he got out of the mess he was in."

"Ain't easy to do that. And he slipped bad when he heard Annie and Pablo were a number."

"Greg Dudley told me he helped Barton get a job at the track and that started Barton's climb to become a trainer."

"I suggested the track to Barton. You don't need much to be a hotwalker and you can get training to be a groom. I mentioned it to a few of the guys. Some did good. Barton got to the top—that's unusual."

"But he cheated. You mentioned he'd been suspended six times in the past five years—four times for positive drug tests and twice for abuse."

"Awesome memory. You must have some of Hercule Poirot's little grey cells!"

"Some things stick. Others are lost. Why did he cheat?"

"Poirot wouldn't have asked. Obvious, ain't it? He was greedy. He wasn't the most honest of people, surprise surprise."

"Why did he fire you? I still don't understand."

"Coming to that. I'm friendly with some of the jocks—the ones who haven't put themselves on pedestals, you know what I mean. And a couple of them let on Barton had asked them to hold their mounts back. He was trying to fix races. Why would he do that? Has to be into gambling. Something not right. And me being me, I asked him, didn't I? And he lost it and fired me on the spot."

"Why didn't you tell me this before?"

"I dunno. Didn't want to rat on my friends, I guess."

"How come you worked for Barton in the first place?"

"You don't want my sob story. My mom killed herself. I still think I should have been able to prevent it. I was a counsellor. I should have done something."

"What about your brother?"

"He's ten years older. I was still living with our mom when it happened, but he'd got an apartment. It didn't hit him the same way. It messed me up bad, so he took me in, and he's been the greatest. I'm sure I wouldn't be here if it wasn't for him. I try to pay him back by keeping house, you know, doing all the women's work! Haha!"

"You do a good job."

"Talking of jobs, I quit mine just after my mom died. I couldn't deal with other people's problems no more. I knew Barton had done well at the track, so I sought him out and he needed a hotwalker, and the rest is history."

"What about becoming a trainer?"

"I've thought about assistant trainer. Finding the right trainer to learn under, that's the trick."

"Neal might be willing to take you on."

"He's a good guy. Might work. I like his team and the horses he's got. Most of them are yours, aren't they?" His smile smooths out the furrows in his brow.

"No, you know only four of them are mine."

"Only four! Haha! Got time for another cuppa?"

"I'll get it. Do you have any idea who poisoned you?"

"I would've told you, wouldn't I? Nope. It gets me edgy at night. You know, can't settle, cause I'm wondering who, how, why, when, and where—the questions Hercule would ask."

"You're telling me to get on with it."

"Haha. Maybe."

"Have you heard about Primula Mokka?"

"Has she been spray-painted again by that goon, Kenny?"

"What makes you say it was Kenny?"

"Linda says it was."

"Ah. No, it's much more serious than that. Someone tried to kill her." The kettle puffs steam and boiling bubbles threaten to spew out. I can't hear what Les says. "Sorry, I couldn't hear you." I fill the teapot for the second time.

"You don't want to hear it. I should wash my mouth out."

"Any ideas on who or why?"

"Primula's a nice person. I didn't get why she was spray-painted, and I sure don't see why anyone would want to do her in. How's she doing?"

"She's conscious, but that's all I could find out. She was hit on the head and left face-down in a stall. Whoever tried to kill her, turned on the shedrow taps, and there was a terrible mess. She would have drowned if she hadn't been found soon after it happened."

"What about the cops?"

"They're treating it seriously. And they hope Primula will be able to help. Perhaps she saw something before she was hit."

"So, whoever poisoned me could be your man."

"Perhaps. I'm not sure what's connected to what at this point."

"Get those little grey cells working. I don't feel safe. It's worse than being a counsellor working on the streets 'cause I don't know who the bad guys are."

* * *

I wake the dogs up as I open the pickup door. The street outside Les' brother's house must be devoid of sounds and smells—at least according to Kelly and Jake. My mobile pings—a text message from an unknown person. I'm about to delete it, but the first four words draw me in. It's a brief note: *you will be next if you keep snooping.*

I should report this to Detective Valeska, but it's probably nothing—just an empty threat.

Almost before I finish this thought, Detective Valeska calls me and I'm tempted to tell her about the text after all, but decide not to.

"Meg, there's something I'd like you to do."

"Before I agree, I need to know what it is."

"I've been to visit Primula Mokka. She's not doing well. Her memory's affected and her speech is hard to understand. I'd like you to see if you can help her recall more of what happened. Will you talk with her?"

"Okay. I'll try to visit her this afternoon."

"Good."

* * *

Kelly struts beside me, wearing her therapy vest, as we enter the hospital. Her tail is curled up and she exudes a sense of pride and purpose.

Dr. Milton told me this morning that Primula has gained consciousness, but he didn't have a chance to find out any more than that. Perhaps I should have waited until tomorrow to visit her, but Detective Valeska is keen to move forward, and it seems the police have little to go on so far.

One of the Detective's officers sits on a chair outside Primula's private room. His chin rests on his chest. Kelly trots past him. Something has her on edge. I pick up my pace. Kelly yaps. She knows she's not allowed to make noise in the hospital. A nurse grabs my arm.

"What's your dog playing at?"

"Something's wrong."

I yank myself free from her grip, and as I turn into the doorway a figure dressed in black slams me against the heavy open door and then sprints away along the corridor.

"Kelly, after him!" The nurse trots into Primula's room. I follow Kelly.

Kelly's nails skid on the shiny vinyl flooring as she navigates a corner. She stops at a fire door that opens onto a stairwell. I catch up with her, gasping. We dash down the stairs and reach an alarmed exterior door. The alarm has been activated by the intruder. I push the panic bar and open the door. The black figure is racing across the parking lot clutching what must be a balaclava or something similar. It had likely hindered his breathing.

"Kelly, catch him!" It's probably too much to ask of her, but Kelly can run like the wind. A black and white blur darts away from me as I struggle to keep running. Sweat drips into my eyes and my feet are hot. I'm not as fit as I thought I was. I dodge between cars and people as Kelly streaks ahead of me and now she's disappeared out of sight. I'm not sure what to do. Jake makes the decision for me. He's barking in the truck which is two rows away. I run over and let him out.

"Find Kelly." He must have seen her run across the parking lot because he takes off in the same direction and I follow. There are heavy footsteps behind me but I'm not wasting precious time to see who it is. I can guess. It'll be the police officer who nodded off. His future won't be a bright one. He'll be back on traffic duty.

There's a busy road at the end of the parking lot. Didn't the fugitive have a vehicle? Perhaps he parked out of sight. He probably didn't want to pay for a ticket and risk being caught on camera. Perhaps he even came by bus. This is a heavily populated area of Vannersville and there's good public transit.

I'm puffing now and getting more worried about my poor decision to send Kelly and Jake after the figure. And I'm wondering how Primula is. Whoever it is, could only have been there to finish her off.

Kelly must have lost him because she and Jake are trotting back to me. But Kelly has what looks like the balaclava in her mouth. What a clever dog!

The officer catches up with me. He's more out of condition than I am. Sweat drips off his nose and he's gasping for air. He bends over with his hands on his thighs.

"This is your lucky day. My dog got the man's balaclava. There'll be DNA on that. Hopefully, this person is in your system." I hold it by a thread or two, and hand it over to the puffing officer who can only nod. "Sorry about the dog saliva." Kelly's tongue is as long as it gets, and her sides are heaving. "What a wonderful dog you are! You need water." The police officer takes a few gulps of air and then talks to someone on his device while holding the balaclava gingerly at arms-length. It might just save his job.

I text Dr. Milton.

He responds immediately.

Kelly, Jake, and I walk into the hospital after I grab a leash for Jake from the truck.

We find a large stainless-steel bowl filled with water just inside the automatic doors. The noise of the two dogs lapping almost drowns out the questions from staff and patients who form an impromptu gathering in the lobby. The whole hospital seems to know what happened. And then they burst into applause. Jake is taken aback but Kelly seems to know she's the star and visits with anyone who wishes to congratulate her. Dr. Milton beams and tells anyone who'll listen how wonderful Kelly is, and that Jake will soon be a therapy dog in training. You'd think they were his dogs. I smile and hope that this celebratory atmosphere means that Primula is okay.

"I'd like to see Primula," I say to Dr. Milton as soon as I get the chance.

"We're going to visit a patient," Dr. Milton announces to the group.

Jake's beginning to enjoy the attention and is reluctant to leave. But Kelly is in work mode and struts ahead of us.

Detective Valeska stands outside Primula's door. Her posture is stiff, and her hands are clenched. My heart flutters. Surely Primula is okay?

"Good afternoon, Detective," Dr. Milton says. They must know each other, but the detective is in no mood for a polite exchange.

"It seems I have to do everything myself. The nurse says my officer was enjoying a nap when you showed up, Meg."

"The nurse didn't like me being here with my dog. Kelly has her therapy vest on, as you can see. She sensed something wasn't right and yapped. The nurse tried to prevent me from going into the room. That's when a figure rammed into me, and I sent Kelly after him."

"The nurse believes that the intruder attempted to smother Primula, but he wasn't able to finish the job because you and Kelly arrived."

"Kelly would have heard the scuffle. Primula must have put up a bit of a fight."

"I've got another officer coming under strict orders to drink a large coffee on the hour, to use the washroom in the room, and to secure Primula's door while in there. And to sit in the doorway— against fire regulations apparently—but there's a life at stake, so unless the Fire Chief shows up, we're okay. As an added precaution Primula will be moved as soon as they can manage it. For Christ's sake, I shouldn't have to babysit people. This will not look good in the press."

"I think the press will focus on Kelly. She's the star and people love dog stories."

"We'll see. They love to point fingers at police services."

"I hope you can get a match for the DNA on that balaclava."

"So do I."

"Perhaps Primula knows who it was?"

"Perhaps, but I've been told we can't interview her. She's heavily sedated."

Kelly's in the room, sitting by Primula's bed expecting to be petted. Primula is breathing, but she's not awake. Dr. Milton checks with the nurse and looks at Primula's online records.

"I can't give a prognosis," he says. "But she'll need at least forty-eight hours before anyone will be able to talk with her."

"Dr. Milton," I say, "how do you think this guy got into the hospital without being noticed?"

"There are so many access points, for deliveries, staff, volunteers, funeral homes, and I'm sure there are more. One thing's for certain, they'll be reviewing security. All hell will be breaking loose in administration. I'm thankful I won't be part of that."

"I'll be doing my own review, and it's not going to be pretty." Detective Valeska says. "The only hero in this story is your dog, Meg."

"She's truly amazing. She deserves a treat or two, so I'll take the heroine home along with her assistant, Jake." I pat both dogs and they wag their tails.

Most of the impromptu gathering is still lingering in the lobby when we walk through, and Kelly gets another round of applause. Kelly wants to visit, so we stop for a while, and she's petted by some of her admirers. Jake gets some pats too and looks proud but also a little confused.

16

Throttled

Melissa and Candice are sitting at the kitchen table when the three of us barge in. The dogs trot over to the water bowl and lap furiously, sending globules of water in all directions.

"What's up with them?" asks Candice.

"There've been two calls from media," Melissa says. "Is Kelly taking interviews?"

"You've heard then."

"Well, we'd still like the full story."

"Treats for Kelly and Jake first."

"I assumed you hadn't eaten and told William to get enough for four of us."

"William's coming?"

"He's bringing food and some information for you. His visit won't upset you, will it?"

"I'll cope." I'd rather not have anyone here other than Melissa.

I'm tired and grouchy. Grouchy partly because I wonder if I could have prevented Primula from going through the trauma of attempted murder a second time, or perhaps even at all. My reluctant sleuth attitude has got to stop. Either I'm investigating or I'm not. I can't do a half-assed job. I must get some rest so I can get going tomorrow.

While we wait for the food which I'm now eagerly anticipating, I tell Melissa and Candice as much as I know about what happened at the hospital. They are in awe of Kelly's heroic chase and her successful snatch of the balaclava. They pet Kelly and Jake and give them more treats.

William's timing is perfect. He strolls into the kitchen holding brown paper bags emitting aromas that make my stomach growl with anticipation. He serves mushroom risotto and salad in silence. He's put on weight and his face has more wrinkles. My heart skips a beat, and I feel a pang of guilt even though I know I don't want him to live here again. I need to have control over my life, and I don't want decisions made for me. No doubt the abuse I suffered under my stepfather has caused me to fear being controlled by others, especially men—both mentally and physically.

"It's ready." William brings plates of salad and then large helpings of risotto over to the kitchen table. Melissa brings cutlery and napkins. Candice pulls a bottle of red wine out of another large paper bag that sits on the counter.

"I'll get glasses," Candice says. "It's not posh wine, but I hope you like it."

"Thanks, Candice," I say.

Not much is said during the meal. It's as if no one knows what to say to warm the cool atmosphere hanging around us. The animals come to our rescue. Kelly starts to snore. Jake is the one who excels at snoring, so that's a surprise and Melissa laughs.

"Kelly's worn out from her escapade," she says.

And then Cooper jumps up onto the table next to Candice

who squeals in surprise and leans away from the precocious cat. I guess Cooper thinks the party needs livening up. Melissa picks up the purring cat and puts him on the floor after a few tickles under his chin.

"How did things go at the track today?" I ask Melissa.

"I stayed late because Neal and Russon said they were going to look at the camera footage from when Primula was attacked. Primula's assistant trainer gave them the link. It's saved online for a few days—but I can't remember how many."

"I wondered about that. I guessed Primula would have upgraded the security since two of her horses had sponges put up their nostrils."

"She did, but she still doesn't have cameras in the stalls. By the way, Detective Valeska has already seen the footage, such as it is."

"I haven't heard anything from her."

"The person was wearing black and had a hoodie hiding his face. I hadn't thought about how good those hoodies are at concealment. So, there wasn't anything to go on. The cameras are set up at points along the shedrow, but as I said, there are none in the stalls. So, there's nothing showing the attack. Neal told me the assistant trainer knew we wouldn't be able to see what happened. In a way, I was relieved. I couldn't bear to see someone beating Primula." She shudders. "I'm sick with anger and shock." She thumps her clenched fist on the table making the wine jump in our glasses.

"It's horrific," I say, "and I keep wondering if I could have prevented it all from happening."

"What do you mean?" Candice asks.

"I've been a coward and reluctant to investigate." The wine is loosening my tongue. "If I'd been more diligent and committed, perhaps Primula would not have been hurt."

"It's not your responsibility to catch criminals," William says. "That's clearly the role of police services."

"Well, I still feel bad."

"Primula would be gone if you and Kelly hadn't shown up," Melissa says.

"Anyway, back to the camera footage. There was nothing helpful, then, Melissa?"

"No. We saw a black figure turn on one of the taps. The other two are just out of range of the cameras, but we could see the water. Those taps don't have water-saving devices, but I was still surprised at how fast the water spread."

"He must have blocked the drains under each tap then."

"I forgot to mention that Neal said there were pieces of rubber covering each of the drains. It was cold-heartedly preplanned. The attacker must have brought them with him.

"The attempted murder of Primula Mokka," William says, as he places his wine glass on the table, "was an egregious act. It was premeditated. It was violent and vicious."

"What are you saying?" I ask.

"That it was an act borne out of fury—perhaps driven by a powerful desire for revenge."

"So, the key is to find out who Primula's enemies are," Melissa says. "But she's liked by everyone in the backstretch, as far as I know. I haven't heard a negative word said about her. Linda even speaks highly of her—she's checked on Hector a few times and, told me he's being well looked after. Amazing! So, who'd want to beat Primula up in a fury, for heaven's sake?"

"There's something we're missing," I say. "For some reason, I keep returning to Barton. That's how all this started, with Barton being poisoned. Les told me Barton was a member of a gang called the Blackbirds Gang and, more recently, frequented that illegal casino. I'm going to focus on those two things. I think there could be a link."

"That doesn't make sense," Melissa says. "Primula wouldn't have anything to do with a gang or an illegal casino, nor would Les."

"According to Bobbie Knightscourt, Orlando was a member of the same gang Barton belonged to."

"And, as I mentioned to Meg," William says, "while I'm not aware of evidence to support the theory that Pablo was shot by a member of the Blackbirds Gang, he did belong to a rival gang, so the possibility exists. And it's interesting to note that Annie, Bobbie's sister, was a member of the same rival gang. As I think you all know, Annie was accused of shooting Pablo but was acquitted. Part of her defence was that she was in a relationship with Pablo at the time, which the jury believed."

"I found out the rival gang was called the Pitbulls Gang", I say.

"If the jury was right, then Annie could be the one seeking revenge for the killing of her lover," William says.

"Perhaps she believes Barton shot Pablo, but why kill Orlando, poison Les, and try to murder Primula?" Melissa asks, not expecting an answer. She opens another bottle of wine and refills our four empty glasses. "It doesn't make sense to me."

"I agree with Meg," William says, "that there could be a link to the gangs and perhaps the casino, even though on the surface it appears unlikely. I'll see what I can find out, but I'm not optimistic I'll learn anything useful."

"How did that bloke Les know Barton was a member of a gang?" Candice asks. "Isn't he a groom at the track?"

"Les worked as a counsellor," I say, "helping people on the streets who were in trouble and needed support. Barton was one of those young men and Les steered him towards the racetrack. Barton worked his way up with Dr. Greg Dudley's help."

"Pablo must have got shot a long time ago then," Candice says. "So, why's all this rotten stuff happening now?"

"That's a very good question, Candice," I say.

"I don't think we're on the right track," Melissa says.

* * *

Linda and I rest our arms on the top of the wooden fence and watch the colts play. They can be rough at times and halters regularly get damaged. But I can't help smiling when I see animals having so much fun.

"Dirk has entered all the yearlings into the sale," I say.

"Why?"

"I don't know exactly, but he said his and Bobbie's lives are unsettled. He also hinted that finances are tight. He probably doesn't have the budget to pay for five horses to be broken in and then kept all winter to be followed by months of training only to find out that most of them won't be ready to race next year. You know what it's like."

"Yeah. Some owners don't get it. They like think they're going to make money with every horse."

"There's a lot of luck involved, as you know. They can have everything going for them, the breeding, conformation, size, good health, and so on, but not want to be a racehorse."

"Yeah, that's the hardest."

"It's probably for the best that he's selling them."

"Who's going to get them ready for the sale? It's like a lot of work."

"I know, and I can't do it. Not enough time. They need training on how to walk, trot, and stand straight on a lead-rein. And they must have daily grooming. They should be out of the sun since buyers are put off by dull, bleached coats. I can't put them out at night and bring them in for the day."

"You don't want to try?"

"No. I've just bought some sun protection spray stuff that I'm going to put on every morning."

"You don't want them?"

"Linda, I don't have that kind of money. I shouldn't have four at the track as it is."

"What about Bella?"

"He wants to board her here. I don't like the responsibility because I have no experience with foaling. Melissa says Russon has promised to drop everything and run if I need assistance, which I definitely will."

"I can help. I worked for a bit at a farm and assisted in foaling."

"That's great, Linda. Thanks. I feel better knowing I'll have support. I'd hate anything to happen to the mare or the foal because I don't know what I'm doing".

"Yeah."

"I have to go and meet with Suzie now—the woman Barton knew at the casino."

"She worked there."

"She did. And she wants to meet with me again. So, I'd better go. Thanks, Linda for all your help."

"No problem. I'll drop by early this evening if I can."

* * *

Suzie asked me to meet her in Three Cherries, a coffee shop in the basement of the casino where she works. It's used mostly by the employees. That works out well for me because the casino is adjacent to the racetrack, and I want to visit my horses and check on Hector.

As I sip on a reasonably decent cup of tea, William sends me a text to let me know he's learned the police have failed to find a match in their database for the DNA on the balaclava that Kelly cleverly snatched. I won't tell Kelly! It's deflating news because I assumed the identification of the person who attempted to smother Primula in the hospital would advance the investigation considerably—perhaps even bring it to a resolution.

197

Suzie walks towards me with ease—on four-inch stilettos. Her sleek black dress and updo make her appear almost elegant but the ace-of-hearts tattoo on her upper arm diminishes her otherwise sophisticated look—at least in my eyes.

"Thanks for coming. I'm a bit tight for time—working the day shift."

"You have something you want to tell me."

"I remembered two things."

"Okay. Do you want a coffee or something?" I stand up ready to go to the counter.

"Thanks, but I haven't got time. I'll be quick. I hope this helps to catch Barton's killer."

"So do I."

"Barton never paid for his drinks. I was told they were on the house. I guess that's partly why he drank too much."

"Could be. Interesting. I suppose you don't know why they were free?"

"Sorry. The other thing is that the company running the casino had the initials A.N.E., but I don't know what they stand for".

"Great information. Thanks. Anything else? I'm wondering if there's a link between the Blackbirds Gang Barton was once a member of and the casino."

"He never mentioned a gang to me."

"Nothing odd went on at the casino? It was run as you would expect a legitimate one to be?"

"The only thing different was that there was a room with a huge television screen, and they'd have live horse racing. I think it was just from the racetrack here."

"Betting on the races?"

"I wasn't involved in that, but yeah. Barton was never there 'cause he was usually at the track when the racing was on so it's likely not important."

"I think it is. Did you ever see anyone give him a package?"

"What sort of package?"

"I'm thinking cash in an envelope."

"Mm. Now that's got me thinking. He got lots of chips—you know, for the tables—and I don't remember seeing him put any cash down. I wonder if he paid for them?"

"I suppose I won't be able to find that out."

"Sorry, but got to go. Hope I've helped a bit."

"For sure. Thanks. Have a good shift."

As I walk towards the garbage bin with my empty cup my mobile pings again. It's another text from an unknown number—*you have been warned*. But I can't pay it much attention since I'm on my way to see Hector.

*　*　*

The horses are restless. I don't see Hector's head hanging over his mesh stall door. Perhaps he's having a rest. I expect he was out on the training track earlier this morning and he may still be recovering from his ordeal, although he looked great when I last saw him. Nevertheless, I mustn't forget he was in the stall where and when Primula was beaten, and he was standing in over a foot of water for a long time.

I peer into his stall and startle as I notice a dark figure standing just to the left of the door. Hector has shrunk back into the far corner. He's trembling. This person must be someone strange to the horse.

"What are you doing?" I yell, hoping that Yuki, the assistant trainer will hear. No one seems to be around. Training is over for the day and most of the staff has left. I open the stall door. Without warning, the man shoves me against the breeze block wall so violently that I get an instant headache and am nauseated. I scream, hoping someone will hear, and kick out with my arms braced against the wall. He hits me across the face with the back of his hand and my nose trickles with something that tastes like blood. I scream again but with less gusto. And before I can collect myself and retaliate, he grabs me around the neck. I'm quivering but I can't let this violent bully get the better of me. Despite my terror, my adrenaline gives me some gumption, and I knee him in the groin as hard as my disadvantaged position will let me. But he doesn't let go. The assailant's hands are large and he's wearing black leather gloves—I can smell them. He has a balaclava so I can't see his face. I try to knee him again, but I'm dizzy and light-headed and my attempt is feeble. Tears stream down my face.

And then the sweetest sounds burst into the stall—my dogs' barks and growls. Kelly and Jake leap up at the intruder's arms, flashing their white teeth—yanking, biting, and snapping close to my face. The man lets go of my neck and I fall onto the soft straw bedding. He scrambles to the doorway of the stall with two dogs holding onto his pant legs. He's lashing out at them as I fade away.

17

Casino

My eyes don't want to open but questions and fears are building to a fever pitch. I need to know if Kelly, Jake, and Hector are okay. So, with what seems like an enormous effort, I open them. The bright lights are painful. The last place I want to be is in a hospital, but it appears that's where I am—I suppose I should be thankful I'm alive and being cared for.

"Meg, how do you feel?" Dr. Milton asks.

"How are Kelly, Jake, and Hector?" My voice sounds raspy, and my throat is sore. My neck is stiff and must be bruised. I'm sure I'd feel better at home. Dr. Milton stands up and I have trouble turning my head to see where he's going. I fear the worst but then Kelly's suddenly on the bed licking my face (breaking the rules), and Jake is sitting and whining, wagging his tail. Tears and chuckles at the same time. I don't think I've ever felt so relieved. Melissa and William appear beside me, smiling.

"Kelly and Jake saved me. He tried to strangle me." Ironically, I choke on my words.

"We know," Dr. Milton says. "Your neck tells the story." He isn't smiling.

"Kelly and Jake deserve medals—again," Melissa says.

"How's Hector?"

"Yuki is amazing. And crazy," Melissa says. "He heard the dogs making a terrible racket in the truck. You'd left the windows down a few inches, so he could hear them barking and carrying on, as he put it. He thought the truck was on fire, so he let them out and they flew towards Hector's stall. That made him realize something was up. He followed them, but he wasn't too alarmed until he heard you scream. Then he ran. By then the man was beating off Kelly and Jake. Yuki found you on the ground and called 911. Kelly and Jake eventually came back and lay next to you. Yuki says Kelly whined until the ambulance arrived."

"I don't deserve such wonderful dogs." More tears grow in my eyes and a couple escape down my cheeks. I fondle Kelly's ears and pat Jake's head. "No one knows who my attacker was?"

"Not yet."

"What about Hector?"

"Yuki was great. Because of Primula being attacked, and now you, and the flooding and stuff, he was suspicious of what the man had been doing in there. He moved Hector to another stall once the ambulance had left and then did a thorough inspection. A couple of police officers helped check things out and said they'd have the water analyzed. Guess what?"

"Poison."

"That's what it looked like. Yuki said strange bits were floating in Hector's water. But because you showed up Hector hadn't drunk any."

"He probably wouldn't have anyway if it wasn't tasteless and if the stuff hadn't dissolved. Hector doesn't like medicine. He can sense it a mile off. Is he okay, though?"

"Yuki said Hector had squished himself into the corner of the stall and he was quaking, as he put it. Russon examined him thoroughly and couldn't find anything physically wrong, but we think these recent events have terrified him. He went off his feed, which isn't surprising, and he's very spooky."

"Where is he? I hope he's not still at the track."

"No. He's at our farm. Yuki asked if we would look after him. He needs lots of TLC. I knew you'd agree. Hector knows our place."

"Good. He can stay as long he wants and needs to."

"I knew you'd say that."

"What about his new owners though—the ones who claimed him?"

"A syndicate—a bunch of friends. They're in it for the excitement of going to the races with their buddies. Yuki's guess is they'll want to sell him because he may not race again this season."

"Oh." I sip some water using a bent plastic straw. I would much prefer a cup of tea at home. "So, what was the poison?"

"The results haven't come back yet," William says. He picks Jake up and puts him on the bed with Kelly. I get another face wash. It's so great to be able to stroke them and rub their ears. I feel better already.

"Are the other horses okay?"

"Yuki emptied and cleaned all the water and feed buckets," Melissa says, "and replaced the hay for each horse. He says all the horses are fine."

"Good. How long have I been here?"

"About thirty-six hours," Dr. Milton says.

"I want to go home."

"Perhaps tomorrow, but you need a few days of rest."

Everyone leaves at the same time, and it's as if the air has been sucked out of the stark room. The off-white walls and bright lights make my eyes ache, so I close them, but I won't be able to sleep—there are too many thoughts and questions spinning in my head.

"How's the patient?" asks Detective Valeska.

"Ooh."

"Sorry to startle you. I thought I'd check on how you're doing."

"Thanks. I don't have any useful information on what happened."

"You're probably not supposed to be talking. Your voice sounds as if your throat's sore and I hear you have bruising around your neck. I must say I'm surprised you were attacked."

"He was attempting to hurt Hector, not me. But I got in the way. I don't know who it was. He was wearing a balaclava."

"Kelly didn't manage to snatch it this time, I suppose."

"No."

"We've interviewed everyone in the vicinity, but no one saw him."

"I've just remembered something."

"Ah. Good."

"As my attacker was scrambling out of the stall with Kelly and Jake pulling on his pant legs, I noticed his large feet. I know that's not a unique feature, but I happen to remember that Kenny from Animal Equality and Freedom has large feet."

"It's worth looking into. But what about motive?"

"I know. It doesn't fit." My voice is failing me. The detective moves closer so she can hear. "Poisoning a horse isn't consistent with animal rights. But I think he stole Bella—Dirk Knightscourt's pregnant mare. There's something not right about him—and something awful occurred to me—he could want horses to die so he has proof that horse racing kills. I know it's bizarre."

"But you say he wore a balaclava. The man who attempted to smother Primula Mokka wore one. That doesn't mean they're necessarily the same person, but I should consider it. What would be

Kenny's reason for wanting Primula dead? It's hard for me to connect an animal rights organization's modus operandi with either incident."

"Perhaps you're right and neither of the attackers was Kenny. Anyone can get a black balaclava."

"Anyway, you rest. We'll connect later."

"How's Primula?"

"Somewhat improved, I hear. But she's not able to give a description. She was sedated and sleeping when the attack started. As far as we can determine, she fought with her attacker as best as she could, but she would have been dead if it wasn't for you and your dogs showing up at an opportune time. The officer on duty is on sick leave, in case you're interested."

"Ah."

"She's being discharged tomorrow. She's going to stay with her mother at her condo in the city for a while."

"If you have a moment, there are a couple of things I learned that you might not know—if my voice will hold out."

"Shoot."

"Barton was served free drinks at the casino. And they showed live horse racing in one of the rooms. Presumably, betting was involved. And another thing—Barton may not have paid for his casino chips."

"We know about the horse racing."

"Barton might be involved in race fixing so I wonder if he was being rewarded for that with free drinks and casino chips."

"Possibly."

"Also, the company that owned the casino had the initials A.N.E.."

"Suzie told you all this, did she? We don't consider her to be reliable."

"Oh."

*　*　*

William is grovelling. I don't like it. It's almost worse than when he was making decisions for me and not respecting my opinion. But I shouldn't be too harsh. He's the reason Dr. Milton was persuaded to support my early discharge: William promised to look after me—whatever that means. I had a burning desire to come home, so I accepted his offer. I'm certain I'll recover faster here.

Even Candice has stepped up. My first impressions of her were not positive especially since she seemed unable to relate to the animals. I was dumbfounded that she could resist Kelly's big brown eyes, Jake's wagging tail, and Cooper's purrs—although she's been caught with the cat on her lap at least twice and has been seen patting the dogs. She didn't show any interest in the horses at first, but going to the track with Melissa and working on some minor chores at the farm have, I like to think, made a difference in her life—enriching her experience and helping her to relate to animals.

She's sitting in the other recliner in the family room and we each have a mug of tea she made. And Cooper is on her lap.

"How is your work going with William?" I ask.

"Pretty good. Actually, very good. I thought I should get some training, and William has told me he'll pay half of the cost of the legal office assistant program offered at Vannersville College. I can do it all online. He's found out that the one year I took at Nottingham University plus my GSCE results are enough to qualify me for entrance into the college. He's helping me with the work permit process too. I'm excited about my future for the first time ever."

"Well, I hope it all works out well." Candice's face has more colour, and her lovely smile has become less rare and is a pleasant sight.

"As soon as Melissa gets back from the track, I'll go to Milkweed Farm to finish setting up William's office and organizing my desk.

I think it's going to be awesome there."

"You don't have to wait for Melissa. I don't need a babysitter. Please go."

"Okay. If you're sure?"

"I am."

Cooper jumps down from Candice's lap, stretches and yawns, and leaps up onto me. His purrs rumble as he turns around and curls up. Kelly and Jake don't stir when Candice leaves.

A couple of seconds after she's left my mobile tells me Les is calling.

"Hello, Les."

"Hi, Meg. Good to hear your voice. But you sound croaky. You okay?"

"I'm fine. How about you?"

"I'm good. Dirk's contacted me about these yearlings. He's asked me if I'll get them spiffy for the sale."

"Okay. I was wondering what was going to happen. Are you sure you're well enough?"

"Yep. It's just groundwork. I don't have to ride."

"I know, but still."

"I'm okay. Can I use your place?"

"I don't have an arena, just paddocks and large fields."

"An empty paddock would work. And a driveway, if you've got one."

"Yes, and it's gated. When do you want to start?"

"Like yesterday. Dirk's fussing. He wants them to shine but things are tight—bucks and time."

"Just let me know when you're coming. A text is fine."

"I'll text you now. Coming tomorrow morning."

"Funny. I'll make sure I'm here to show you around. You've got my address?"

"Yep."

"What about working for Neal?"

"Three hours six mornings a week followed by training Dirk's horses each day."

"Okay."

"See you tomorrow. And thanks."

*   *   *

Candice has moved out and is staying at Milkweed Farm—helping William to get settled in and organized. She says William is considering putting his office up for sale, including the flat above it—in other words, the whole old house. He's moved most of the office furniture out. Candice tells me he's fallen in love with Milkweed Farm and doesn't see why clients can't meet him there—but he would go to them if they don't like the idea of a drive into the country. So, Milkweed Farm may not be empty again for a long time and that's okay with me. In fact, it feels good.

Candice says William's connecting with colleagues, acquaintances, and professional contacts as he works to rebuild his business. He must also have been doing some digging. He texted to ask if he could bring breakfast—he has some information on Kenny. He'll be arriving soon, but I'm not lying in this recliner any longer this morning.

"Come on dogs, we're going out for a walk to see the horses." Linda has done all the chores, so the horses are fed, the stalls are clean, and everyone's outside. I've been thinking about the investigation (or investigations) and breathing in fresh air and exercising my legs will give me a clearer head.

We walk around the paddock Bella's grazing in. She barely lifts her head to check us out. Her coat is sleek and shiny with beautiful dapples. The pasture suits her well. And she's smart to stay out of the direct sun—standing either under the trees or in the run-in

shed when the sun is at its brightest—so her coat hasn't become
bleached and dry.

"Hi, Meg." Les' voice jolts me out of my admiration of Bella.
He parks his e-bike by the barn and hops off. "Nice temp. Can I use
your grooming stuff?"

"You'll find it in the feed room in the barn. The horses will need
some work. I was just enjoying watching Bella who's smart enough
to stay out of the bleaching sun's rays at least for the brightest part
of the day. Doesn't she look good?"

"Dirk's prize mare. Nice and round. She'd look good in the mixed
sale."

"She's staying here."

"Good luck with that. Gotta get going."

"I just want to ask you something. Do you know who the members of the Blackbirds Gang and the Pitbulls Gang were?"

"Those little grey cells think the murders have something to do
with those gangs?"

"I'm considering anything at this point."

"All I know is what I said. Barton was in the Blackbirds Gang
and one of them shot a guy called Pablo in the Pitbulls Gang. That's
all I've got."

"Okay. Thanks."

"Who tried to do you in?"

"I don't know."

"You got ideas, I bet."

"Maybe. Would you like me to help you get the horses in?"

"I'm good. I'll text when I'm done. Could be a while. Which
paddock can I use?"

"The one behind Bella's. Let me know if you need anything."

I wander over to another paddock to visit with Hector. He's
tossing his head and nipping at the three young colts—they're geldings but I find myself calling them colts. They're in the field next

to Hector and interacting with him over the fence. It seems like harmless play, and it looks like Hector is enjoying himself. Linda tells me he's eating well and loves to graze. The syndicate wants to sell him, and Neal is certain I'm going to buy him. I haven't made up my mind—at least that's what I'm telling myself. They've given me the first right of refusal. I don't know if there's a deadline. The colts amble away from the fence and Hector puts his head down to graze. Les walks towards the field with a lead-rein. I'm sure he has mints in his pocket. It's easier than I thought it would be for him to clip the lead-rein to one of the colts' halters and lead the young horse to the gate.

This short foray outside to see the horses has healed more wounds inside and out than hours of sitting in a recliner has. I gaze around me and soak in the beauty of the old maple trees tinged with the beginnings of fall colours, the lush green grass tamed by the horses, and the large daisies with their happy faces standing in the garden. And a special treat—two bluebirds settle on the fence rail about twenty feet away. They fly off as William's jag shows up. It stops by the house much to the delight of Kelly and Jake who tear over to greet him. The dogs get lots of ear rubs and pats, and then they run around the car in pure joy.

"You're out and about—obviously back on your feet. That's good to see."

"I've turned a corner today."

"You look better."

"Anyway, you said you have some information."

"Yes, I do. I hope it'll be helpful."

"We could sit on the verandah. I don't want to go back indoors yet."

"I'll make tea and coffee and bring it out. Is that okay?"

"Good idea."

It's shady on the verandah but warm enough to sit. The

information William has can't be urgent otherwise he would have at least given me a hint as soon as he arrived.

Kelly and Jake lie on the lawn and watch the road. The birdsong is sporadic—not like the incessant chirping of the cheery sparrows in the backstretch. I miss their music—I haven't visited my racehorses for a few days.

I feel out of the loop generally. I suppose people haven't contacted me because they know I was attacked and in poor shape. And I haven't connected with anyone. But now I'm feeling restless and want to get going again.

William appears carrying a tray with two mugs and a paper bag. Kelly and Jake sense that there are treats. They both sit in front of William, and he hands them each an oatmeal raisin cookie.

"I got a muffin for you. I thought carrot would be appropriate."

"That's great. Thanks."

"To get to the point. You recently told me about Kenny and said you thought his behaviour, even for an animal rights activist, was bizarre."

"Ada told me he was the one who spray-painted my truck. I don't know why he did. I can't prove any of this—but I think he put sponges up two of Primula's horses' nostrils, and Dr. Dudley is sure he was the one who threw a stink bomb into his office trailer, and I'm pretty certain he kidnapped Bella but I don't know why, and his large feet make me think he was the one who tried to poison Hector and kill me when I showed up unexpectedly".

"Couldn't that all be consistent with the behaviour of an over-zealous animal rights activist?"

"I'm not sure. Even though AEF displayed posters saying 'horse racing kills'—and he may have wanted to prove it, what he did was targeted and not effective in getting his message out in my opinion. In other words, his actions don't make sense to me."

"Then the information I have could be more useful than I

thought. As you know, I have valued contacts who trust me to be discrete. By the way, you must know the police want to talk to Kenny because of your statement about the attack. They haven't unearthed him yet."

"Oh. I wish they had."

"And I've heard there are no promising leads on the murders of Barton or Orlando."

"Oh."

"Meg, I hope you're well enough to follow up because this is all going nowhere fast."

"Is this what you wanted to tell me?"

"Of course not. It's about Kenny. What you've just said about his actions makes this more significant, although it's not going to lead to a breakthrough."

"William, just tell me for crying out loud."

"He was seen entering the illegal casino located in the mansion where Dirk and Bobbie Knightscourt were living. The police had it under surveillance and have several photos".

"I would never have guessed there was a connection between Kenny and the casino. That means it would have been possible for him to poison Barton. But why?"

"Knowing the motive can make all the difference."

"I must ask Suzie if she saw Kenny and what he did when he was there."

"Suzie's the woman who worked in the casino and was with Barton when he died?"

"Yes. She told me Barton went to the casino several times a week and got drunk—he was probably suffering from the effects of poisoning as well as too much booze. She admitted he didn't drink all that much, as she put it. Perhaps the poison was the main issue all along. Anyway, she usually made sure he got to the track okay on the bus in the early hours of the morning. She lives nearby."

"You believe her?"

"I do. I'd love to see at least one of those surveillance photos."

"I'll see what I can do."

"Thanks, William. It's great to get new information that might lead somewhere."

"I hope it does. This next piece of information will be disappointing, I think. Detective Valeska said the Crime Scenes Officers took endless samples from the stall where you were almost killed and snapped hundreds of photographs." He rubs his hands over his face. "I apologize. I'm just relieved you're okay." He hesitates, looking down at his leather loafers. He's not one to show his emotions and neither am I. Kelly puts her head on my lap and saves me from an awkward moment. I didn't know what to say to him. "The good news is Kelly and Jake are stars again."

"I suppose I shouldn't be surprised."

"The investigators found a small fragment of black material just inside the stall door. You mentioned that the last thing you saw before you lost consciousness was Kelly and Jake holding onto the assailant's pant legs as he scrambled out of the stall. The results of the analysis show that the DNA on that scrap does not match that found on the balaclava snatched by Kelly in the parking lot."

"That sounds like bad news to me."

"Perhaps, but it's useful to know it wasn't. You might be right that Kenny is the person who tried to poison Hector and strangle you. My problem is I have trouble coming up with a plausible motive."

"Can't the police search Kenny's home and get some DNA so we can prove it was him?"

"I've not been able to find that out, but I assume that's the next step. As you know, there's been a press release and posts on social media with Kenny's photograph. They're hoping someone will see him and call."

"I haven't seen any of that."

"What are your thoughts about the murders of Barton and Orlando?"

"I think someone else is responsible but have no clue what the motive would be for those crimes, and then there's the brutal attack on Primula."

"I agree that's a tough one."

"Well, thanks for the info and the muffin."

"You're welcome."

18

Fire

The first thing I want to do this afternoon is visit my racehorses, so the dogs and I are on our way to the racetrack. I have my truck back and there is no sign of fluorescent orange swirls. Its clean, shiny finish and the odour of fresh paint remind me of when it was new.

The afternoons are quiet in the backstretch although busier on race days. The sales barns are even quieter than I anticipated. If it wasn't for the pigeons and sparrows, there wouldn't be a living thing in sight as I park nearby. But there are only a few horses stabled here and those will soon be gone to free up the stalls in preparation for the yearling sale.

The dogs are settled behind me but I'm jittery. Disturbing memories of large, black leather gloves around my neck invade my thoughts and refuse to be quashed. I sit for a minute and take two deep breaths. Perhaps I should leave. I don't really need to visit. Just as I'm about to restart the pickup, Yuki walks out of the barn leading a large chestnut that reminds me of Hector. He's seen me so I venture out of my truck.

"Hello, Yuki. Just a brief visit to see if the horses are okay." I catch up and walk beside him.

"Doing fine. How's Hector?"

"He's happy."

"Good."

"How's Primula?"

"I get more calls and texts now, so I guess that means she's healing. That reminds me, she wants to chat with you when you're up to it. She was cut up about you being attacked."

"Okay. I'll give her a call."

"Feel free to visit with the horses. There's a pot of mints on top of the chest."

"When will you be able to move back into your barn?"

"We're in the process. That's where I'm leading this handsome guy."

"Would you like some help?"

"Primula would shoot me if you helped. Too soon after what happened to you."

"I'm sure I'd be fine, but you may be right. It's a big responsibility leading other people's racehorses."

"Don't remind me." He smiles and picks up the pace as I turn back and walk towards the sales barns. The horses look great and don't show any signs of stress. Yuki must know what he's doing. I have a quick visit with each one and listen to them crunch noisily on mints.

Rather than walk to Neal's barn, I drive. Something catches my eye as I pass the row of office trailers. I stop and back up. Steam or smoke is coming from one of the veterinarian's trailers. Perhaps it's an optical illusion. I roll down the passenger window and take a closer look. Kelly growls. That's not a good sign. It's a warm day, so I rule out steam. And now a whiff of foul-smelling smoke stings the back of my throat.

It's Dr. Greg Dudley's trailer. I hope he's gone for the day. Most of the veterinarians will have left by now. It's likely to be faulty wiring. I don't know what makes me let the dogs out—perhaps it was Kelly's unexpected growl. She leads the way to the trailer door. Sometimes I think she's smarter than I am. Jake follows because that's what he does most of the time. And I make a hasty call to security and ask them to call the fire department.

I skip up the wooden steps although my legs are not as responsive as I'm used to. I'm glad neither Melissa nor William can see me now. They'd want me back in that darned recliner. The doorknob is not hot, and the door is not locked. I hesitate. I know that opening the door will provide oxygen to the fire and I should probably wait for the experts. Kelly makes the decision for me. She scratches at the door. I take that to mean she thinks someone is inside. I open the door with caution. The acrid smoke makes my eyes run. I cough. Just as I say "stay" to Kelly, she rushes in and yaps. Jake holds back just inside the door which I shut hastily in hopes of preventing the fire from suddenly erupting.

There's a cloud of smoke in the trailer and Kelly is below the bottom of the cloud. She looks at me and then turns her gaze to an office chair. Someone is in it, slumped over—probably a man. I crawl over to him on my hands and knees so I can stay out of the worst of the smoke and breathe. But my eyes water so much I can barely see. He's tied to the chair with baling twine. I need a knife. I scan the floor for the source of the smoke. I can't see flames.

I wish the firefighters would show up, but there's no time to lose. I must get this man out of here. Kelly coughs. I don't want to open the door and use precious time arguing with her to get out—she won't want to leave. Besides, it will let more fuel in for the fire. I need to act quickly. Knife. Where is there a knife? I stand up by a desk and there's a yellow click knife I can barely see in the haze. Nausea and dizziness begin to creep into my body which is also attacked by a fit of coughing. I get back down onto my knees and crawl to the chair. It's less noxious down here.

What if the man is dead? I tell myself to focus on the job at hand and not to think about 'what ifs?'. I cut through the baling twine. There isn't a lot of it. As I cut through the last piece that's around the man's middle, he collapses onto the floor as if in slow motion. I crawl around to his ankles, grasp them and pull. I wish my hands were bigger and I was stronger, and I didn't have a sore arm.

"Kelly and Jake, pull!" Kelly catches on to what I want and grabs a mouthful of denim above his ankle. "Jake, come and help!" He slithers over as we slide the man over the vinyl tiles—I'm glad there's no carpet. Jake's not keen, but Kelly must have glared at him because he suddenly grabs and tugs. His effort makes an appreciable difference. The dogs are working hard on either side of me.

I hope I'm not imagining the man's moans as we yank and pull him towards the door. I desperately want him to be alive. Kelly's determined and is working hard. She's probably right—he is alive—I trust Kelly's instinct. I pull even harder but when I reach up to the doorknob, I wonder how on earth we'll manage to get him over the threshold.

As I open the door there's a whoosh and sudden heat. Flames burst into life at the back of the trailer. I yell "pull!" at the dogs. Kelly and Jake arch their backs before each tug. It's probably a coincidence but they're in synch with each other and I try to time my pulls with theirs.

We get his body over the threshold, but his head is still inside the door.

"Wait!" I tell the dogs. They let go of his jeans and pant so rapidly it makes me anxious for them—it's as if their tongues have doubled in length. I move to the man's head and lift it. We can't let his head bounce on the metal ledge. "Pull!" With my pushing and their pulling, we get him out. I shut the door, but I can still feel the heat. Now we have the wooden steps to negotiate. My vision is blurry and I'm coughing. The dogs cough now and then, but they're primarily panting—it's as if we're in a horror movie that's been sped up. The thought of more pulling and lifting makes my legs tremble. I don't think I can do it.

"Let us help with that," a security officer says. How long does it take them to get from their offices to here? Two burly security guys lift the man and place him on the patchy grass near the bottom of the steps. My legs are now wobblier, and I'm concerned they may give out on me. If I faint, I'll be doomed to sit in that recliner for another two or three days. I lie down on the cool grass next to the man as Kelly licks my face with a slimy tongue. Jake sits and watches all the sudden action. Fire engines, an ambulance, and a police vehicle all arrive simultaneously. My eyes are sore, and it's as if there's grit in my throat and my lungs have lost some capacity, but otherwise, I'm fine. The dogs have sneezed and coughed a few times, but I think they're okay too. They were able to stay below the smoke for the most part. But we're all exhausted.

What about the man?

The sign on the trailer lists Dr. Greg Dudley as one of the veterinarians. Despite us helping the man, I'm not absolutely certain it's him. But seeing his name on the plaque makes my stomach flutter. There must be a link to all the other horrific things that have happened. I wonder if the connection is that illegal casino. That's where Barton was likely poisoned, Kenny was seen there, and Dirk and Bobbie lived in the same building. Orlando worked in the barn on the property and that's where Dr. Dudley provided veterinary care for Dirk's horses—those that weren't at the track. That must be the connection. But why Primula? My head aches too much now to ask any more questions. They want me to go in the ambulance to be checked out at the hospital. I'm signing a form to decline.

* * *

"You all smell disgusting. Where have you been?" asks Melissa as the three of us walk into the kitchen. Kelly and Jake trot over to their water bowl and lap with gusto, splashing each other's muzzle. I sit down and rest my head on my folded arms. "I'll make a cup of tea. What have you been up to?"

"I thought you might have heard. Someone set fire to Dr. Dudley's office trailer."

"Don't tell me you went in there to put out the fire? Honestly, Meg!"

"For some reason, when I saw what I thought could be smoke I let Kelly and Jake out of the truck and Kelly made a beeline for the door and started scratching. She knew someone was in there and we had to do something. I don't know for sure, but I think it was Dr. Dudley."

"Meg! You should have waited for help."

"He would have died."

"He wasn't conscious?"

"No. He was tied up. I cut the twine, and the dogs helped me to drag him out of there."

"Your eyes are bloodshot, and your voice sounds raspy again. They should have taken you to the hospital to be checked out."

"They wanted to. I declined."

"Meg! And the dogs. What about them?"

"There's no need to be so upset. We're all fine. I just need a cup of tea."

"It's coming."

"You look nice. Are you going out?"

"Yuki and I are going to have a drink at a new pub in Vannersville."

"Oh. That's great."

"Before you ask—no I haven't heard from Edwin. And it's over."

"I wasn't going to ask. I hope you have a nice time this evening."

"I don't think I should go."

"What do you mean? Why?"

"Because you look terrible."

"Thanks."

"I'm being serious." Melissa grabs her mobile.

"Please don't cancel your date, Melissa. I'll feel even worse if you do."

"I'm not cancelling."

"Who are you texting?"

"Meg!"

"Okay. I'll have a bath. You'll be gone by the time I come back down."

Relaxing in a hot bath surrounded by the aromas of lavender and sweet oranges, I let my mind soak in all that's happened since Barton was found dead. I can't decide if everything is connected. Kenny's behaviour puzzles me. Could he be responsible for Barton's death since he was seen entering the casino? Is he an animal rights zealot or are his actions a smoke screen for more lethal intents? Is animal rights the link? Or is the illegal casino at the bottom of it all? I suppose there could be a connection between the illegal casino and an animal rights agenda, but I can't imagine what that could be. And I'm perplexed by the two shootings—a shot at me when I was at the side entrance to where the Knightscourts lived, and two shots at the horse trailer while it was here. I can't see what was achieved by either assault.

Barton and Pablo were members of rival gangs, and Pablo was allegedly shot by a member of Blackbirds Gang. Pablo was Annie's partner at the time—she'd split up with Barton. This must be at the root of it all. I need to dig deeper into who the members of those gangs were. And I must remember that Annie is Bobbie Knightscourt's sister. This could be important.

And, in the midst of my rambling thoughts, I receive another nasty text—*you shouldn't have saved him. You're next.* I don't have the energy to deal with it.

* * *

Melissa invited Yuki to the farm yesterday evening so she could keep an eye on me. She pretended it was the dogs she was concerned about, but I knew better. Yuki was friendly and upbeat. He even got us laughing. He says he loves horses more than people, and I can relate to that—although I'd say I love my animals more than <u>nearly</u> all the people in my life.

We didn't stay up late. Yuki had to leave early since he was due to get up at 4 am. He says Primula won't be back for a while, so he has a lot of extra work to do. But he seems to be enjoying it and talks of getting his trainer's licence soon. He repeated that Primula wants to have a chat with me and as soon as I've had my morning tea and the fresh carrot muffin Linda brought me earlier, and after I've visited Dr. Dudley in the hospital, I'll be visiting Primula. I've asked Candice to come with me because Melissa says Candice feels at a bit of a loose end—William hasn't many clients at the moment. She has organized his office including her working area at Milkweed Farm, so they're ready for action.

My mobile rings as I'm getting ready to leave for the hospital. It's Ada.

"Hello, Ada. How are you?"

"I'm fine. I heard about Dr. Greg Dudley on Facebook. Is he okay?"

"I'll find out soon. I'm just about to leave for the hospital. Why are you asking?"

"Because I found notes in Kenny's stuff he'd left behind, you know—when I was clearing out the AEF office. I thought I should tell you."

"Okay. Thanks. What do the notes say?"

"He has Dr. Dudley's name on a piece of paper with a thick black line around it. And he's written down the names of some drugs. I looked up a couple and they're banned in racehorses. He must believe Dr. Dudley supplies performance-enhancing drugs."

"So, you think he could be Dr. Dudley's attacker?"

"I hate to think that, but I guess so. I started AEF to help animals but that doesn't mean I wanted people to be hurt. I feel sick about it."

"We don't know if it was Kenny, and if it was, we don't know that his passion for animal rights was the reason."

"I guess. Oh, and there was another piece of paper with the names of herbs and plants. I couldn't figure out what it was about. I Googled one and it came up as being poisonous to horses, so I checked another one and it was too. So, I'm worried he could be planning to poison horses. He wants to get across his belief that horse racing kills but killing the horses to prove the point is so cruel and absolutely insane. It's too ghastly to think about. I hope you can stop him."

"I believe Kenny tried to poison a horse with something that was floating in his water bucket, but luckily I showed up and the horse is okay. He's now safe at my farm."

"I'm so glad. I couldn't sleep last night. I didn't find the papers until yesterday because I packed everything up and thought I'd go through them here, at my mother's house, when I'd have no deadline."

"Did you get a job with Greenpeace?"

"I'm so excited. I start next week."

"Congratulations. And thank you for sharing what you found out."

"You're welcome. I feel better having told you."

"Have you any idea where Kenny might be?"

"I've been thinking hard about that. I don't want any more animals or people hurt. He let drop once that he has a half-brother somewhere. Perhaps he's there. But I don't know where."

"That will help to track him down. Thanks again. You've been very helpful. I hope you get a good night tonight."

"I think I will."

*   *   *

Kelly, Jake, and I reach the hospital parking lot as the rain starts. The sky is slate grey, and the wind is forcing the large drops to hammer down at a forty-five-degree angle. Puddles are forming as I pull into a parking space as near to the front entrance as possible. I've had a special vest made for Jake embroidered with 'therapy dog in training' because I don't like leaving Jake by himself in the truck when Kelly and I go into the hospital. The way Jake wears it you'd think it says 'gold medallist'. I put my rain jacket hood up, and we tumble out of the truck into the downpour and trot to the entrance. My feet get wet in short order.

The dogs have a thorough shake as we step into the vestibule. I hope they dry off quickly so patients and staff can enjoy their visit.

"Dr. Milton. How nice to see you."

"Meg, I'll walk with you."

"Is there bad news about Dr. Dudley?"

"He's not under my care, so I don't know. I haven't had a chance to follow up. No, I wanted to talk to you about Kelly and Jake."

"What about them?"

"Hospital administration, in its wisdom, has decided that therapy dogs cannot be permitted in the hospital for health and safety reasons. I wanted to give you a heads-up so that you're not taken off-guard when you're approached—which I'm certain you will be. And it might not be handled tactfully. This administration is not known for its diplomacy."

"Oh."

"I want you to know that Kelly and Jake have my full support."

"Is there anything I can do?"

"You can't do anything yourself, I don't believe, but there's an active Patient Council you could approach once they are aware of the new policy. I'm sure they would take up the cause. The patients love Kelly, and she has a remarkable and faultless history here. That's all I can suggest."

"Thank you. I appreciate the advice."

"I have to run, but I'm glad I caught you."

19

More Bullet Holes

I'm relieved there's a police officer stationed outside Dr. Dudley's private room—and he's awake and alert. No doubt Detective Valeska is squirming—her budget must have evolved into a thing of fiction.

The sight of Dr. Dudley lying in a hospital bed with a white bandage around his head which covers part of one eye, tubes everywhere, and an intravenous drip, makes shivers go down my spine. His skin is grey in the unforgiving light, and it's as if he has a painted dark blue Nike swoosh under each eye, which I'm sure wasn't there before his ordeal. The bed is inclined so he's almost sitting. Perhaps that's to help with breathing, or lung drainage, or something.

He looks vulnerable and dependent. He must hate it.

"Visitors are not allowed," snaps a nurse dressed in what they call scrubs—what a horrible name. Hers are plain and pale blue. She has grey hair pulled back severely from her face as if she'd rather have none. The impression is of efficiency and professionalism at the expense of humanity and compassion. Perhaps that's not fair. I don't know the woman. "And those dogs are not allowed either. New policy."

"Stay," says Dr. Dudley with a grunt. He pats the bed with a hand that looks bruised and as if it could do with some moisturizing cream.

"Is there a problem?" The police officer stands in the doorway.

"I'm not sure," I say. "I'm Meg Sheppard."

"I assumed it was you. I was given orders that no one could visit but you, Mrs. Sheppard."

"What about those dogs?" asks the nurse in a nasal voice, almost as if she's afraid to breathe the same air as Kelly and Jake.

"I'm not familiar with hospital policy, but I was informed that Mrs. Sheppard and these two dogs saved this gentleman's life. He might want to thank them."

The nurse turns on her heels and brushes past the police officer as she leaves the room.

"Thank you," I say.

"As far as I know, you're not breaking any laws. And your dogs are getting quite the name." He stoops down and strokes their heads. "They're the best. And don't worry, the detective told me to be alert at all times because we have a nutcase on the loose. There will be three of us doing shifts, just so you know."

"Thanks."

He returns to the corridor and sits on a plastic chair.

Dr. Dudley coughs and I sense his pain. He has an oximeter attached to one of his fingers, so they must be monitoring oxygen levels in his blood. Perhaps he's been receiving oxygen therapy. He probably has considerable damage to his throat and lungs from smoke inhalation. I can hear his breathing over the clatter and chatter coming from the corridor. Hospitals can be noisy and far from restful.

"Kelly, say hello to Dr. Dudley." She knows what that means. She puts her front paws on the bed and places her chin on his arm. He turns his head towards her.

"Good dog." She wags her tail. Jake sits and looks up at him with bright eyes as he sweeps the floor with his fat, black tail. Dr. Dudley's eyes shine with tears and his mouth quivers. "Thank you."

"I hope you don't have to stay here for long."

He nods. "Caught Kenny?" He coughs.

"It was Kenny, for sure?"

He nods.

"The police haven't got him yet, but I just got a lead. I'm going to text Detective Valeska now." I let her know that Ada told me Kenny has a half-brother. Perhaps he's staying with him. The police shouldn't have any trouble tracking him down if he is. "I heard that Kenny believed you were supplying performance-enhancing drugs, perhaps even manufacturing them. Don't talk. It must be painful. I just want you to know."

"I knew." He coughs.

"Did he assume that because you were Barton's veterinarian and he was a cheat, you must have had some part in that cheating?"

He nods.

"Barton was suspended six times in the past five years, four times for positive drug tests and twice for abuse. But I've also heard he fixed races."

He nods.

"But none of this had anything to do with you?"

He rolls his head slowly from side to side.

"Do you think Kenny killed Barton?"

He doesn't move his head.

"You don't know."

He nods.

Is there anything I can do for you?

"Catch the bugger." His cough sounds like a wretch and the pain makes him close his eyes. Kelly sits down. He stops coughing and gazes at the dogs and then at me. "Thank you."

"You're welcome. I hope you get out of here soon and recover quickly. We'll get back to work. Come on dogs."

As I approach the exit, I hear heels clicking at a rapid pace behind me. The three of us turn. I know what's coming. A young woman dressed in a dark trouser suit and white silk blouse hands me a printed copy of the new policy on animals in the hospital. They are banned. We have a brief conversation, and I see no point in prolonging it.

"Meg Sheppard. It is you, isn't it?" asks a man in a wheelchair a few feet away. He must be from the chronic care part of the hospital. We walk towards him.

"Yes. Have you met my dogs before? This is Kelly and this is Jake."

"Ooh, aren't you lovely? I used to have a border collie called Dickens. We loved him to bits." Blue veins bulge out of his gnarled hands as he pats the dogs. "You know, they're darned stupid with that policy. I'm a lawyer. I eventually specialized in mediation. God knows I do a lot of it now because this administration is all about rules and they've lost their way. But there could be a compromise if you're willing to contemplate that. You know—the dogs only visit the chronic care wing and this lobby, and don't go into the surgical wards, etcetera etcetera. Would you permit me to pursue this? I sit on the Patient Council, and we get an audience with the bigwigs once a month. I have no doubt in my mind that the Patient Council will want to take this on. What do you say?"

"We say thank you very much, and here's my card. Your name?"

"Edward Bergerstein. By the way, I heard about you and your dogs saving lives. You should all get medals or be knighted or something. Good show."

"Thanks. And thank you for being willing to advocate for the therapy dog program."

"My pleasure. Lovely dogs. Good boys. I hope to see you all again soon."

"We'll be sure to visit you once this is resolved."

"Good show."

I hope Kelly doesn't understand that the therapy program is threatened. I'm sure she would be disappointed. She has brought many patients a taste of joy and she loves her visits. And I was looking forward to Jake's training—they would make a wonderful team.

Back in the parking lot, Kelly and I dodge the puddles which are now larger and more frequent, but Jake paddles through them. It's as if the raindrops are bouncing up at us as water spurts back upwards on impact.

The windows in the truck fog up quickly. Kelly and Jake shake off as much as they can as soon as I let them in behind the front seats. They spray the inside of the truck with a myriad of droplets. I hope there's no mud. Cleaning the inside of vehicles is one of my least favourite things.

Before we get moving, I call Detective Valeska and let her know that I've had a visit with Dr. Dudley. I tell her he wanted to know if Kenny had been caught, so he must be sure he was the attacker. He knows Kenny believed he was dealing in performance-enhancing drugs, but Dr. Dudley denies any involvement with Barton's cheating. And he doesn't know if Kenny killed Barton.

Primula is expecting me in about an hour. I have time to check in on Dirk and Bobbie since I'll be driving past the farm where they're staying. I haven't heard from them in a while. I want to ask them more about the casino. It's hard to believe they knew nothing about it—after all, they were under the same, albeit enormous, roof.

There are no visible vehicles in the driveway or by the old farmhouse. The curtains are drawn making it appear that no one is home.

The rain continues its relentless torrent, so I leave the dogs in the truck.

I trot to the front door, knock, and stand under the small portico. My ankles are getting wet. I knock again. The rain's intensity increases and the noise of its pummelling on the portico and into the puddles drowns out other sounds. Nevertheless, I hear a voice raised above the din. Shouting. I think it's Dirk's, and he sounds angry. I knock again—this time with extra vigour and determination.

The door opens enough to show a red-faced Dirk. Beads of sweat decorate his upper lip.

"It's Meg Sheppard, Bobbie," he shouts before I can say anything. The light in the hall goes out and it's as if someone sprinted up the stairs. But I can't be certain. I have serious doubts that I saw anything at all because when we enter the living room Bobbie is reading a magazine.

"We weren't expecting you," Dirk says as he invites me to sit—by pointing to the sofa which is sagging with age, and which I sank into the last time I visited.

"I can't…"

"You can't stay long. Do you have news about who killed Orlando?"

"No, but…"

"You want to ask us something."

"For heaven's sake let the woman speak, Dirk. Sit down. Okay, Meg, what is it?"

"I'm trying to establish if there's a link between the murders of Barton and Orlando and the casino operating out of the mansion you were living in. As you know, Barton visited the casino regularly and it seems likely that's where the poison was administered to him, and Orlando worked in the barn on the same property. Did Orlando visit the casino at all?"

"No, he wouldn't do that," Dirk says.

"So, your theory there's a link to the casino is incorrect," Bobbie snaps.

"You sound very sure."

"I am," Bobbie says.

"Okay. Thank you. The other theory is that there's a link to the gang that Barton was in. It was called the Blackbirds Gang. Pablo was in a rival gang and your sister, Annie, was accused of killing him. Although I know she was acquitted."

"Which means she was innocent."

"Yes. But, if the connection isn't the casino, then it must be the gangs."

"What makes you think there's a connection? Orlando was shot in the head. Barton was poisoned. There's no common thread there."

"What's that noise? I heard a thump. I'm sure it came from upstairs."

"We have mice. We've done everything we can to get rid of them, but no luck. We're going to move shortly. In any case, I don't think we should stay in one place for long until this is all sorted. Dirk agrees, don't you hun?"

"I guess so. Meg, I wish you could find out who killed Orlando."

"The police are investigating it," Bobbie says. "I'm sure there's no need for Meg to get involved."

"I'm already involved."

"You must have other things to do. We'll keep in touch," Bobbie says as she stands and walks towards the front door. I struggle to extract myself from the sofa—I seem to have sunk almost to the floor.

As I leave the house, I realize Bobbie ushered me out. I wonder if they're hiding something or even someone. The thought unsettles me.

I drive to Milkweed Farm because William has offered to look after the dogs while I'm visiting Primula. And Candice is coming with me. She said she'd love to help when I asked her if she'd come. William admits there isn't enough to keep her busy in the office yet.

He's promised to take the dogs out for a run around the weedy fields at Milkweed Farm. I'm sure they'll love it. There'll be lots of smells and places to explore—they haven't had a chance to venture into the unkempt pasture before. I haven't decided whether to let it all revert to nature or if I should assume some control over the rampant weeds.

Candice is wearing her short skirt but has flat shoes on. She pulls herself into the truck.

"When I've earned a bit of money I'm going to get some new clothes," she says.

"I have some I used to wear to work at the humane society that might fit you. Some of them are almost new. You can have a look at them sometime. Remind me when we get back and I'll get them out."

"Thanks awfully."

"Have you got a notepad or a mobile or something? For taking notes?"

"I've got a notepad in my bag. William is getting me set up with a laptop and smartphone."

"Great. It would be helpful if you'd take notes. I'm willing to pay for any work you do today."

"Oh no. Gosh. I'd rather not take money. Honestly, you're all being so nice. I'm not used to 'nice'." She sniffs. "If I can have a couple of your outfits that would be super."

"Okay." Candice is growing on me. She's trying hard to fit in and be useful.

I give her an overview of the events that affected Primula, including the spray-painting, the sponges up the nostrils of two of her horses, and the attempted murder. But I can tell Candice isn't paying attention. She's staring into her side mirror.

"Is there a problem, Candice?"

"I don't know, but I don't like the way that vehicle is so close. He's been following us like that since we left."

"He's probably just impatient."

"He's pointing something at us out of his window."

"Maybe he wants me to stop for some reason."

"Meg, mind out! I'm sure it's a gun."

Candice ducks, I put my foot down and spin my back tires on the gritty road. As I pull away there's a whizzing sound and a loud, startling pop. The windshield now has a small hole in it under the rearview mirror and three cracks have appeared as if in a flash. The top of my right shoulder stings.

"Stay down," I say. Candice is shaking. She's got her head between her knees, but I can't see any blood on her from where I sit. I keep my foot down even though we're snaking. Unfortunately, the dirt road is wet from the rain so I'm not creating a dust screen. The pickup isn't on our tail, but I think it's trying to catch up.

"Hold tight. I'm going to try something." Perhaps the dangerous bend ahead can help me get out of this. It owes me. I'm travelling at seventy miles per hour which is far too fast for this road, but because I know the layout of the entrance to the parking area at the head of the walking trail—which leads off the infamous bend—I take a chance and swerve into it. My pickup snakes as I turn at high speed, and we almost hit a tree and then a rock. But the truck that's been following us misses the entrance, skids off the road and slams into a tree making a resounding crunching sound.

I don't hang around. I already have my pickup pointing its nose out of the parking area. The engine screams as I get us back onto the road.

When we reach the highway. I slow down to the speed limit and hope my heart rate will settle down too. It all happened so fast—I can hardly believe it. But the hole in the windshield and the broken rear window make it frighteningly real.

"Candice, I think we're out of danger. Are you okay?"

She sits up. Her face is flushed, and her mascara is smudged below her eyes. Her hair is damp and stuck to her forehead and her teeth are chattering. She must be in shock.

"Candice, I think your clever and careful observation saved our lives."

"Meg, there's blood. You're bleeding!"

"It's okay. I probably got grazed. Don't worry. I'm going to call the police and an ambulance, okay?"

"Yes, of course, of course." She bends over again, hugs her knees and rocks. I text Primula to let her know that I'm deeply sorry, but something has come up and I can't make it. She sends back a sad emoji. I reply that I'll get there in a day or two at the latest.

Then another strange text pops up—*I won't miss next time.* I chuck my mobile behind the seat—out of sight, out of mind.

20

More Fire

"We're fine," I say for the tenth time.

"Well, I'm not," says Melissa.

"I am not either," says William.

"That's twice you've been shot." Melissa's voice is high-pitched and squeaky. "Someone wants you dead and gone. It must be Kenny. He's the one who tried to strangle you. What's wrong with that man?"

"I don't think it was him.'

"My assessment," William says, "is that this investigation or investigations—we're still not sure if we're dealing with two parallel situations—has become too dangerous. And don't forget there was a shooting on this farm when the horse trailer was hit."

"You're telling me I should stop?"

William hangs his head and stares at the kitchen table. He realizes I'm sensitive to being told what to do, especially by him.

"Meg, are you alright?" Candice asks again—I've lost count of how many times she's asked. "It's like the wild west here. I can't believe it."

"It truly isn't, Candice," I say.

And I haven't told them about the threatening texts. I finally reported them to Detective Valeska and gave her all the information, but I wouldn't part with my mobile. Nevertheless, she's taking the messages much more seriously than I am. I'm simply furious at being a target just because I'm hunting down a brutal murderer, and I think his actions put him more at risk of being caught.

"I can't believe you've been shot again! A second time!" Candice says as her large hazel eyes open even wider than usual.

"Candice, I'm fine. It was just a graze as I said. The weird thing is it's made me angry. I don't feel intimidated or scared. I'm just livid. And thank you, Candice. You were observant and kept your cool and were helpful with descriptions for the police."

"I suppose I shouldn't be surprised at being shot at since I'm in North America."

"Canada doesn't have the same relationship with guns as in the US, and they're not as prolific here."

"That reminds me of something I wanted to tell you," William says as he lifts his head. His eyes look sad. My guess is he doesn't know how to behave around me anymore.

"Before you get into that, we need brandy or hot chocolate or something," says Melissa as she stands up. "Meg, have you eaten anything today?"

"I probably had a carrot muffin this morning. Linda always brings one."

"That's it? I wish you'd take better care of yourself. Candice, what about you?"

"I can't remember. It's sort of a blur. Sorry, they gave me a sedative and it's messed with my thinking."

"You both need food. I wonder what we have. Oh yes, I almost forgot. I bought some bagels and cream cheese, will that work?"

"Thanks, Melissa," I say. "How about some tea?"

"That would be nice," Candice says.

"Okay, I'm on it. Now, Meg, you said you don't think it was Kenny. Who do you think it was?"

"Someone connected with Dirk and Bobbie. I'm sure there was someone else in the house when I visited them just before we left for Primula's place. But it's hard to believe there's a connection when Dirk keeps asking me to find out who killed Orlando. Whoever was in the house with them couldn't be Orlando's murderer."

"That makes things more complicated," William says. "What I wanted to tell you, by the way, is that the police completed their forensics examinations of the bullet found at the side entrance to the building where the Knightscourts were living, and the bullet found in the horse trailer."

"So, they found a bullet where I was shot the first time?"

"Yes. They have determined the bullets came from the same gun, and what is particularly useful is they found the bullet extracted from Orlando is also a match."

"Wow."

"And they have evidence that the gun has been discharged in other crimes. It seems it's one of those firearms that has been resold more than once within the criminal network. My guess is that the same gun was used today."

"I suppose that's not a big surprise," I say. "But it helps because it suggests the same person was likely involved in the three shootings as well as Orlando's murder. It's helpful, but also disturbing. There's a nasty bad guy at work then."

"Didn't you say that Orlando's body was found in a Knightscourt Funeral Home?" Candice asks. She yanks at her short skirt—it wants to ride up her thighs. I must remember to dig out a couple of outfits for her.

"Your brain is working better than mine, Candice," I say. "That's a good point. It connects the murder back to Dirk and Bobbie or their accomplice if there is one."

"But perhaps we can deduce they are victims rather than perpetrators," William says.

"I'm not sure," I say. "They could have placed Orlando's body there deliberately to make us assume just that."

"But I remember you saying they were forced off the road," Melissa says.

"They could have staged that," I say. "That's been known to happen before."

"Really?" Candice asks. I give her a brief overview of the incident that involved my late husband, Frank. She stares at me, unblinking, with her wide eyes.

"What are your thoughts about all these happenings, Meg?" asks William as Melissa places warm bagels on the table along with plates, knives, napkins, and cream cheese. I dive in, realizing, that despite the day's dramatic events, I have a strong appetite.

"Right now, I'm leaning towards there being two people on two completely different paths." The bagel is delicious. I finish a welcome mouthful. "One is Kenny and he's a fanatical, almost maniacal animal rights activist who's on a warpath and out of control. I know that it's hard to swallow, but it's the most likely theory I can come up with."

"Do you mean," asks Candice, "that he's trying to murder horses to prove his point that racing kills?"

"I'm certain he spray-painted trainers' doors and my truck, and Dr. Dudley's trailer—and threw a stink bomb in there. He also attempted to kill Dr. Dudley. He believed that Dr. Dudley was dealing in performance-enhancing drugs. And he tried to poison Hector and to murder me when I turned up unexpectedly."

"If he's a maniacal animal rights guy he must have poisoned Barton," Melissa says, "because Barton was a cheat and that involved abusing horses by giving them drugs—Barton had even been suspended, right?"

"If he poisoned Barton, then he is the most likely suspect concerning the poisoning of Les Joseph," William says, "since it's unlikely that two different suspects would use the same poison. And what about Primula Mokka? He probably was the one who targeted her horses, but why would he want her dead? She is held up to be an ethical and humane trainer."

"You have a point, William," I say. "But he may not have been discriminating. It could be he views all trainers as evil."

"And who has a gun?" asks Candice. "Do you think Kenny does?"

"Actually, I think that's unlikely somehow," I say. I sip on my tea. I can almost hear the cogwheels of our brains spinning as we mull over the confusing events. "The murders and attempted murders don't strike me as professional jobs, but perhaps it all goes back to the gangs, and Pablo's murder. But then I get pulled back to the illegal casino."

"I agree the casino is part of the puzzle," William says.

"Anyway, I'm going to visit Primula tomorrow."

William opens his mouth and closes it.

"I'd like to come," Candice says. "If you get another truck." She smiles.

"I like your spunk, Candice," I say. "I've arranged to pick one up tomorrow morning, and I'd like your company. Thanks." I'm pleasantly surprised that Candice is emerging from her shell. And I hear she has the makings of an effective assistant for William.

"I have to get back to Milkweed Farm," William says.

"I'll come with you," Candice says. "I want to get some rest for tomorrow."

After they leave, I call Detective Valeska.

"Hi, Meg. Are you and your friend okay?"

"Candice and I are fine. Did your officers find the truck or a bullet?"

"There was no sign of the truck except minor damage to a tree. The description of the truck is probably not sufficient. When questioned, your friend couldn't be sure it was a truck and not an SUV. But there would be damage and we're following up."

"The person is probably going to hide it somewhere if they can."

"Or abandon it and set it ablaze."

"What about a bullet?"

"Nothing so far, but the search is ongoing for now. You need police protection. And I'm saying this as my budget is crashing and burning before my eyes. I don't like those texts. He's a dangerous menace and carries out his threats—they should not be ignored. I will post an officer or two to monitor the situation, despite your protests. Keep me up to date on developments."

"Okay, I understand. Thanks for your concern. What about Kenny, by the way?" I'm not happy about having police officers on my tail, but it's better than being restricted to my home with a police officer at the gate. And perhaps I'm not taking the threats seriously enough.

"Kenny's half-brother lives in Newfoundland. We're working on it. The Royal Newfoundland Constabulary is cooperating, and I expect to hear soon."

"Thanks for telling me."

"Any more news?"

"Not really."

"Keep safe. Even with the assignment of my officers, I can't guarantee your safety under the circumstances. I'd prefer you to keep out of the line of fire. I mean it."

"I'll do my best."

*   *   *

Getting shot for the second time has shaken me up more than I want to admit. The wound didn't cause me much angst last night, but

242

I was revisited by disturbing and fitful dreams I've had in the past. They focused on my stepfather's sexual abuse when I was growing up in England—I have been haunted by memories of cruelty and torment, and feelings of helplessness, for many years. These dreams woke me up four times and it was hard to get back to sleep. So, it was not a good night.

But I'm up as the sun rises—it's hazy in the mist and peeping above the horizon. Oranges and pinks are streaked across the sky. Everything else is in shades of black and white.

Linda is at work in the barn. She puts a bucket down, grabs a brown paper bag, and gives it to me. I peek inside and find a warm, aromatic carrot muffin. These muffins have become a crucial part of my somewhat meagre diet. I make sure she knows how grateful I am—for everything. The horses are in excellent hands. But I must leave her to it.

The car rental company was very obliging and delivered a rental truck yesterday evening, and the driver took my damaged truck to the auto glass repair place. So, I'm ready to hit the road first thing this morning. I'm on a mission.

I wonder if there's a police officer around, but I doubt they'd expect me to be in action this early in the day.

Kelly, Jake and I head down the driveway in a sparkling pickup. I pull off moist chunks of muffin—they taste sweet and delicious. The dogs are interested but I'm not sharing.

I did some reconnaissance of the farm where Dirk and Bobbie are staying using Google Earth and discovered an old bank barn and another large outbuilding on the property. There's a laneway parallel to the driveway to the house, but about two hundred feet distant—that's what I'm aiming for.

This rental truck is dark grey—I hope it's not easy to see. I drive cautiously up the rutted, stony laneway. The pickup lunges into some large puddles that are deeper than I expected. My hands have a firm grip on the steering wheel and my teeth are clenched. I feel exposed. There's no screen between me and the house except for the partial protection of long grasses waving in the breeze.

A couple of crows fly up from the ground in front of the truck and startle me. I must be a bag of nerves. The dogs sense that something's up and walk backwards and forwards on the back seat. The laneway curves behind the large, weathered grey outbuilding. The roof has collapsed at one end and several boards are missing, leaving sad holes of neglect. I stop the truck behind the building and sigh when I turn the engine off. We all get out. The weeds and grasses are tall and dense between us and the broken doors, but I see what I hoped I'd see—evidence of a vehicle having entered. My heart skips a beat.

One of the double doors is easy to open—it still has functional hinges. The dogs rush into the semi-darkness. The morning sunshine beams in through the vertical gaps where boards should be. And there it is—the truck with a broken headlight, crushed front bumper, and crumpled hood.

"Meg! What are you doing here?"

The dogs' barks resound in the almost empty derelict building. The three of us are taken off-guard.

"Dirk!"

He enters the building. I tell the dogs it's okay, but Jake still has his hackles up. He doesn't like surprises and neither do I.

"Is this your truck?" he asks. He stares at it as if he's never seen it before.

"I was…"

"You were going to ask me the same thing. It's not mine and I know nothing about it. It's been in some kind of accident."

"Someone shot…"

"You were shot at again, but not in that grey truck you're driving. It looks brand new. You think the person doing the shooting was in this one?"

"Yes."

"How come you thought to look here?"

"Google Earth…"

"You must have a greater reason than that. Do you suspect Bobbie and me of being involved in any of this? I can't believe you would. But you've found this truck here, so I can see why you'd be suspicious. But why did you come in the first place? Are you going to tell the police?"

"I must."

"I'll leave that to you. Bobbie will be as surprised as I am when I tell her. The stress of what's been going on has got to me. I was telling Bobbie about it, and she said a walk in the fresh air would do me a lot of good. Well, it hasn't because this damn truck has just added to my worries. Who would dump it here?"

"Who else lives…"

"No one else. You'll tell the police, then?"

I nod, but my gaze drifts back to the abandoned truck. It raises a lot of questions, but it also holds the potential to provide some answers.

Dirk leaves the building and steps into the bright sunshine. The sun has fully risen and is like a spotlight shining on the farm.

I take photos of the truck and send them to Detective Valeska along with coordinates. She texts back and tells me to leave. The police will handle it. An officer is in the vicinity. She thinks the shooter may return and the detective doesn't want me anywhere nearby.

The dogs and I bounce down the rutted, potholed laneway—I'm driving faster than I should under these conditions, but I've heeded Detective Valeska's warning—I don't want to be shot again.

We arrive safely at Milkweed Farm to pick up Candice, who's waiting at the end of the driveway. Her short brown hair sparkles in the sunshine. Her makeup highlights unblemished skin and her hazel eyes. I don't wear makeup, but if I did it wouldn't look as neat and subtle as Candice's—it would be smudged and uneven.

Despite recent events, Candice has a broad smile as she climbs into the truck. She's not wearing her short skirt. It looks like she's wearing loans from Melissa. The black pants and pale blue sweater look familiar.

"You have a new jacket on," she says. "I guess it couldn't be mended."

"The bullet shredded the top of the sleeve and part of the shoulder, and I was surprised at how much blood had soaked into it. I had to throw it away along with the top I was wearing."

"How's the wound?"

"Most of the time I don't notice it. The first bullet that hit me when I was by the Knightscourt place gave me more trouble. But I'm fine."

I give her a brief recount of my morning adventure and one-sided conversation with Dirk. We both agree it's suspicious that the truck involved in the shooting incident started following us shortly after I visited the Knightscourts, and that it was subsequently found in a building they're renting. I've learned it can be dangerous to assume such occurrences are simply coincidences.

"What's that horrid noise?"

"Sirens. We must pull over and let them pass."

"The sirens sound different than in England."

"Two fire engines, and now police vehicles. I wonder what's going on."

"There's smoke ahead. Look, it's almost black."

"I have a thought. We'll find out soon if I'm right."

"You think someone's set fire to the truck?"

"Yep."

"Dirk must be the owner. He must be the murderer."

"I still don't think so. He returned to the house and told Bobbie and, as you know, I'm convinced someone else is with them. I'm going to park here at the side of the road out of the way and call Detective Valeska." I put my mobile on speaker.

"I'm here. I can see you," Detective Valeska says. "You have a different truck already."

"I give the car rental company regular business, so I get good service. What's happened?"

"We got here too late. The truck and building have been torched as well as the farmhouse. There's no sign of the Knightscourts or any vehicles other than the burning truck. The Vannersville Fire Department will be conducting a full investigation, but I already have their preliminary, unofficial assessment. Arson. Don't come any closer. You don't need to breathe in the toxic fumes."

"Where are you?"

"I'm parked further up the road. I'm leaving the firefighting to the professionals. Thanks for the photos of the truck. They could be helpful. Got to run."

She ends the call.

"The Knightscourts must have moved quickly," Candice says. "You didn't leave long ago."

"That could be their downfall. Everything now points to them, although I still have trouble with that probability. Anyway, we need to keep alert as we drive to see Primula."

Candice takes this seriously and constantly checks her side mirror and looks behind us. Her neck will be sore once we get back.

We park in the visitors' parking area next to an older colour-less condominium building. The windows display an eclectic mix of drapes and blinds, mostly closed to shut out the sun's relentless rays. A few of the small balconies provide splashes of colour with flowers, some have garden chairs, others have bulging garbage bags, and some appear not to be used for anything. The overall appearance is one of discordance and untidiness.

The security system appears to work, and we are buzzed into

the lobby. We take the elevator to the third floor. I hope this isn't a waste of time. Primula's mother opens the door to her condo, and we are welcomed into heavy, warm air.

"I'm Rosalie, Primula's mother. Thank you for coming. You must be Meg."

"And this is Candice."

"Lovely to meet you both. Primula is waiting for you."

Rosalie leads us into a stuffy room shrouded in semi-darkness. I think there's a lingering aroma of curry spices which would be pleasant if it wasn't for the thickness of the air.

"Primula is still not feeling well, are you dear?"

"It was a terrible attack," I say.

"She almost died. I could have lost my only child—my beautiful daughter who's everything to me." She strokes Primula's long sleek dark hair. Primula was skinny but now she's skin and bone. Her honey-coloured skin has a greenish tinge, and her lips are purple. She sits in a large armchair that accentuates her petite frame.

"Thank you for coming," Rosalie says. "Primula has something she wants to tell you. I think she'll settle better if she can share this with you. The recovery is slow and frustrating for her. She has mental and physical challenges to overcome. But I know she will get better. She is a fighter. She is much loved." She sits on the arm of the chair, takes one of Primula's hands, and caresses it. "You'll have to be patient. Her speech has been affected although it's much improved thanks to speech therapy. We are grateful for the health care system in Ontario. We have had much help and kindness."

"I'm glad to hear that."

"Primula, do you feel up to talking to Meg Sheppard?"

Primula nods and pushes herself into a straighter upright position as if in preparation for a heroic effort. Candice is crying softly beside me. I glare at her. Rosalie gets up and offers her a box of tissues. Candice wipes her eyes.

"There's no need to shed tears for her, dear. She's going to be fine, aren't you Primula?"

Primula doesn't respond. She points to a tablet that's sitting on a coffee table covered with medication bottles, books, a teapot, two mugs, two half-empty water bottles, a pot of drooping mums, newspapers, and a magazine. I can't see any of the table's surface.

I pick up the tablet and hand it to her. She stabs at the screen with jerky movements and then hands it back to me. It must have taken her hours to enter the information that's in front of me which was obviously prepared before we came. Most of her brain must be functioning otherwise she wouldn't have been able to record this.

"Primula, this is very helpful."

"It's hard for you, dear, to remember your past, isn't it? Those were dark days. I thought I'd lost you then too. But you came back, as you will this time."

"Can I print this off, or send it to my email address?"

"We don't have a printer, and Primula doesn't want to send anything over the internet. That's used just as a word processor. She can write when she can't speak. Sometimes the words won't come out of her mouth, but she has them in her brain, right dear? She wants you to have the information but doesn't want anyone to know she gave it to you. She's frightened that someone will hurt her again. She's scared. She's open about it, which is most of the battle and we'll get over it, but that's how she feels right now."

"Candice, this is where you can be very helpful."

"I'll copy it into my notebook."

"And I'll make some tea while you do that," Rosalie says.

* * *

"You'll get carsick," I say as Candice pores over the information she's copied into her notebook.

"I don't get carsick. The clue to solving the murders is in these names."

"I agree."

"I'm sorry I cried. I got so emotional when I saw Primula. And her mum is so nice and loves her so much. Life is unfair."

"It is."

"Rosalie is the opposite of my mum."

"Oh."

"But she wasn't as bad as your mum. Melissa told me she was given up for adoption and was bounced from one foster home to another. And you told me you were abused. You must be bloody angry about the hurt. Sorry, I shouldn't have said that."

"I'm much better than I was, but there are still scars."

"Was your stepfather charged? What did your mum do about it?"

"Nothing."

"That's much worse than I suffered. It wasn't abuse—it was neglect. My stepfather nor his family wanted me around and my mother travelled with him on business. I was left on my own a lot from the age of about twelve. The headmistress at my school helped me a lot. If it wasn't for her, I wouldn't have been accepted into Nottingham University. But my stepfather didn't provide his share of the funds like he was supposed to. So, after a year I didn't have enough money to keep going even though I worked whenever I could. I got some temp office jobs, but I couldn't save much. The pay was low. But it's nothing like you and Melissa have been through."

"Neglect is a form of abuse."

"I wish I had a sister." She resumes reading her transcription. "Okay, so Primula was a member of the Blackbirds Gang. I was shocked to find that out. I didn't think girls belonged to gangs."

"I'm sure they're in the minority, but there are examples in history of gangs with exclusively female members."

"I must look that up. Anyway, I think it took courage for Primula to tell us. And her notes say Rosalie looked after her when she came out of rehab. How horrid it must have been for them both."

"The only other names I recognized from her list of members of the Blackbirds Gang were Barton's and Orlando's."

"Primula had those underlined. Then there's the Pitbulls Gang. Two names are underlined—Annie's and Pablo's. She hasn't included last names, but perhaps she doesn't know them."

"She's told us their real first names at least, not their gang names, which makes it easier. What do her notes say about them?"

"I'll read them out: '*Barton had been Annie's boyfriend. Annie left him and the Blackbirds Gang to join Pablo in the Pitbulls Gang. I don't know how they met or what caused this. Barton was consumed by rage, and he set up a confrontation between the gangs. Orlando and I thought Barton shot Pablo, but we weren't sure. It was a messy situation. And I'm almost certain Annie didn't see who pulled the trigger. Annie was infatuated with Pablo and bent over her lover, stricken with grief. Although I was a gang member, I'd never seen anyone killed before. We got away. Annie was arrested. She was the only one left. Others who have since been hurt, and could be part of this, are Les Joseph and Greg Dudley. Les helped me, Barton, and Orlando get on our feet. He encouraged us to consider working at the track. Greg was a mentor to me, and I believe he also helped Barton. He could also have introduced Orlando to the Knightscourts. To muddle this, Kenny from AEF was involved in the Pitbulls Gang for a short time. I don't know why he joined or why he left. Who attacked me? It could have been Kenny. I honestly don't know.*'" Candice closes her notebook. "You've said Kenny is fanatical. We have OTT animal rights activists in England. They do the strangest things sometimes. All this horrid stuff could be his doing."

"I'm not sure."

"Do you think this is all about Annie out for revenge?"

"That's a real possibility."

"But it's been a few years, hasn't it? Why now?"

"Good question. Anyway, it's helpful to know who was in which gang. It gives us something to work on. I can't follow up this afternoon because I must go to the races. Fay is running."

"Can I come?"

"William doesn't need you in the office?"

"I'll check." She retrieves her new mobile from her small knapsack. "William got me this smartphone. It's brilliant."

21

A Scrap

The dogs are in the truck which sits in the parking lot adjacent to the grandstand at the racetrack. Candice isn't here because William needs her in the office. He has two appointments with potential clients this afternoon. Although Candice is disappointed that she won't see Fay run, she's excited to be working for William.

The weather has turned from warm, bright sunshine to gusts of wind and fine rain. Fay doesn't like any kind of inclement weather. She prefers cool, calm, partly sunny days, and definitely not rain. And the turf will be yielding rather than firm which could also cause her to back off.

"Here you are," says Neal as he reaches the rail and leans his forearms on it.

"How's Fay?"

"Good. She's been training well. And the slight swelling in her ankle came down nicely. There wasn't ever any heat, so I wasn't worried. She probably had a minor sprain. There's been no sign of it for a couple of weeks."

"Great. What's the competition like? I haven't studied the past performances of any of the other horses."

"It's tough again. The horse that was in a dead heat with her a while back is in this race—and she's probably the toughest, but there are a couple of others to watch. Oh, and good news—Hector's owners have agreed to your terms."

"That's great. He can have the rest of the season off."

"And we'll be sure to give him some preliminary training before the track opens next year so he's fit enough for the schedule here."

"Sounds good."

"And the other news is there's a rider who'd like to own Basil. I know you suggested Four Rs, but this guy approached me. He's an eventer and I like him."

"If you believe he's suitable, I'm fine with it. It would save Four Rs from having to retrain Basil and get him ready for adoption. As you know, I'm a supporter of that charity and if I can save them some expense, I'll do it."

"Basil will be going to a barn with a good reputation, and you can visit. I made sure he agreed to that. I'll give you his contact info later. Do you want to talk with him before he takes Basil?"

"No, I trust your judgement and I don't want to hold things up. Basil must be going crazy being stuck in a stall with no training happening."

"And this guy knows he needs some R & R. He has some nice paddocks for turn-out. He's respected in the eventing community. He coaches and competes. He'll do the right things for Basil. You can follow him on social media."

"I'll do that."

"The horses are here. The post parade is about to start."

Fay's fine bones make her look elegant and her radiant coat adds to her beauty. I'm fortunate to own such a stunning athlete. She's 'on her toes' as if she wants to dance to the starting gate and isn't happy about being held by the pony rider.

"Neal—you and Linda are doing a wonderful job of looking after Fay. She looks fantastic."

He nods. He has his binoculars up so he can watch Fay moving towards the starting gate.

"And she doesn't seem to mind the drizzle," I say.

"I'm here!" Candice says—almost out of breath. "William told me I could come. The second man postponed until tomorrow. Tell me what's happening."

"Candice, this is Neal Carvey, my trainer, well, the trainer of my horses."

"Ha! Hello, Neal, I'm Candice Burley. Pleased to meet you."

"The horses are now being loaded into the starting gate."

"I don't know anything about racing, but I don't think they use starting gates in England."

"They do in flat races," Neal says. "The starting gate will open soon—the last horse is being led in. The gate crew are perched on the partitions ready to let each horse go when the gate opens. Fay is number six."

"The announcer will tell us where each horse is placed during the race," I say.

"Number six is called Fabulocity," Candice says. "Isn't she called Fay?"

"Her racing name is Fabulocity," Neal says. "Watch the big screen. It'll tell you how she's doing. The numbers at the bottom show the racing order."

Candice has become engaged and is taking an interest in what's going on around her. It's as if she's burst out of her cage and is spreading her wings.

We watch the race in silence until the horses turn for home. The numbers disappear from the bottom of the screen and Neal is peering through his binoculars. The horses are bunched together except for one straggler—fortunately, it isn't Fay. The group straighten out into one almost straight line across the track. Divots fly up behind them. The ground reverberates with their footfall as they come closer. I can't tell how she's doing—it's not clear from where we're standing. Neal and I yell with as much gusto as we can muster. Candice has her mouth open, but nothing is coming out.

We're positioned before the finishing line. They thunder past us wet with the drizzle and breathing in rhythm with their strides. Fay is perhaps third. We keep yelling—I think my voice is closer to a scream. Candice jumps up and down with her mouth still open.

We can't tell who's won. The announcer says it's close. Usually, he makes an accurate call, so when he says, "photo finish, looks like Tumbleweed won," I turn to Neal and shrug. You can't win them all.

"Did she come third?" asks Candice.

"No, they've posted the third-place finisher," Neal says. "Unofficial. Fay and Tumbleweed crossed the finish line together, so there'll be little in it."

"I hope it isn't a dead heat again," I say. "Perhaps she thinks she's supposed to cross the finish line with one of the other horses."

"No, Meg." Neal doesn't laugh. He wants a win. Not only does he get a percentage of the purse, but it would improve his winning statistics and this matters to owners looking for trainers. Although Neal gets better than average results, in this business you can never sit back and take it easy. He and his team work hard every day.

Neal walks onto the track to greet Fay. The horses were not brought to an abrupt halt immediately after the finish line—they galloped on for a short distance and now they're trotting back to the grandstand. Linda is there ready to lead her back to the barn, but we're all waiting to hear the official result of the race.

"Fabulocity won!" Candice screams into my ear which rings from the shock.

"Come on, we have to get into the winners' circle for the photo."

"Am I allowed in? Really?" Candice is so excited. I haven't seen this side of her personality. She reminds me of Melissa and how exuberant she can be at times.

Fay is puffing a little with the exertion, and the veins along her neck are swollen. She's damp with drizzle and sweat—small clouds of steam rise around the jockey who wears a wide grin. Fay holds her head high and doesn't want to stand still. The photographer somehow manages to get us into a reasonable grouping. I rub Fay's face, and she nudges me twice. She's as excited as we are.

"Linda, thanks for taking such excellent care of her. Your TLC makes an enormous difference. I can't come to the backstretch right now, but I'll see you tomorrow morning at the farm I expect."

"I'll be there."

"And I may not be able to bring the usual celebratory goodies to the backstretch tomorrow, but I'll be sure to make up for it soon."

"No worries. We all want you to do your like sleuthing stuff so we can feel safe again." Linda throws a light blanket on Fay and leads her away from us.

It's a long day for the barn crew. They start in the early hours of the morning and when they have horses racing in the afternoon, they don't finish until the evening. And now Linda must take Fay to the testing barn for drug analysis—because she won—before she can settle the winner into her stall.

"Neal, I have time for a quick drink. The dogs are waiting in the truck so I can't be long. But we should celebrate."

"Candice," Neal says, "don't get the idea we win every time."

"I know."

"This is where owners and trainers hang out," Neal says as he scans his trainer's licence at the entrance to a lounge.

There are several interruptions while we're having our drinks—fellow owners and trainers congratulating us. They pat Neal on the shoulder, hold their glasses up, give the thumbs up, and generally help us to enjoy the moment.

"Candice, how did you get here?"

"William paid for a taxi, which was super kind of him."

"So, you'd better come with me. I've got to leave now."

"I do too," Neal says. "I'll let you know how Fay comes out of the race."

"Thanks."

Both Candice and I have damp hair, but we don't notice until we're clambering into the pickup.

"This has been the best day! And not just because Fay won which is fabulous. But I just received a letter from the Canadian Government authorizing me to work while they process my work permit application."

"That's good news but what happened to your Canadian citizenship application?"

"William confirmed I'm not eligible right now. I don't know who my father is, and my step-grandfather is no blood relative obviously, so him being Canadian doesn't help. I was really cheesed off when William told me."

"Oh."

"But I can apply for immigration status and once I've lived here long enough, I'll be able to apply for citizenship."

"So, you're planning on staying for sure? You haven't been here very long to make such a big decision."

"I know I don't want to go back."

"You don't think your stepfather is looking for you, and could even turn up?"

"He probably won't even notice I've gone."

"Does he know Melissa is his half-sister?"

"I don't think he cares and probably doesn't believe it in any case. Remember the lawyer's letter I told you about? He's only interested in himself. I know that sounds critical, but it's the truth."

"So, you don't have any blood relatives you're aware of?"

"No. But I really, really wish I was the third sister."

* * *

"How's Dr. Dudley doing?" asks Melissa. The four of us—Melissa, Candice, William, and I are enjoying a curry William picked up. He went out especially because Candice said she likes curry and we're all starving—well—extremely hungry.

"I haven't connected with him since my visit," I say. "I expect he's still in hospital. Part of my reluctance to see him again is they now have a stupid new policy banning dogs."

"Even certified therapy dogs?" Melissa asks.

"Yes. I talked to a charming man—he must be a chronic care patient—who said he'd talk to the Patient Council. He was sure the Council would take it to the 'bigwigs' as he called administration. He thought a compromise could be negotiated. I even remember his name—Edward Bergerstein."

"I know him," William says. "He was a powerful, well-respected lawyer in his day. We used to call him 'The Rottweiler' because he was such an accomplished and renowned litigator, but he was also an effective and successful mediator. If there's a reasonable compromise to be had, he will get it. Meg, would it be okay if I followed up with him? I'd enjoy having the opportunity to meet him and chat. He's an icon."

"That would be helpful. I have too much on my plate but it's important to me that Kelly and Jake can perform their therapy roles—I've seen so many faces light up when Kelly has visited over the years. Some patients, who staff told me were non-verbal, actually spoke to Kelly. It can be so heartwarming to see the reactions."

"Right. I'll do that. It'll be my pleasure."

"Candice, do you have a little time to do a job for me?" I ask.

"I think I do." She looks at William and he nods a bit too enthusiastically. He's trying too hard to regain my trust.

"Okay. William you may have to help with this, if you're able and willing that is. Your name might be enough, or you may need to use your contacts at police services, to find out who accessed the back-stretch through the security checkpoint on these dates." I mention the dates I'm interested in. "I hope security can print off a list of names. Then, Candice, it would be great if you could review it and look for these people." I tell her which ones. "And let me know if they entered, and on what date and at what time. That could be extremely helpful."

"I'd love to do that," Candice says.

"Of course we'll do this," says William.

"I have to talk to Suzie now before she starts her night shift in the casino," I say. "Melissa, will you be here so I can leave the dogs? They've been in the truck a lot today."

"Sure, but I'm going to bed soon."

"Thanks."

* * *

Suzie is dressed in a tight-fitting black dress. Her long red nails dig into a Styrofoam coffee cup as she stares at the table.

"Suzie, you look stressed."

"It's that obvious? Not good. I have to put on a cheerful smile at all times in this job."

"I take it you're not enjoying it."

"Nope. It's a drag and two of the regular customers harass me. I don't like it."

"You should report it."

"That's what's got me. Should I, or shouldn't I?"

"You should."

"Perhaps."

"You wanted to chat?"

"Yeah, sorry, it's not about that. It's something I remembered. You showed me photos of a guy called Ken?"

"Kenny."

"Kenny, right. Well, it suddenly came back to me out of nowhere—he and Barton got into a scrap in the casino. I'd forgotten all about it. They shouted at each other and Kenny pushed Barton off his bar stool. I thought Kenny was going to hit him. And he might have, but one of our tough bouncers was right there and threw Kenny out. So, I'm betting Kenny was the one who poisoned Barton."

"That's unlikely because the poisoning happened over an extended period of time according to the analysis of Barton's hair. Did you hear anything that was said?"

"It's hard, you know, to remember. Barton called Kenny a raving lunatic, or something like that, and Kenny told Barton he was killing horses, but that could be wrong. It doesn't sound right, does it?"

"You could be remembering correctly. Kenny believes racing kills horses and seems bound and determined to prove it—even by taking some extreme measures that could lead to horses dying. His behaviour is bizarre, and I could call it hypocritical because he's putting the lives of horses at risk—the very animals he professes to protect."

"Whacko. But I don't think Barton was a saint. I say that 'cause another thing came back to me. The evening before he died, he bragged about fixing a race that afternoon. He raked in a lot of dough from betting on it. He showed me a roll of cash. I thought it was odd that he had real money, but I was too busy to do any more than think about it."

"Thanks for the info. You mentioned the name of the casino was ANE, right? But you didn't know what it stood for?"

"Nope."

"I've just thought of something. Did you ever see the owner or owners?"

"Could have, but not sure. She never talked to me—this woman I'm thinking of. She drifted around the casino sometimes, but not often."

"What did she look like?"

"Blonde hair."

"Oh. Anything else?"

"She wasn't pretty. She had a big nose and thin lips. Silly, but I couldn't imagine her being the owner and manager—no way. They want pretty people in these places. And yeah, she walked funny, like she wasn't used to heels. It made me look at her feet. They were so large they could have been a man's."

"Could she have been a man dressed in drag?"

"No. I'm sure she didn't have an Adam's apple. I would've noticed. I stared at her a bit one time 'cause she seemed odd and I didn't know who she was. You said you were thinking of something?"

"The initials ANE. I thought they could be every other letter from the name Annie."

"I guess they could. Who's Annie?"

"Bobbie Knightscourt's sister. But your description doesn't fit with the pictures I've seen of Annie. Bobbie has a large nose and thin lips, but she has longish curly brown hair."

"A wig?"

"You have a point. Thanks, Suzie, this has been great. I wish you luck with reporting the harassment. You shouldn't have to put up with that."

"Thanks, I'll think about it. I don't want to lose my job."

"Look after yourself."

22

Unarmed

An early frost sparkles in my flashlight's beam as Kelly, Jake, and I walk to the barn. I called Linda last evening and told her not to come. She'd be so tired from her long day yesterday. I'm well enough to feed the horses, clean the stalls, and lead them out. I'll miss the carrot muffin though. I suppose there's always the option of picking up one myself.

As we enter the barn I sigh and relax almost immediately on listening to the horses' nickers. They blink their eyes as I turn on the lights and pick up their volume as I near the feed room. The barn cats stretch and yawn in unison. I stroke them despite the demands for food coming from the stalls.

I scoop the sweet-smelling grain into their feed buckets. Sometimes this can be tricky because a horse's head is in the bucket giving me little room to tip the feed in. I check that each of them has enough water to last until I lead them out.

A cup of tea would be welcome. I have time to grab one while the horses eat their breakfast. The three of us wander out of the barn as the sun peeks over the horizon. It shines its early rays on a car which pulls up at the end of the driveway. The dogs bark for a few seconds but then they recognize Les as he uses the key I gave him to unlock the gate. I wait for him to drive up to the barn.

"No e-bike?"

"I don't like riding that thing in the dark."

"Yes, it's only just getting light—you're early."

"I couldn't sleep. I saw Yuki yesterday. He said Primula is bad. Yuki talked to her mom. She said it's got to do with the gang she was in. Gang! I told him, you've got it wrong, man."

"Come in. I'm going to make a cup of tea. It won't meet your exemplary standards, but it'll be okay."

"No worries. Thanks." He's not smiling but I'm sure it's not because of my tea—he's genuinely upset about Primula.

Kelly and Jake are restless. I give them each a large dog biscuit and tell them to lie down. Cooper jumps up on the table. Les picks him up and puts him on his lap.

"My brother's allergic to everything. I have to put my barn clothes in the wash as soon as I get home, but I love cats."

"Primula was a member of a gang. I thought you knew."

"Barton was in the Blackbirds Gang, I knew that, and one of them shot a guy called Pablo in the Pitbulls Gang."

"Les, you must know more than that. You said you worked on the streets"

"A girl called Annie was Barton's girlfriend."

"But she left him and joined the Pitbulls Gang. She and Pablo became a couple. And then Pablo was shot and killed."

"Shouldn't talk ill of the dead."

"What's that got to do with it?"

"Barton killed Pablo. That was the word on the street."

"That doesn't mean it was true. It was likely just a rumour."

"Maybe. All this bad stuff happening gotta be about Annie getting revenge."

"But Primula thinks Annie doesn't know who shot Pablo."

"I bet Annie is a serial killer and is out to get all the Blackbirds Gang members. But why me?"

"Perhaps because you helped Barton and Orlando."

"I was just doing my effing job."

"I know. It does seem over the top."

"You're telling me. And what about Primula? Why try to kill her?"

"She was in the Blackbirds Gang. If your theory is right, Annie would want her gone too. But I'm not convinced."

"What about that dumb spray-painting stuff and putting effing sponges up horses' noses? Yuki told me the whole stinking story."

"I think Kenny and his fanatical animal rights stance is more likely to be what's behind those incidents."

"Cruel."

"I know. It looks like he's gone off the rails. But I don't think he attacked Primula."

"He tried to wring your neck."

"I'm not even sure about that anymore."

"He'd be crazy enough."

"Perhaps, but I'm having doubts. This is a confusing mess of so many incidents that I'm seriously thinking it's not the work of one person. I think there are two parallel sequences of events perpetrated by at least two different people."

"You mean Annie and Kenny?"

"I'm sure of Kenny, but for some reason, as I said, I'm not as sure about Annie. Nobody seems to have seen her anywhere. Even the police haven't been able to track her down. But I'm not certain if that's significant."

"Gotta be Kenny. When I think about it, a woman wouldn't do

all that stuff—killing people, I mean."

"How's the tea?"

"Not bad. It's the first tea I've had out of my home since I was sick. I daren't have anything that ain't in a bottle."

"I don't blame you."

"I saw a lot when I worked with the homeless, but poison and all the other effing stuff has got to me."

"It's tough to see animals and people hurt."

"Sure is. It's gotta stop. We don't feel safe at the track no more. Fire up those little grey cells and catch them monsters."

I laugh, but he's being serious—he has a deep frown that looks as if it's in danger of becoming permanent. The poisoning has rattled him. I understand. I feel rattled myself by all that's happened to people and animals, including me.

"I'm trying, Les. Tell me, how's it going with the yearlings?"

"Good."

"They look like a million dollars."

"Thanks, but they won't get that much in the auction."

"Haha! No, they won't. I've got to lead the horses out. You can help."

Les says he'll let the yearlings graze while he gets his grooming things ready and plays with the barn cats who follow him around. It's as if he's a cat whisperer and in turn, perhaps, they help to uplift his spirits.

Kelly, Jake, and I wander back to the house under cloudy skies. As we enter the kitchen my mobile makes noises alerting me to two texts. Detective Valeska wants me to call her, and Candice wants to visit—she has some information—we agree on her coming here in fifteen minutes.

"Hi, Meg. Thanks for calling. I have some good news."

"You've solved the murders."

"No, but we have Kenny in custody. He's talking but there are questions I'd like to ask you. The sooner you can meet with me the better."

"I could be there in an hour."

"I'll be expecting you."

I clear up the mugs and wipe the table. Kelly and Jake bark but soon stop when Candice walks in. We told her she didn't need to knock—she could just come in—and she said it made her feel like one of the family. Tears threatened. That was a few days ago.

"William helped me get access to the security records at the racetrack for that gate. And the only person who entered consistently on the dates and times that you asked me to check was Bobbie Knightscourt. Don't you think that's interesting?"

"It is, but now I'm wondering if someone stole her pass. It doesn't prove it was her."

"But there's a photo on the pass."

"Security doesn't look at the photo anymore. You just scan the pass, and the gate opens. You could use anyone's pass, as far as I can tell."

"That's barmy."

"Don't be disappointed, Candice. This is still helpful. I need to follow up with Bobbie and if she hasn't got her licence or pass, I'll ask her who could possibly have it. I'll also ask her where she was at the times when the pass was used."

"I suppose if she doesn't want to talk, that will speak volumes."

"I'm sure I'll find out something. Thanks for doing the work. I'll pay you for your time."

"No. I want to help. It makes me feel as if I'm one of the family. Paying me will make me feel like an employee. What else can I do?"

"I'm not sure right now. I wish we could track Annie down."

"Aren't the police looking for her?"

"I assume so, but they've not found her yet."

"You never know, I might be able to find something on social media. People make mistakes and reveal things."

"Well, if you don't mind checking it out. Don't spend a long time on it though, because you could just be going down a rabbit hole."

"Ah, but I could be Alice and end up in Wonderland and find out all sorts of things."

"Thanks, Candice."

"I'll get on it right now. William doesn't have anything for me to do until this afternoon."

"Thanks again for your help."

*　*　*

Bobbie nor Dirk have answered my calls. I've called each of them twice and tried texting. Nothing. I don't know where they've disappeared to.

The dogs have come with me to police services and are waiting in the pickup. Just as I arrive at the elevator, William calls.

"Hello, Meg. Dr. Milton called on your landline. I had to retrieve something from Frank's office, so I picked up the phone. I hope you don't mind."

"Okay. Did he tell you what he was calling about?"

"He said he was told by one of the staff that Dr. Dudley has suffered a stroke but was able to convey he wants to speak to you."

"That's terrible. How serious is it?"

"Dr. Milton didn't say."

"I wonder how he found out."

"He didn't expand on that."

"I'm glad he called. Thanks for letting me know."

"You're welcome."

We end the call.

I hope the meeting with Detective Valeska will be short. I want to get to the hospital as soon as possible.

"Good morning, Meg. Have a seat."

"I'm glad you found Kenny."

"He was, as suspected, living with his half-brother in Newfoundland. He didn't do a good job of flying under the radar."

"Has he admitted to anything?"

"He's confessed to a few minor offences. He admits he spray-painted some trainers' office doors and has given us particulars. He denies he has ever owned a gun."

"What about attempting to poison Hector and strangle me?"

"He has come up with alibis for everything else we've questioned him about. Naturally, we are checking those out."

"I hoped he'd be more cooperative."

"The primary reason I want to talk with you is that he is alleging you harassed him."

"What?"

"You went to the Animal Equality and Freedom offices and accused Kenny of vandalism, of stealing a mare, and of kidnapping Orlando. And another time you visited you accused Kenny of putting sponges up horses' nostrils—that sounded so bizarre to me that I had an officer look into it, and there are documented cases of that abuse. Anyway, Kenny stated you directly accused him of animal cruelty. He's full of rage and says he's going to make sure you go to jail. He thinks he can sue for defamation because his colleague was present at the times you visited, and he believes you have told others. He also stated that the accusations have caused him harm in the animal rights field and jeopardized his chances of finding suitable employment. He says he'll be seeking significant compensation."

"His colleague was Ada Burkfield and yes, she was present when I visited. I hope you have a chance to check with her about all this. She's living with her mother and will be working for Greenpeace next week."

"We're tracking her down. But how do you respond to Kenny's allegations?"

"Did he admit to spray-painting my truck?"

"I can't tell you that."

"Well, I was told he did. And Ada found a piece of paper in Kenny's stuff he left behind at the AEF offices when he left. He'd written Dr. Dudley's name with a thick black line around it. And there was a list of drugs that made Ada think Kenny believed Dr. Dudley was supplying illegal performance-enhancing drugs."

"Where is this piece of paper?"

"I hope Ada has it. She was already at her mother's when she called to tell me she'd found it. That's not all. Ada also found a list of names of herbs and plants Kenny had written on another piece of paper. She Googled a couple of them and found they're poisonous to horses. As you know, there were bits of something floating in Hector's water."

"The results of the analysis revealed it was poison hemlock."

"I'm sure Hector wouldn't have touched it. He's fussy about clean water and I don't blame him. But it's obvious there was intent to harm him. Poison hemlock couldn't have just dropped into his water bucket."

"No. So, we need to talk to Ada and find those pieces of paper. Why would he have used paper and pen?"

"I expect Ada knew his passwords. It was probably an office laptop."

"You must realize, though, that having those pieces of paper is not sufficient proof that Kenny was responsible for the attack on Dr. Dudley or the attempted poisoning of Hector."

"I know."

"You haven't given me a response to Kenny's allegations of harassment."

"I don't know how to respond. I suppose he'll have to sue me."

"In alleged defamation, it's usually hard to prove that what has been said is the truth. If it's the truth, then obviously there is no case. In this situation, you'd need proof Kenny vandalized, stole the horse, put sponges wherever, and so on. Then the case has no validity. But I'm not a lawyer. You should consult William."

"What about Annie? Have you got any leads on her whereabouts?"

"No."

"You must want to talk with her."

"We do."

"I think she should be a suspect. I keep coming back to her, but something's niggling at the back of my mind. I don't know what exactly, or why."

"At the moment, she's a person of interest, and we have alerted the Ontario Provincial Police."

"Oh. And I should tell you, but you've probably already done this, we checked out who went through the gate into the backstretch at the dates and times of the various incidents, and the only pass consistently scanned at security was Bobbie Knightscourt's."

"But you can't prove it was her."

"No, because they don't look at the photo anymore."

"They should."

"I know. I'm going to raise it with officials at Vannersville Racetrack."

"Good."

"You're aware Kenny had an altercation with Barton in the casino, right?"

"Yes. We talked to Suzie. Kenny denies it was an altercation, as you put it, but he can't deny he was there because we have surveillance photos to prove he went in."

"I think he must have thrown the stink bomb into Dr. Dudley's trailer."

"I can't confirm that. I have a meeting—got to go."

* * *

A shuddery sigh escapes as I get into the pickup. The dogs give me an enthusiastic welcome as if they feared I wouldn't be seen again. I rub their ears, gently pat their heads, and tell them to get back behind the front seats. The next stop is the hospital.

Kelly shows her disappointment when I don't put her therapy vest on. She knows where we are. She has her ears flat on her head and looks at me with mournful eyes.

"I'm sorry, Kelly. Let's hope you can both come next time."

As I walk into the hospital I hear my name.

"Mr. Bergerstein. How nice to see you again."

"Do call me Edward. I've made some progress. God knows things are always slow around here, you know. But I've already made a presentation to the Patient Council and the vote was unanimous. They all agree we should tackle the matter of that darned stupid policy and knock some sense into administration. I'm sure we can reach a compromise as I suggested to you in our earlier conversation. We've formed a task force to draft an alternate policy for consideration by the bigwigs. I'll send you the draft so you can add your two cents. I've got your card. And I'm delighted that William Porter has offered his help. He's a fine man that one. I have a lot of respect for him. I know he's gone off the rails a couple of times, but that doesn't change my opinion of him as a lawyer. Very capable. Good man."

I nod.

"It's such a shame I can't say hello to Kelly today. How is she? She reminds me of my border collie, Dickens. I'll tell you about him one day when we have time for a chat."

"Thanks for taking this on. I, Kelly, and Jake appreciate what you and the Patient Council are doing. It makes us feel good to visit with patients here and I hope we'll be able to return."

"You will, I'm sure of that. Just leave it with us. But, as I said, everything takes an eternity here. It's like molasses. But we have a lot of families as well as patients on our side. Kelly has a fan club—did you know that? She truly does. I'm optimistic, you know."

"Well, thanks again Mr. Bergerstein."

"Edward. My pleasure."

It must be a gloomy existence living in the hospital day after day. It seems to me he should be able to manage in supportive housing of some kind.

It doesn't feel right to be walking the corridors without Kelly at my side—her tail curled upwards with pride as she wears her therapy vest. I have her with me during nearly all my visits.

A police officer stands when I catch his eye.

"Meg Sheppard come to see Dr. Greg Dudley," I say.

"I need to see some ID."

"Okay." I fumble in my bag for my driver's licence. He makes a little show of checking the photo against my face, to the point that my cheeks redden for some reason—I hope imperceptibly.

"Go ahead."

Dr. Dudley looks frailer, and one corner of his mouth droops down. But the bandage has gone and the dark Nike swooshes under his eyes have faded.

"The rumours of my death have been greatly exaggerated." His speech is somewhat slurred but understandable. I'm relieved that he's doing much better than I feared.

"How are you?"

"I'm doing better than expected."

"I'm glad to hear it."

"I'm in physio now and walking with help. I want out of here like yesterday."

"I can understand that. Do you have an anticipated discharge date?"

"I've told them I'm leaving next week."

"Do you have someone to help you at home?"

"Let me worry about that. I'm glad you came. I want to tell you something."

"Okay." Although his speech is unclear at times, his voice sounds better. Most of the damage from smoke inhalation must have healed.

"I've been having bad dreams about what happened."

"I'm not surprised. You could have died."

"Where's Kelly?"

"The hospital has implemented a new policy banning animals."

"What? I thought the nurse was joking last time you came."

"No. But Edward Bergerstein is working with the Patient Council to try to negotiate a compromise with administration."

"Good. I'm a believer in animal therapy. I volunteer at a centre— therapeutic riding for children with autism." He coughs. Perhaps his lungs aren't completely healed yet. "It's amazing."

"Anyway, you wanted to tell me something about the bad dreams?"

"They haunt me at night, but I'm haunted by daydreams too."

"Oh."

"You asked me if it was Kenny who attacked me, and I nodded."

"Yes."

"I've gone over it many times. I'm not sure it was him."

"Do you have any idea who it was?"

"No."

"Could it have been a woman?"

"No. Would a woman do such a thing?"

"Why not?"

"If there's sufficient motive, I suppose. But I don't think so."

"You know that women can be members of gangs—Primula, for example."

"It doesn't mean they're murderers."

"I know, but I'm keeping an open mind because of some things that have happened."

"It wasn't Primula."

"I wasn't suggesting it was her. As you know, she was the victim of a vicious attack and is still a long way from recovery."

"I was very sorry to hear that."

"You shook your head when I asked if you had anything to do with Barton's cheating. Can you confirm that you didn't supply him with drugs?"

"I did not. Barton was a greedy fool."

"But you continued as his veterinarian."

"Yes. But he knew I wouldn't cross the line". He clears his throat. "Whatever he did to cheat he did without any help from me."

"Why did you continue working for him?"

"Because he would have had a tough time finding another veterinarian willing to work with him and I wanted to be sure the horses received quality veterinary services. And—stupid of me—I thought I could get him to smarten up." He fidgets as if to try to get more comfortable in the hospital bed. The top part is raised and he's sitting almost upright. "After all, I'd been in college with him and got him his first job at the track as a hotwalker. I've helped him a lot over the years."

"But you weren't having much luck with him?"

"No. I wasn't."

"Okay. So, is there anything else about what happened to you that could help?"

"I'm not sure."

"Tell me, even if you're not certain."

"I caught a whiff of something. I was turning around to see what it was when I was hit. I didn't hear the door opening." He coughs. "I remember a balaclava, that's the other thing I wanted to tell you." He leans over to his side table and picks up a plastic tumbler of water with his left hand. "My right hand is a bit weak, but I'm recovering well. Lots of physio."

"Good."

"What was I saying?"

"You caught a whiff of something."

"Ah. It was a sweet, fruity smell. It reminded me of a laundry detergent I've used sometimes."

"Could be useful."

"When I go home, will I have police protection?"

"I don't know."

"That guy has got to be stopped."

"I agree. You focus on getting well and keep up the physio. There are several of us working on this. We'll get him soon."

"He's probably a serial killer."

"I'm not sure only one person is involved."

"That doesn't make me feel better."

"Mm. Assuming the person or persons wants to kill you, Primula, and Les, they haven't done a good job, thank goodness."

"But Barton's dead. And Orlando."

"Barton was poisoned, and Orlando was shot. There are still lots of questions."

"Answers. That's what we need. Will you keep me posted?" He closes his eyes as if exhausted.

"Of course."

"And bring Kelly if I'm still here."

"If she's allowed. Thanks for talking with me. Bye." There's no answer. I think he's already snoring.

I leave his room and nod at the police officer who's reading. My stomach is unsettled—reflecting my mood. Dr. Dudley looked like an old man. Only a little while ago he'd been a vibrant, sometimes cantankerous, middle-aged veterinarian who was well-respected at the racetrack as far as I can gather. I believe him—he had nothing to do with Barton's bad behaviour or his death.

As I walk towards the pickup, frantic barking reaches my ears. It grabs my attention and I'm immediately on high alert. It is not hard for me to discover what has unsettled the dogs—someone is crouched beside my truck. The sight of the dark figure makes my legs wobble, and my palms sweat. It's as if he's taken Kelly and Jake hostage. What do I do? He's seen me. I'm three rows of vehicles away. I can't let my dogs be hurt but I don't want to die—especially in this parking lot and for no good reason.

Whoever the person is will eventually get caught. I don't see the point of killing me. How is that going to help them? The police are on this. I'm an amateur sleuth with no authority or powers, doing an amateurish job. And who could possibly believe that shooting two innocent dogs is a smart tactic? Who could be that inhumane?

My brain's going a mile a minute but I'm not coming up with a strategy. I duck behind a large SUV but it's obvious where I am. I text Detective Valeska—SOS, hospital parking lot. Help.

I have no weapon. I have no way of protecting my dogs or myself against an armed man. Perhaps I can draw him away from the dogs—how? I pull out my key fob for the truck and press the panic button. I peek around the side of the SUV as the headlights flash and the horn blasts.

The dogs have steamed up the windows—they must have been barking for several minutes. The person in black stands and points what looks like a gun in my direction. I'm relieved that he's not aiming at my pickup and its precious cargo. I duck back behind the SUV just as I hear a loud bang. A tire of the SUV deflates with an alarming whoosh.

It's as if the gunshot disturbed the heavens because the clouds suddenly dump torrents of water. I wipe wet hair out of my eyes and dare to peek out again. The person has gone—at least I can't see him.

A police car races in with sirens blaring and lights flashing. It skids to a halt on the wet asphalt in front of my truck.

Despite my whole body shaking, I dash in a wobbly line to the pickup as the rain splashes up around me and yank a door open to let the dogs out. They're both panting in between hacking coughs and their enthusiasm in greeting me is dampened by their obvious exhaustion.

If it hadn't been for Kelly and Jake's frantic barking, I wouldn't have realized someone was lurking by the truck. My two heroes!

23

Showdown

A morose band of people stands by the backdoor watching us as Kelly, Jake, and I slither out of a police vehicle. The dogs trot into the kitchen. They're desperate for a drink, and so am I. I'm not a drinker but I'd like one now.

Melissa and Candice wipe the dogs down with old towels while Kelly and Jake feverishly lap up water. Despite my exhaustion, a warm tingle makes me smile inside to see Candice drying Kelly with such tenderness.

I leave the kitchen, take my sodden body upstairs, and turn the bath tap on. Nobody has said a word, but the air is heavy with unspoken concern and worry—and perhaps criticism.

Aromas emitted by Italian food waft up the stairs, and I inhale their deliciousness as I descend towards the kitchen. Both dogs are flat on their sides and Cooper is licking Jake's face.

"Why didn't you tell us you were getting threatening notes?"

Melissa's high-pitched voice makes her sound hysterical.

"Why don't we eat first?" William suggests. "We can have a debrief afterwards. Meg must be famished."

Candice opens a bottle of red wine and pours me a generous glass for which I express sincere thanks. I sigh as the tangy rich fruity taste washes over my dry tongue. I collapse onto a chair as if my bones have lost most of their rigidity and I've become a ragdoll.

We eat in near silence. Candice attempts to engage the rest of us in conversation about Milkweed Farm, but no one responds except with the occasional nod or grunt. The lasagne and salad are delicious, and I surprise myself by eating a larger portion than I usually would.

Melissa won't let me help. The three of them soon have the table and counters clean and clear of dishes. We each have a fresh glass of wine thanks to William finding another bottle.

"Meg." William looks at me with such a serious, intense look that I almost break out into laughter. Thank goodness I can control my emotions (most of the time). "Detective Valeska informed me about the threatening notes and her decision that one of her officers is to remain here at all times."

"Obviously there'll be different ones," Candice says. "They'll be on shifts."

"Of course," William says with a soupçon of rare irritability in his voice. Candice peers into her wine. "Detective Valeska says a different prepaid phone was used each time. You must have sent her screenshots of the texts."

"Do you realize how serious this is, Meg?" Melissa asks. "Someone's determined to kill you."

"You've been shot at four times and injured twice," Candice says as she continues to stare into her drink.

"Four times?" I ask.

She looks up. "They shot at the horse trailer, they injured you by the entrance to the casino, they shot you when we were driving to see Primula, and they aimed at you today at the hospital."

"You and the dogs could all be dead," Melissa breaks out into sobs and Candice moves her chair closer so she can put her arm around her.

"But we're not," I say. "We're very much alive."

"We'd like you to stay that way," William says.

"So would I. Honestly, I don't see the point of this person killing me. I'm just an amateur sleuth and the police are going to catch them—it's inevitable. I don't understand it."

"What's your current theory?" asks William.

"I'm not sure."

"Promise you'll stay at home tomorrow," Melissa says as she dries her tears with a tissue.

"The dogs and I need a break, and I need to think."

"Good."

*　　*　　*

The rain has stopped but the breeze is shaking the sodden trees, and water comes down in curtains of droplets underneath their branches. Kelly, Jake, and I stay dry except for boots and paws as we wander around the large field while keeping a wary eye on the rambunctious young horses.

It's late afternoon. William and Candice are at Milkweed Farm, and a police vehicle kitted out in full regalia is parked at the end of the driveway.

Melissa's car has come home, but she's not in the house.

"Kelly and Jake, find Melissa". I'm sure Kelly understands, but I'm not certain that Jake does. As we leave the field, Kelly dashes off towards the barn with Jake on her heels. Sure enough, Melissa is there, with Yuki.

"Hi, Meg," Yuki says.

"Yuki helped bring the horses in. Linda nor Les can help this evening, and I thought you'd like to rest."

"Thanks. That's very thoughtful of you. Both of you must have had a long day. What do you think of the yearlings, Yuki?"

"Les must be doing all the right things. They have good manners and their coats shine. They'll show well in the sale. I'm not sure they have enough pedigree to get the big bucks, but they're all a decent size and have some nice markings which buyers like. And I don't see any conformation issues. They'll have x-rays done of course and I don't know what will crop up there, but I'd say Dirk Knightscourt will do okay."

"Les asked me to take some videos of them so he can post them," I say. "Some people will bid online, and videos are important."

"I can help with that."

"Thanks, Yuki."

"Meg, I don't know if you've heard, but Primula won't be coming back this racing season. Her recovery is so darn slow. Her mom called me. She tries hard to put a positive spin on everything, but she told me she's starting to give up hope that Primula will ever fully recover. I tell you—I was close to tears talking to her and I prefer optimism, just as she does."

"Where does that leave you?"

"Now that Primula is officially out of the picture, I need a licenced trainer to attach to—I'm only an assistant trainer. Neal has agreed to do that for me. He's a great man, isn't he? Meanwhile, I'm studying like mad so that I can take the trainer's tests. I've got the basic requirements, but I must get over ninety percent to pass. There are written and practical tests. Melissa is helping me with my studies which is great because I have attention deficit issues."

"Are the owners keeping their horses with you and Neal?"

"Only one has told me she's leaving. That's too bad, but I'm not losing sleep over it. She's one of those absentee types. I haven't even met her in person. I don't know why she has two racehorses she never visits even on race days. It blows me away. So, no loss there."

"Well, I'm glad Neal's willing to help out, but he's very busy."

"I know, but he won't have to do much. I've got a great staff, and we have a solid training program. We have good vets and an excellent farrier. We have two of the best exercise riders and I've got relationships with several of the top jockeys. We'll be fine. And I'm going to keep Primula's mom up to date with everything. I don't want to leave Primula out. She's laid the foundation. Have you got any leads on who beat her up yet? I feel sick when I think about it."

"Meg," Melissa interjects. "I bet you haven't eaten, and we haven't either. It's been a long day for us, as you said. Let's call Candice and see if she wants to join us at that Italian restaurant. Okay?"

"Good idea," I say.

"Sounds like a plan," Yuki says.

"We can fit everyone in the rental pickup," I say as we all walk towards the house leaving the nickering and munching behind us. Yet another truck was delivered this morning. A forensics team is examining my previous pickup in case the shooter left any DNA or other evidence during the fearsome parking lot incident.

I pick up my mobile from the kitchen table. There's a text from William. It says he forgot to tell me the police traced the truck that was set ablaze to one that was reported stolen. It took a while for the police to get the information because the owner was reluctant to admit it had been stolen from the illegal casino's parking lot.

Annie comes to mind.

The police vehicle follows us to the restaurant and the officer parks in a disabled spot so he can monitor the entrance.

During dinner, Candice gives an overview of her social media dive, and it's disappointing. Knightscourt Funeral Homes is on Facebook and Instagram, but I knew that already. They've been inactive for a while and what they have posted is humdrum. Candice says

Annie has a profile picture on Facebook, but that's all she could find. She follows a handful of people, none of whom we've come across in the investigation so far. Bobbie is on Instagram and has posted pictures of peacocks and chandeliers which have received an average of six 'likes' and no comments. Candice dug deep, even checking out darknets with William's help. There was nothing helpful and, surprisingly, they couldn't find anything on the illegal casino—the operators must have relied on word of mouth.

*   *   *

Linda came this morning and we both worked on barn chores in the early light. I asked her what she thought about Neal helping Yuki out, and she's fine with it, she says. So, Yuki must meet with her approval as a horseperson. She's left for her primary job at the racetrack, and I said I would be there shortly with celebratory treats to thank the barn team for their tender loving care of Fay. The police officer will have an interesting trip to Vannersville Racetrack, and I plan to stop at Vannersville Inn on the way. I hope he doesn't follow me inside. I'm on a mission to find Bobbie. I want to ask her about her licence or pass that was used to access the backstretch at the times the attacks took place. My phone calls and texts haven't been answered. I've checked with Detective Valeska and—of course— police services are also looking for her and Dirk. I'm puzzled about their disappearance but also suspicious.

Detective Valeska confirmed that no human remains were found in the charred ruins of the outbuilding, truck, or farmhouse where they lived for a brief time. There's no trace of their SUV despite police services checking camera footage, alerting traffic cops, and even setting up a few checkpoints on ramps exiting major highways.

The dogs are in the pickup, and the police vehicle is parked near the automatic sliding doors. I enter the Inn armed with photos of Dirk and Bobbie downloaded from the Knightscourt Funeral Homes website. Dirk is wearing a suit and is barely recognizable, and Bobbie's brown hair is swept off her face showing no trace of her curls. Her nose looks bigger than I remember.

I show the photos to someone at the reception desk but they're not willing to comment. I realize my mistake in thinking I could unearth them here—especially if they're using assumed names. And I could be wrong about them wanting to stay in Vannersville, or thereabouts—but Dirk's funeral home business is centred here, and he manages the staff and operations. He isn't a hands-off owner as he is with his horses. Even so, Detective Valeska says Dirk hasn't been seen near any of his funeral homes recently.

Although I'm reluctant to bother Detective Valeska on a vague hunch, police services has authority I don't have, so I text her to let her know they could be staying here. She answers immediately 'they're not'. So, I presume they've checked it out. Feeling defeated, I leave the building and look forward to a warm greeting from the dogs. They don't disappoint me—their love raises my spirits.

So, we're on our way to congratulate and thank Fay's team.

"How's Hector?" Neal asks as I walk towards his office.

"He's doing well." I put donuts, muffins, and coffee on the table that's outside his door. "How's Fay?"

"She thinks she's a star."

"Well, she is."

"She's come out of the race well. She's eating and drinking. And she was bucking and squealing as she was walked around the shedrow this morning. She's not happy having days off."

"I've brought some carrots. I'll go and visit with her."

"Don't give her too much praise, she's already pumped up."

"Haha!"

"Thanks for the goodies. I'll let everyone know."

Linda is folding clean saddle cloths close to Fay's stall.

"Hi, Linda. I've come to visit the winner."

"She's been a handful."

"So I gather."

"I hope you find who nearly killed Primula. Yuki is that upset."

"I'm not surprised. It's tragic."

"It's not just that, it's like scary 'cause we don't know who or why."

Fay munches her carrots as I feed the pieces to her one by one. Her loud crunching makes it hard to hear Linda.

"If it helps, I think I'm getting closer. The list of suspects is shorter. I didn't realize Yuki was concerned about more attacks."

"Not just him. All of us."

*   *   *

My plans for the morning have changed because Kenny has been true to his word and is suing me for defamation. I need a lawyer to help me fight this case—but perhaps I should offer a settlement—although something tells me that Kenny wouldn't accept it. He's such an angry young man.

William heard about Kenny's lawsuit from Candice and offered to find me legal counsel. Candice has emerged from the cocoon spun out of fear, loneliness, and poverty. She's wonderfully enthusiastic about her role in William's law firm and her new life here. Melissa is embracing her and supporting her—it's as if helping Candice is giving Melissa renewed strength and a sense of purpose.

Yet more cold, steady rain splatters on the sidewalk as I stride towards the office of the law firm William has introduced me to. I'm not happy to be using valuable time meeting with a lawyer when I'm close to solving the puzzle of who did what to whom and why. There are a few unanswered questions and more work to do, but I'm almost there.

Charlene Brookes shakes my hand with vigour and beckons me

to sit in a padded leather chair—one of four surrounding a shiny solid wood table. We exchange a few brief words of greeting. She's a woman after my own heart—she gets down to business as soon as we're seated.

"Meg, I've reviewed Kenny Linseed's allegations, and, in my opinion, they would not stand up in court. No doubt you agree."

I nod.

"However, if you're not determined to fight the allegations for reasons unknown to me at this point, I suggest you offer a modest settlement. It will cost you less in the long run, will get this business out of your hair quicker, and will save us both a lot of unnecessary aggravation and work. Don't get me wrong, I'm here to work for you and am most certainly willing and able to do what you wish, but my recommendation is that you offer him $10,000."

"I appreciate your directness and I've been wondering about this myself. But if he refuses it, can he use the offer as evidence of my guilt?"

"The offer would be presented 'without prejudice' and would therefore not be admissible in court in the event that he decides to decline the offer and proceed with his case."

"Would it do my reputation any harm to make an offer?"

"No. We will require Mr. Linseed to sign a confidentiality agreement. But, in any case, your excellent reputation, of which I'm aware, will protect you from negative ramifications from such a minor case involving a relatively unknown, and to be frank, insignificant person. I'm sure he thinks he's an important player in the animal rights movement, but my staff have not found evidence to support that. He has demonstrated inconsistent and inappropriate behaviour and lacks credibility and integrity. That's why I think there would be no risk of damage to you if you take this approach."

"I appreciate your directness. I would like you to make an offer on my behalf."

"You don't have to make the decision right now. You can take time to think about it."

"No, that's fine. Thank you."

That wasn't as painful and frustrating as I had anticipated. My steps are lighter as I return to the pickup, despite the large and persistent raindrops. The dogs are glad to see me and are both doing their best to lick the rain off my face and I'm not stopping them even though there's serious doubt as to whether I'm getting any drier. I'm not an umbrella person—it comes from being around horses so much—most of them think umbrellas are alien spacecraft plotting to abduct them, or worse.

My mobile rings and brings an end to the face-licking.

"Suzie! How's the harassment situation?"

"I reported it, and the short story is I'm looking for work."

"Suzie, that's terrible. I'm so sorry."

"I wasn't a union member 'cause I was 'casual', so I was hanging out there on my own and the powers that be said if I didn't like it there I was free to leave, or something like that."

"That's not fair."

"My mom always said, 'Life's not fair—get used to it'. I'm still not used to it. I wasn't calling about that and this is probably silly, but I remembered that woman's hands. You know, the owner with a big nose, thin lips, and large feet. You thought she could be a man in drag. I'm still sure she was a woman, and I remember her long fingers and the horrible bright pink nails. I can see them now. She seemed to, like, flash them around as if she was proud of the ugly things. I sure don't like bright pink polish."

"That's so helpful, Suzie. It's important."

"Great. I wondered if I should bother you with it."

"I'm glad you did. I suggest you contact the Italian restaurant in town. You can use my name if you like. I'm almost certain I heard the owner saying he's looking for help. I don't know what kind or if it would suit you, but you may want to check it out."

"That's nice of you. I will."

"Thanks for the info."

"You're welcome. Have a great day."

"You too."

While I'm parked, I text Detective Valeska and briefly let her know my theory. Perhaps she's already on it. Surely police services is making progress.

* * *

The rental truck has new windshield wipers and they're swishing backwards and forwards in a blur, but the relentless rain continues to obscure my vision. Kelly doesn't like extreme weather—I glance behind me to see her lying down on the floor with her ears flat on her head. Jake is sitting bolt upright with his ears pricked.

The pummelling rain drowns out all other sounds, so I miss my mobile's ping. It's not until I pull over—because visibility has diminished to almost zero—that I realize someone has tried to connect with me, but I don't recognize the number. It's another unsettling message: *You've run out of luck.* I let Detective Valeska know before I resume the drive home.

The police vehicle that was following me must have lost us in the downpour. I can't see him anywhere.

We're all eager to jump out of the pickup when we reach the farm, even though it's still raining. We trot to the kitchen door and sprinkle raindrops on the mat. The dogs shake in unison, sending only a little spray in all directions—but enough to affect surfaces which I make a mental note to clean later.

"Meg, you haven't been out in this awful weather, have you?" asks Melissa.

"I thought the rain was scary it came down so hard," Candice says. "It was something like I imagined a tropical storm would be—like a monsoon."

"I had to pull off the road at one point, but we're fine." I hang up my wet jacket in the laundry room and return to the kitchen. "So, you both have the day off?"

"No, I've got to go soon," Candice says. "William has two important meetings with potential new clients today."

"And Russon said he couldn't make it in this morning, but he's working this afternoon, so I'm also going soon."

"Is Russon okay?"

"Yes, other than he's working too hard."

"Hark who's talking," Candice says. "I'm the one who has it the easiest at the moment."

Melissa says she's going to have a shower before going to work and walks towards the stairs with Jake following. Cooper scampers in from the family room and leaps up at Jake's wagging tail. Candice puts her jacket on.

A loud knocking startles us, including the dogs who bark. Cooper disappears in a flash. Jake rushes back into the kitchen with his hackles up. Before I reach the door, the knocking erupts again—even more frantic than the first time. I'm somewhat leery as I turn the knob. The person pushes the door open wide with enough force that it hits the closet.

"Dirk, what's the matter?" Despite his obvious agitation, I sense the tension being released in the room. The dogs stop barking—after all, they've met Dirk before—Candice puts her mug in the sink.

"She's after me." He's red in the face and breathless.

"Sit down." I pull out a chair. He's unsteady on his feet and his hands tremble as he reaches for the table for support as he sits down. "Who...?"

"Bobbie."

"Ah."

"I've been a fool. I've ignored so many things. I've made excuses.

I've played along. I've done everything wrong, and people have died."

"What…"

"You probably know. You've worked it out. You saw the truck at that farm."

I don't have a chance to answer—and not because Dirk won't let me get a word in, but because the backdoor is flung open hitting the closet again. Torrential rain is the backdrop to the figure standing on the mat with a gun pointed at Dirk who collapses onto the floor. Candice screams. The dogs growl and keep growling as they sit on either side of me—having responded to my hand signal.

"Put the gun down," I shout. "Killing more people is not going to help you or Annie."

"You wouldn't understand. You've got no idea what we've been through." Bobbie's voice sounds deeper and stronger.

"I know you need to stop."

She waves the gun around as if circling my face. I'm at a loss to know how to handle this confrontation without someone getting hurt or killed. I hope Dirk is breathing. I can't tell. Most of him is under the table.

"I'm an avenger."

"For Annie's sake? Does she know this?"

Candice stands by the sink like a statue and her face is as pale and shiny as a piece of cold marble.

"She knows I love her. All this is for her."

"Let's talk about it. I'll make some tea. Sit down."

"No. Annie and I are going away after I've tied up these loose ends. You'll all be found here, and the cops will assume you committed suicide after killing everyone else. It's easy to set it up that way."

"What about the dogs?" Where's that police officer when I need him, or her?

"They can fend for themselves. I don't care for dogs, but I won't waste bullets on them."

"What motive would I have to kill everyone?"

"That doesn't matter."

"Wouldn't I leave a note? People who commit suicide usually leave a note. The police might suspect something else happened if there isn't a note."

"You're just wasting my time." She aims the gun at my forehead. I'm losing my nerve. The dogs lean against me as if on cue. That's all I need to spur me into action.

"Go!" I yell at the dogs. But it isn't just the dogs that respond. Candice springs forward and Melissa appears as if by magic. We all rush at Bobbie simultaneously as if we're part of a rugby team. The dogs grab her pants and pull while Candice, Melissa and I slam into her, pushing her against the open kitchen door which crashes into the closet yet again.

Bobbie pulls the trigger.

No one slumps to the floor. The dogs are okay. Can I hear sirens? I can't hear anything. I can't see. I'm falling, falling.

24

Truths Revealed

Flowers of all colours of the rainbow and all shapes and sizes crowd a huge vase that leaves no space for anything else on my bedside table. The perfumes make me sneeze causing me to wonder why the administration here hasn't banned flowers. After all, they've banned dogs.

I'm not a happy camper. I want to leave but Dr. Milton has persuaded me to stay until tomorrow. It seems that Bobbie banged me on the side of the head with the gun and then shot me while Melissa, Candice, Kelly, and Jake tackled her. They eventually wrestled her to the floor and tied her arms behind her back with a stray thick cotton lead-rein I'd left by my boots intending to return it to the barn on the next trip.

I didn't regain consciousness until I was loaded into an ambulance. I tried to convince them I didn't need to go, but I wasn't making much sense—so they say. Someone had put a large patch on my shoulder, and it felt wet. The good news is that it's not the same arm that was grazed by a bullet when I was at the side entrance leading to the casino and injured when Candice and I were on our way to see Primula. And I didn't feel pain until today—two days later. I've little recollection of yesterday.

I've been told not to move or use my left arm. And in my mind, I'm a caged animal pacing up and down but getting nowhere. No one has sent me any news. Dr. Milton said he didn't want me to be disturbed but I'm deeply distressed because I don't know what's going on. When I threatened to leave, Dr. Milton finally relented, and I'm permitted to have visitors this afternoon. I'm expecting Melissa and Candice soon.

A kind volunteer gave me a cup of tea, although Les would be disgusted with it—it's not close to being as delicious as his brew. But I'm grateful. It's more pleasant than the chlorine-tasting water I've had to drink. If I was used to town water I wouldn't notice, I'm sure, but I'm accustomed to well water or spring water.

Time passes slowly and my anxiety creeps up in intensity. Are Kelly and Jake okay? I know Melissa and Candice are okay. Dr. Milton told me that.

I try to shift my position to be more upright but the pain in my shoulder makes it challenging. I sneeze. I don't know what to do about these flowers.

Melissa and Candice trot into the room with huge smiles.

"Are Kelly and Jake okay?"

"You mean these two?" asks Melissa as the dogs run into the room and put their front paws on the bed. I pat their heads with my right hand. They seem to understand I can't give them the exuberant welcome they deserve.

"They've allowed them into the hospital, then? I thought it was against their new policy."

"Ah," says Edward Bergerstein as he's wheeled into the room by

Dr. Milton. "The Patient Council was successful. The administration has withdrawn the policy and is going to study the matter further. They will be surveying other hospitals, interviewing patients and families, and conducting a literature review. I think Kelly and Jake will be safe to visit for some considerable time."

"Which is excellent for all concerned," Dr. Milton says.

"I hope you don't mind me coming," Edward says, "but I wanted to tell you that good news myself, and Dr. Milton advised me that you were allowed visitors this afternoon."

"Thank you for all you've done. I appreciate it and so do Kelly and Jake." I turn to look at Melissa and Candice. "And how are you two?" They still have wide grins on their faces.

"I thought you'd never ask," Melissa says.

"We're fine," Candice says.

"How's Dirk? The last time I saw him he was lying under our kitchen table. I wasn't even sure if he was breathing."

"I'm alive," Dirk says as he limps into the room using a cane. "It was stress. My doctor's got me on some drugs. I'll be okay. I'm sure sorry I didn't help you. I can't believe what Bobbie's done. I feel so bad I didn't stop her. I hope you recover quickly. Do you like the flowers? They were left over from a big funeral, and I thought you'd like them. They were too nice to throw in the trash. I suppose that's not very tasteful of me, but I wasn't up to flower shopping, so I asked my staff to get me some. Sorry, rambling, not feeling the greatest." His hands are trembling. He's not wearing his gold chain and medallion. Perhaps that was a gift from Bobbie.

"Here, sit down," Dr. Milton says. He points to the chair near my bed.

"Thanks, doc. I get shaky sometimes."

"Dirk…"

"You know most of it, Meg."

"But…"

"Do you want the whole, sad story?"

I'm not the only one who replies 'yes'.

"And I'd like to hear it too," Detective Valeska says as her heels click on the glistening vinyl flooring. "Hello, Meg. I'm glad to see you're more or less in one piece. Before you ask, the officer was called away. It was a hoax, and I owe you an official apology." Before I can respond, she turns and faces Dirk. "Mr. Knightscourt, I'm Detective Sandra Valeska." They shake hands. "I've heard Meg's theory on what this has been all about, but I would very much like you to add your perspective. This isn't official, of course." She smiles but Dirk frowns.

"So many horrible things. I told everyone before you came in that I should have stopped her. I've been worse than a fool and people have died."

We're all looking at Dirk. Kelly and Jake have their heads on his lap and he's absent-mindedly stroking them. They must believe he's a patient and needs their attention. I'm thrilled that Jake is learning the role of a therapy dog.

"Okay. I'll try not to get muddled. It's not simple. Help me out, Meg. I'll add to what you say. I'm not up to telling the whole thing. I'll interrupt—I'm good at that—and add stuff."

"I'll give it a shot." I take a big breath, which I immediately regret because a stab of pain shoots from my shoulder up my neck and down my side like a lightning strike. I cough to quash the gasp I know is threatening to erupt. "Here goes. Everyone knows Bobbie and Annie are sisters. They had a very close relationship."

"That's because their mother left them when Bobbie was fifteen and Annie was ten. The father wasn't part of their lives. They lived in the basement of their drunken uncle's house. I don't know how Bobbie made enough money to feed them both. But I do know she's super protective of her sister. Annie means everything to her."

"And that's the key to this whole story."

"It is. But things got tough and, jumping a few years ahead,

Bobbie joined the Blackbirds Gang."

"You should have told me Bobbie was in the gang."

"I know." He hangs his head.

"Later, Annie must have joined Bobbie," I say. "It probably started off being a gang of young people shoplifting and stealing wallets and so on."

"You're right. They had to do it to survive." Dirk looks at me with dewy eyes. "And when they became young adults, they got involved in drugs." He coughs. "I don't have any details. What I know is mostly from Annie. Bobbie has been secretive about their past. I'm her husband and helped get her off the streets and out of that gang business, but she never told me this stuff."

"And then Annie became Barton's girlfriend."

"Yes, but there was a falling out. I guess it resulted in Annie breaking up with Barton. And then, somehow, Bobbie and Annie became members of the Pitbulls Gang. Horrible name."

"Drugs could have been at the root of the altercation with the Blackbirds Gang, perhaps."

"I honestly don't know. It could have been Barton seeking revenge for Annie leaving him, or it could have been drug-related."

"And Pablo—Annie's new boyfriend and a member of the Pitbulls Gang—was shot and killed."

"I don't know how it happened. But Annie loved him and was cut up so bad. I guess Bobbie was as mad as hell to see her sister consumed by grief."

"But it was a few years ago. That's the part that confuses me. Why did Bobbie seek revenge several years later?"

"I don't know for sure, but I reckon the opportunity sort of came up. Barton showed up at the casino. Although it was Annie's casino, Bobbie took control. She can be downright autocratic about things. I don't know if Annie saw Barton, but Bobbie did. I learned this later. I honestly didn't have a clue at the time." I nod.

"But Bobbie would have known Barton was training your race-horses," Melissa says. "Why didn't she act earlier?"

"Annie told me they had gang names. I guess Bobbie didn't know Barton's real name. She never came to the track with me, even though she was officially part-owner of the horses, and she never ventured into our barn, so I guess she didn't meet Barton until he went to the casino. Seeing him is what triggered her to seek revenge on behalf of Annie. That has to be it."

"Bobbie came up with a plan," I say. "I would love to know if my theory about this is right—perhaps Bobbie will talk, and Detective Valeska will be able to confirm this. I think Bobbie realized that Barton hadn't recognized her, but she put on a wig and dressed up, including having her nails painted a bright pink, to make it harder for him to identify her. Then she plied him with free drinks in the hopes he would talk. She wanted to know the real names of all the other members of the Blackbirds Gang who were present when Pablo was shot. My guess is that Barton gave her the information she wanted and more. He must have mentioned Greg Dudley and Les Joseph as people who had helped him. So, she added their names to her list."

"I can't disclose what Bobbie Knightscourt has told us," Detective Valeska says, "but you're not wrong."

"So, she planned to murder all those people," Candice says. She looks like a startled deer. "I can't believe it."

"She started with Barton and added arsenic to his drinks when-ever she got the chance, making sure no one saw her, including Suzie who worked as a bartender. It was easy to do, and she probably thought it wouldn't be discovered."

"This is too awful," Dirk says. His cane drops to the floor with a clatter and Dr. Milton picks it up. "But I suppose that's what must have happened. My god. It's even worse thinking she planned it all." He stops petting the dogs and holds his head in his hands.

"It's not your fault, Dirk," I say. "Anyway, Barton got sicker and sicker. Suzie would, when she could, make sure he got on and off the bus okay, but that morning he fell into the path of Linda's car which happened to be driven by Les Joseph."

"He was dead before that incident," Detective Valeska says.

"The police might not have found out that Barton was poisoned if he hadn't hit the car."

"But I should have suspected something bad was going on much much earlier," Dirk says. "Bobbie made out she didn't like to go out and told me she wanted to be alone in her room, but she disappeared quite often—I know she did—but I ignored it. Oh my god."

"The other part of this that was confusing for quite a while," I say, "were the actions of Kenny Linseed of Animal Equality and Freedom. It was particularly difficult to sort out who did what to Dr. Greg Dudley. Dr. Dudley helped members of the Blackbirds Gang, so was one of Bobbie's targets, but Kenny also thought Greg had supplied performance-enhancing drugs to Barton. Kenny is a zealot and some of his actions have been extreme. But we won't go into that now."

"Kenny didn't kill anyone then?" asks Melissa.

"No. Ironically, he hurt several horses. But he nearly crossed the line when he put his hands around my throat after he'd added some poisonous plants to Hector's water."

"He's been charged with aggravated assault," Detective Valeska says, "and I hope the evidence will stand up in court. That's probably why he's lashing out at you with a defamation lawsuit."

"What?" exclaims Melissa.

"It's okay, I'll explain later," I say. "Anyway, then Orlando is found dead in one of your funeral homes, Dirk. He was shot in the head."

"Forensics has the gun Bobbie allegedly used," Detective Valeska says. "They're checking the bullet that tore the top of your shoulder during the recent assault in your home—it was removed from a kitchen cupboard—to determine if it matches the bullets we previously retrieved, which were all fired from the same gun. One from Orlando's head, one from the incident at the side entrance where the Knightscourts were staying, one discovered in the horse trailer shooting, and another one used in the attack on you and Candice in the pickup. And they will determine if the gun Bobbie had in her possession is the one that discharged those bullets."

"Orlando, poor Orlando," Dirk groans as if he's been stabbed in the heart. "I don't care what he did—he didn't deserve to die. He was a good man. He loved the horses. He worked hard. Why kill him after all this time?"

"I'm not trained as a psychiatrist, but I've been witness to some of their work with suspects," Detective Valeska says, "and some find killing becomes easier to them after they've murdered their first victim."

"You mean to say she was on a roll?" Dirk shakes his head. Detective Valeska shrugs.

"Dirk," I say, "I remember Bobbie saying, 'I'm an avenger'. She had started on a mission to eliminate all the members of the Blackbirds Gang who were around when Pablo was shot. Probably neither Bobbie nor Annie know who shot him, so Bobbie went after all of the ones who were present at the shooting. But I think Dr. Dudley and Les were a stretch. It's as if she couldn't control her vengeance."

"It made Bobbie seethe that Annie was charged with the murder of Pablo," Dirk says. "And I could understand her being angry."

"We made a mistake," Detective Valeska says, "and justice was served. She was acquitted."

"But if that hadn't happened," Dirk says, "then maybe Bobbie wouldn't have been so mad, and nobody would have got hurt or died."

"I'm not sure," I say, "but I suggest it would have happened anyway. She was looking for revenge on Annie's behalf for the shooting of her beloved Pablo."

"Oh, god, this is too much." The dogs put their heads on Dirk's lap again and he pats them as if they're made of wafer-thin glass.

"Why did she shoot at the horse trailer that day—assuming it was her?" asks Candice. "And why did she shoot at us in the pickup?"

"She shot at the horse trailer for the same reason that she drove off the road in your SUV, Dirk, am I right? To make it seem to us that neither you nor she should be considered suspects."

"Now I look back on that crash, yes. It's so effing awful. I'd fallen asleep and I woke up as we hit a damn tree, and the airbags scared me half to death. I thought I was going to suffocate. You're right. Bobbie was driving. I don't know if anyone forced us off the road but that's what Bobbie said."

"We found no physical evidence to support Bobbie's claim," Detective Valeska says. "But we can't prove it didn't happen either."

"Bobbie shot at us, Candice, in the hopes that it would scare me off."

"There are far too many visitors," a nurse bellows from the doorway. "Only two allowed. The rest of you will have to go."

Both Dr. Milton and Detective Valeska hustle towards the male nurse. It takes less than a minute for him to be convinced that he's the one who must leave. He shuts the heavy fire door behind him.

"And she attempted to kill Les," I continue. "He was a counsellor who worked on the streets and as such he helped members of the Blackbirds Gang. Bobbie was certainly on the rampage."

"We don't have proof that Bobbie poisoned Les," Detective Valeska says.

"No. But it makes sense. However, neither Les nor I know how she did it. It may stay a mystery. And next on Bobbie's list was Primula. She was another member of the Blackbirds Gang."

"How could she do that to her?" Candice asks. "It was so brutal.

To beat her around the head and then flood the place, hoping she'd drown, and the water would cover up any evidence."

"I don't think she's ever going to fully recover from her brain injury," I say.

"Her mother must be gutted," Candice says. "And didn't Bobbie try to smother Primula when she was in hospital?"

"I don't like to be reminded of that incident," Detective Valeska says.

"And then there's Dr. Greg Dudley," I say. "I don't believe he's ever had anything to do with performance-enhancing drugs—Kenny got the wrong end of the stick. But Bobbie wanted her revenge because Greg helped Barton and Primula. He'd been to college with Barton and got him his first job at the track as a hotwalker and continued to support him in his career at the racetrack."

"How is Greg?" asks Melissa.

"As far as I know," Dr. Milton says, "he discharged himself."

"It looks like he can tell us himself," I say as all eyes turn towards the door. The male nurse holds it open for Dr. Dudley who's using a cane but looking much brighter. His eyes even have a bit of a twinkle. Dr. Milton beckons him to sit in the only other chair. Everyone else is standing except for Dirk.

"I've missed most of the story if you've got to me."

"I'll tell you another day," I say. "How are you?"

"Great. My rehab's going well. I can speak more clearly. I get about fine with a cane. I plan to go back to work part-time in about a month. This must mean you know who attacked me?"

"I'm pretty sure that Kenny threw the stink bomb."

"Kenny's a messed up young man. He was certain I was dealing in banned drugs and helping Barton to cheat. And I suspect he thought that attacking my office would raise questions and there'd be an investigation, and I'd lose my veterinarian's licence. But who tried to kill me? They would have succeeded if it hadn't been for these lovely dogs." He fondles Kelly's ears as she looks at him with wide, deep brown eyes.

"This won't surprise anyone here, but I believe your attacker was Bobbie Knightscourt."

"Why on earth would she want to murder me?"

"I'll explain later. We need to have a long chat. But something you told me has been in my mind. You said you caught a whiff of a sweet and fruity scent. Dirk, does that mean anything to you?"

"What? A fruity smell?"

"Yes. Dr. Dudley thought it smelt like a laundry detergent he'd used. Could that smell be linked to Bobbie?"

"I don't know. I'm trying to think. The only thing I remember is a giant laundry detergent bottle on top of the washing machine with various fruits printed all over it. I thought it odd—just a quick thought as I was passing through. Aren't laundry detergents usually lemon-scented or herbal or something? Fruit seems peculiar."

"Unfortunately," Detective Valeska says, "that is not sufficient proof it was Bobbie Knightscourt who attacked you, Dr. Dudley. But our team is examining every inch of your charred trailer and if there is evidence that Bobbie was there, we'll find it."

"Dirk," I say, "this is the question I'm sure we all want answered. Where is Annie? And where has she been? As far as I know, no one here has seen or heard from her."

"She's completely innocent. She's done nothing wrong. Well, other than some shenanigans when she was with the Pitbulls Gang, but that was a long time ago."

"We're not pursuing that line of enquiry," Detective Valeska says.

"I helped her to escape from Bobbie's suffocating control. Bobbie was literally holding her prisoner. I don't understand why, so don't ask me. She says she loves Annie more than anyone or anything, but then she doesn't respect her wishes or give her freedom. She was locked in one room or another wherever we were. Bobbie said it was for her own good—as protection."

"Did she think members of the Blackbirds Gang might want to harm her?" asks Candice.

"How do I know what's going on in her crazy mind? She's not the woman I thought I married. Anyhow, when we were at that farm and the fire broke out, I unlocked Annie's door and told her to run. By then I was very uneasy about Bobbie. I had strong suspicions she was, you know, anyway, I was getting scared for Annie and for me."

"Where's Annie now? Do you know?"

"Yes. She's been in contact with me since. I bought her a ticket to Guatemala because that's where Pablo's family live. She's there now and feels safe. She wants me to visit. I might."

"Bobbie set the fires, right?"

"I suppose she must have. Both the outbuilding with the truck and the house—doesn't make sense for it to be accidental or natural causes, does it?"

"The Fire Department found evidence to support arson in both locations," Detective Valeska says.

"Is this the end of the story?" asks Doctor Milton. "Because you need to rest, Meg, especially if you want to go home tomorrow."

Les's face appears as the door opens slowly.

"I missed it," he says. "I missed Hercule Poirot's summing up. Oh no!" His white teeth flash as he gives us a broad smile. "I knew your little grey cells would figure it out."

"I hear you've done a great job with the yearlings," Dirk says as he nods his head towards Les.

"They're good," Les says. "Meg, give me the scoop." Jake rolls on the floor and Les squats down to give him a tummy rub.

"The very short version is that Bobbie is the murderer, and Kenny is the fanatical animal rights activist on steroids."

"And Pablo's death was the trigger for Bobbie," Les says.

"In a way. It was Annie's devastated response to Pablo's death that ate away at Bobbie."

"Pablo's death was the result of that dumb gang rivalry."

"You know more about those gangs than the rest of us, and more than you've let on, I think."

"Yeah, perhaps. All I'll say is if it wasn't for my brother, I'd likely be dead. You gotta take it from me—brothers are the best."

"Okay, it truly is now time for everyone to leave," Dr. Milton says.

"Thanks for coming," I say. "I don't know who invited you all, but it's so nice to see you and get a chance to sort of wrap this whole thing up."

"Ah," Detective Valeska says. "There's a lot of work for me and my team to do but I'm optimistic we'll have sufficient evidence to charge Bobbie Knightscourt with several serious offences, and that the prosecution will be successful in proving her guilt in all cases."

Dirk holds his head in his hands again. I hope he doesn't start crying.

"You must go," Dr. Milton opens the door and ushers everyone out with exaggerated arm movements. Dirk stumbles as he gets to his feet. Dr. Milton takes his arm and leads him into the corridor. Dirk doesn't say a word.

25

The Gift

Finally, my visitors have left—but it's as if they were dragging their feet. They probably have lots of questions and perhaps some comments as well. Melissa and Candice stay behind but now they tell the dogs it's time to go. I give them a last pat on their heads with my right hand.

"You're the heroes, Kelly and Jake. You're incredibly special dogs." They wag their tails as if to agree. The four of them leave, and the room is suddenly quiet and white and empty. But then the nurse returns to push the heavy fire door into its open mode. Despite the babble and rattles that invade my room from the corridor, I shut my eyes as a deep tiredness crawls through my muscles and bones making it seem as if I'm sinking into the hard, plastic-covered mattress.

But my eyes open wide before I can fall asleep because someone else has entered the room.

"Hi, Meg," William says. "I hear you had a lot of visitors this afternoon."

"Hello. Yes, you missed the whole story. We can fill you in—the bits you don't know already—but it'll have to be on another day because I'm beat."

"I'm sorry to come when you're so tired. But it's important."

"Oh?"

"I didn't know what to bring you, so I brought you tea and a carrot muffin although that's probably not the appropriate snack for the afternoon."

"It's always the right time for a carrot muffin. I live on them. Thank you. And a decent tea will go down well." As I accept the paper cup, movement catches my eye. "Is someone with you? Gabriel! You've come to visit!"

I hand the tea back to William and hug his nephew with my right arm. Gabriel's grin couldn't be any wider.

"Meg, I'm here to apologize again for what I did and didn't do." William hands me the cup again.

"Let's not revisit that." Gabriel's leaning against the bed. His face is pale, and he's lost weight.

"I won't go over it again, but circumstances have changed."

"What do you mean?" I sip on the tea. It's wonderful. I'll eat the muffin after they've gone.

"Gabriel will live with me permanently. He's here to stay. Gabriel, do you want to tell Meg what happened?"

"I don't know."

"Do you mind if I tell her? You can correct me if I get something wrong."

"Fine. Where are Kelly and Jake?"

"You just missed them," I say. "They're on their way back to the farm."

"I'm going to be at Milkweed Farm," Gabriel says. "It's next door, isn't it?"

"You mean next door to where I and Melissa live?" He nods. "Almost. It's very near to the farm. I'm sure you'll remember. So, what happened William?"

"You were right. I should have asked you and Gabriel what you both wanted, but more importantly, I should have upheld the wishes of my sister, Elizabeth."

"So, she didn't want your cousin Maddy and her husband to adopt Gabriel?"

"I told a terrible lie. I've talked to Gabriel about it, and I've apologized to him."

"You told this lie because you thought, if I remember what you said correctly, that 'it was apparent I wasn't comfortable with my role of stepmother'. But we didn't discuss it, and you didn't ask."

"I know."

"So, Gabriel, what happened in Saskatchewan?"

He sits on the chair and hugs his knees with his feet on the seat. "They didn't want me. Howie was mean to me." He bursts into sobs, and I rub his back with my hand as best I can while holding the tea.

"Howie is Maddie's son. He's about two years older than Gabriel. From all accounts, he's a bully and likes being the only child. He resented Gabriel joining their family. Maddy said she thought it would improve, but it got worse."

"William, how did you let this happen? I can't get over you acting against your sister's wishes."

"I'm well aware that I've let everyone down."

"It wasn't just about me, was it? It was also because you felt inadequate as his uncle taking on a father role. I'm right, aren't I?"

"It all seemed overwhelming to me. I'm ashamed to admit I believed I wasn't made of the right stuff to look after Gabriel, and I did honestly believe you were at least unenthusiastic. But Gabriel wants to be with us. He says he felt wanted and loved." William's eyes brim with rare and sparkling tears.

"You're going to raise him on your own?"

"With help from you, Melissa, and Candice, yes."

"And this is what you want, Gabriel?"

"Yes," sniff. "I love everyone and the animals here. I didn't want to go."

"How will the adoption work?"

"It'll be fine, and my sister will be able to rest in peace."

"You're not religious."

"No. I suppose it's my peace of mind that's been in question."

"Well, Gabriel. I'll be back at the farm tomorrow. I hope we'll see lots and lots of you."

He looks at me with red-rimmed eyes, but there's a trace of a smile on his lips.

"Good. Now I must get some rest otherwise they won't let me leave tomorrow." Even the carrot muffin lies untouched as I close my heavy eyelids.

*   *   *

The taxi driver won't open the gates and drive up to the house because Kelly and Jake are barking. He tells me he's terrified of dogs. As soon as I get out of the cab, the dogs wag their tails and I'm sure they're smiling, as am I. The driver hands me my small bag and I open the gate. Kelly dances on her front feet and Jake runs in crazy circles on the lawn. It's as if I've been away for months.

There's a crispness in the air as we walk up to the house. My legs are a little wobbly, but I barely notice because I'm soaking in the deep pleasure of being back home. Horses are grazing in the fields, birds are singing, trees have hints of fall colours, and the sun's shining.

After I dump my bag on the kitchen floor, we amble over to the barn.

"Meg!" Linda says. "I didn't know what time you'd be here. I'm late leaving. I wanted it ready for this evening, so you didn't have to do much."

"Thanks. That's thoughtful of you. But don't keep Neal waiting for too long."

"He's okay with it."

"Well, that's nice of both of you."

"Just have a bit more to do. All of us at the track are like super happy Bobbie is locked up."

"Yes. It's a relief."

"Where's Kenny? Someone told me he's gone."

"He's living with his half-brother in Newfoundland. But he'll have to come back here again to face several charges."

"But at least he won't be hurting the horses here."

"No. I'm pretty sure there's a temporary injunction banning him from having contact with any animals."

"I don't get him."

"Neither do I. His fanaticism got the better of him and I reckon he lost his way."

"Good riddance is what I say. But why steal Bella? That's even more crazy than his other stuff."

"I can only guess, but I think it was simply for ransom. He wanted funds so he could grow his campaign against horse racing. But he must have got cold feet because, as far as I know, he didn't contact Dirk. Perhaps he didn't like me being on his case."

"He's a cruel man. He should be locked up for a long time."

"He probably will get a prison sentence. Anyway, thanks again for all you're doing, Linda. I do appreciate it."

She waddles into another stall.

Les is working with one of the yearlings and Dirk is leaning on the fence. I didn't notice his SUV.

"Hi, Dirk."

"Meg. Just the person I want to see."

"Oh."

"Yeah. Isn't Les doing a fantastic job? Look how he's got that colt standing so pretty. I'm sure he'll do well in the sale."

"I hope...."

"I know. The results can be disappointing. Buyers want large horses, with clean x-rays, perfect conformation, nice markings, great pedigree and preferably a halo."

"Will..."

"No, I'm not putting on reserves. I have to sell. But that's what I want to tell you. One of the yearlings is real nice and I want you to have him."

"What?"

"It's not in lieu of payment. I must make that clear. It's a gift. It's my way of saying thank you. The outcome of your investigation into the murders is goddam horrifying and I'm cut up about it for lots of reasons, but you have Bella and you're looking after her, and the yearlings, and you unravelled the animal rights effing nonsense. And you solved the murders. You made me face up to the truth about Bobbie. I was too slow to admit your investigation was making Bobbie edgy and weird. Anyway, he's yours."

"I can't..."

"Yes, you can. And I have a selfish reason. He's the best colt and I want him to have the best chance, with the best owner and best trainer I know, oh, and the best groom. He'll do well for you, I know."

"Why..."

"Because I'm going to Guatemala to see Annie, and I may not return. Too many memories here. Look, Les is bringing him in now for his schooling. See his walk? And see his neck and shoulder? Please take him. You'll be doing me a favour, honestly. I mean it."

"But..."

"Too much. No, it's not. I'm selling my funeral home business.

I can't face it anymore. I'll have more than enough. Enjoy him. All I ask is that you keep me posted on his progress." He pats my arm gently as if it may break, but it's not the one I have in a sling. I smile at him since he's not going to let me say more than one word. "Les, bring that guy over here so Meg can get a good look."

"I've…"

"I know—you've seen him every day, but just take a long, good look at your colt. Let his beauty soak into your soul."

"He's amazing, Dirk, and so smart," Les says as he leads the stunning colt towards us. "I sure like him. You'll do well in the sale with him."

"Ah. Meg's his new owner. So, you can break him in for her when you get a chance."

I wipe a couple of runaway tears from my cheeks.

"Fantastic, man. This will be an honour. Wow, Meg." The colt kicks out with his back legs. He's obviously not one for standing still for a chat. "I'll let him have the day off and I'll start him on more serious work tomorrow. Yay. This will be fun, man."

"I feel so good about this," says Dirk. I'm sure he's choking back tears. Why has this made us all so emotional?

"And, Meg," Les says. "You did it. You've made us feel safe again. Boy, I can't tell you what that means. I don't have nightmares about being poisoned and I can drink what I want."

"I didn't do it alone. I cannot take all the credit. And I wish I'd…"

"Found the killer earlier?" Dirk asks. "That's partly my fault because I couldn't believe Bobbie was capable of murder. I happily buried my head in the sand. It's a terrible thing. I'll be haunted by this for the rest of my life." He grabs the fence rail as if to steady himself.

"Come in…"

"Thanks, but I've got to go. I have a lot of stuff to do. A taxi is coming soon. I don't like driving. I never have. And I don't like being in the front of a vehicle since those airbags got me."

"Thank you…"

"Yeah, he's a beaut." Dirk turns to look at the colt again. "By the way, I told Dr. Dudley he can have Bella. You'll have to talk with him about that. Greg's been through so much. I thought it would buck him up and I think it has. He's going to keep me up to date on the foal and I'll decide what to do later. Thanks for everything. Gotta go—my taxi's here." This driver has dared to come up the driveway. I'm glad I didn't lock the gate.

26

Sisters and Brothers

My legs are even more wobbly as I walk into the house. I flop onto a chair and the dogs lie down. Cooper saunters into the kitchen with his tail in the air and rubs against each of the dogs and my leg. He then starts an elaborate grooming routine. Sometimes I wish I was Cooper—without a care in the world and apparently happy all the time.

I don't have the energy to put the kettle on.

The door is flung open as Melissa, Candice, William, and Gabriel bring chatter and laughter into the room.

"We went out for a late breakfast," Melissa says. "How long have you been here?"

"I've only just sat down."

"You look very tired. I'll make you a cup of tea."

"I don't think I've ever had such a yummy breakfast," Candice says. "Pancakes and maple syrup—super!"

"I like hashbrowns," Gabriel says, "with ketchup."

"And I like it all," William says. "Apologies, but Gabriel and I have to go. Melissa dropped us off in case you were here so we could say hello, and so I could show Gabriel the path from here to Milkweed Farm. Then he can come on his own, but he understands he must tell me, and you, when he does. He knows how to use the landline. He'll come for another visit late this afternoon. We have an appointment at the school this morning."

"That's great. I look forward to lots of visits. See you later." I'm too tired to stand so I reach for Gabriel with my available arm and give him an awkward hug. I feel warm inside. I hold back tears that are threatening to run down my cheeks. William and Gabriel leave, and I take a deep breath.

"How's your shoulder?" Candice asks as I put a lid on my emotions.

"Not bad. I think they've made much too much fuss about it. Just a few stitches. I'm tired, that's all."

Melissa hands me a steaming mug of tea.

"But I'm not too tired to call for a toast," I say. "You'll have to get a glass of water each or something."

"Okay." Melissa fills two glasses with sparkling water. "It has to be sparkling if it's a toast."

"Before I make the toast—which will be to sisters—I'll explain why—and hopefully before I fall asleep."

They both sit down at the table. Candice scoops Cooper off the floor. She has come a long way since she first arrived.

"While Bobbie's love for Annie became controlling and eventually deadly for others, they had been very close and had a deep and caring relationship. Bobbie believed she was avenging Pablo's death on behalf of her sister. Don't misunderstand me—I'm not excusing her murderous behaviour. Now, I'm not just thinking about sisters. I'm also considering brothers. Les says he wouldn't have made it without the love and support of his brother. Kenny—and I know he's gone off the rails—but his half-brother in Newfoundland has taken him in despite his errant behaviour. William had a difficult relationship with his sister, but he has now stepped up to take care of her son—his nephew—Gabriel, and is honouring his sister's wishes. And Melissa, I treasure our relationship. It is very precious to me as I hope you know. Not all that long ago I had no idea you existed."

"I'm so glad we found each other."

"I wish I had a sister," Candice says as she stares down at her glass of bubbles.

"You have two," I say. "We've adopted you, Candice. So, let's have a toast to sisters and brothers." Candice's cheeks immediately get streaked with tears.

"To sisters and brothers!" we shout in unison.

I stand up and stretch out my right arm to initiate a group hug. Melissa, Candice, and I enjoy a warm and loving family embrace. Kelly and Jake wander around us wagging their tails and Cooper spreads cat hair on our jeans.